# A CENTURY OF STORIES
### NEW HANOVER COUNTY PUBLIC LIBRARY
## 1906-2006

# THE MARCELLI

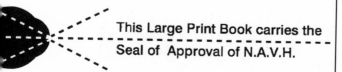

This Large Print Book carries the
Seal of Approval of N.A.V.H.

# THE MARCELLI BRIDE

## SUSAN MALLERY

**THORNDIKE PRESS**

*An imprint of Thomson Gale, a part of The Thomson Corporation*

Detroit • New York • San Francisco • New Haven, Conn. • Waterville, Maine • London • Munich

Thorndike Press® Large Print Basic.

The text of this Large Print edition is unabridged.

Other aspects of the book may vary from the original edition.

Set in 16 pt. Plantin.

**LIBRARY OF CONGRESS CATALOGING-IN-PUBLICATION DATA**

Mallery, Susan.
   The Marcelli bride / by Susan Mallery. — Large print ed.
      p. cm. — (Thorndike Press large print basic) (The Marcelli family saga)
   ISBN 0-7862-8969-4 (hardcover : alk. paper)
   1. Bodyguards — Fiction. 2. Children of presidents — Fiction. 3. Wineries
   — California — Fiction. 4. Large type books. I. Title.
   PS3613.A453M37 2006                                   813'.54—dc22 2006018577

Published in 2006 by arrangement with Pocket Books,
a division of Simon & Schuster, Inc.

Printed in the United States of America on permanent paper
10 9 8 7 6 5 4 3 2 1

# THE MARCELLI BRIDE

# 1

If Darcy Jensen had known she was going to be kidnapped, she would have worn better shoes. Or at least more sensible shoes. As it was she'd dressed in black strappy sandals that weren't all that comfortable for walking, let alone being dragged across a parking lot and thrown into the back of a van.

She did her best to resist. Screaming was out of the question because they'd already gagged her. And the resisting part went badly, what with her hands tied behind her back, although she did nail one guy with a decent head butt.

Even as she landed hard on the metal floor of the van, she wondered how it all had happened. She'd been in Ann Taylor checking out the new clothes for fall. She'd told Drew she needed to use the restroom.

Traveling with two Secret Service agents meant rarely using a public restroom. Drew had consulted with the manager of the store, who was all too happy to have the president of the United States' daughter peeing in her private bathroom. Darcy had done her business, washed her hands — not only because she always did, but also because people checked on things like that when one was in the public eye — and had started back through the stockroom toward the dressing rooms, where she had a pile of clothes waiting for her.

That's when the men attacked. Four guys in Halloween-type demon masks grabbed her. Before she knew what was happening, they'd slapped tape on her mouth. The hand tying came next, then the dragging.

One of them even remembered to pick up her purse, she thought grimly as she stared at her now-scratched Maxx bag bought on QVC lying next to her on the floor of the van.

The rear doors slammed shut, and the vehicle sped out of the parking lot.

Darcy braced herself as best she could on the ribbed floor as the van bounced, swerved, then turned onto what felt like a main road. Two of her abductors had taken the front seats — she could see them through the small grille — while the other two must have had their own transportation. She was alone in the back of the van.

Alone with her purse.

There were no windows, no way to get anyone's attention. And no one to watch her retrieve the panic button that would signal the Secret Service and send them rushing to rescue her.

She inched her way toward the purse, only to have the van take another corner, causing the bag to go sliding out of reach. Two more slip-slides across the dirty metal floor and she was within reaching distance of her purse . . . except for the small problem of her hands tied behind her back. Could she open the zipper with her teeth? Probably not with the gag in place.

Darcy had done her best to stay focused in the moment. If she anchored herself in the now, the terror wasn't so bad. She could function. But if she allowed herself to think about what they could do to her, how it was national policy to never negotiate with terrorists, then fear would explode inside of her, making her want to scream and beg, despite the tape across her mouth.

No! She wouldn't go there. She wouldn't give in. She was strong and determined, and by God, she would get her panic button and push it until dozens of armed agents came storming through the walls of the van.

She didn't have much choice. Drew had been assigned to her long enough to know that the "trying on" part of a shopping trip could take at least an hour, which meant he wouldn't notice she was missing until the van had enough time to cross a couple of state lines.

If only it wasn't so hot, she thought as she went to work on the zipper. August in D.C. maintained the average temperature of a blast furnace with plenty of humidity thrown in for good measure. The front of the van might have AC, but here in the prison part of the vehicle, no such luck.

She ignored the heat, the sweat, the scrapes and bruises, and bent over her purse. Several more turns, some speeding and three failed attempts later, Darcy had discovered she could *not* open the damn zipper with her teeth. Which left her to scoot the purse into a corner, turn her back, and try to open it that way.

Easier said than done, she thought as she discovered she couldn't even hold on to the purse, although she did a lovely job of scraping her arm and banging her head. Why did this stuff always look so easy in the movies?

She tried again, carefully lodging the purse against the wheel well, then rolling onto her back and grabbing for the bag with her fingers. This time she got it and turned it slowly until she felt the zipper.

*Don't make a turn, don't make a turn,* she chanted silently, knowing if they did, she would slide across the van and have to start all over again.

The vehicle stayed mercifully straight.

Inch by inch she pulled the zipper down. Sweat poured down her back and made her fingers damp. Her bare legs stuck to the floor of the van and to whatever crumbs and icky things were scattered there. At last the purse was open. She plunged both hands inside and felt around for the familiar plastic case. Lipstick, wallet, cell phone, pen —

Cell phone? Nearly as good as the panic button. She would have to dial, of course, but she could call the operator and asked to be put through to her father. She could —

Darcy swore. Right. The tape across her mouth would make it difficult to hold a conversation. Back to digging for the panic button.

At that exact moment, the van suddenly came to a stop. Both she and her purse went sliding, although not at the same rate of speed. She had no way to get back to it before the bad guys opened the rear door to find her sprawled in a corner, her skirt up to her waist and the contents of her purse spread all over the floor of the van.

"You didn't take her handbag?" one of the guys asked the other. "Goddamn it, Bill, I thought you were smarter than that."

The recipient of the scolding, a smallish man in a vampire mask, stiffened. "You used my name. Now she knows my name."

The other one, demon-guy, snorted. "Yeah, because there's only one guy named Bill in the whole country. Come on, Einstein, let's get her inside."

Darcy tried to scramble away from her kidnappers, but as she was already in a back corner of the van, there was nowhere else to go. They half carried, half dragged her into what looked like a large warehouse.

She did her best to fight, lashing out at them with her feet. The action caused them to hold on tighter to her upper arms and made her break a heel on her new sandals.

Now she was mad, she thought as they put her into a straight-back chair and began tying her down. They'd screwed with her day, bruised her, thrown her around the inside of a disgusting van, scratched her new leather bag, and ruined the black sandals she'd just bought after waiting four weeks for them to go on sale. There was going to be hell to pay.

She told them so, although the tape on her mouth interfered with the intensity of her message.

"I don't think she likes us," Bill said, stepping back as she tried to kick his shin.

"Gee, I wonder why. Most people love a good kidnapping."

With that, the two men walked off. Darcy tried to hold on to her anger by reminding herself how much the sandals had cost, even on clearance, and how little money she had coming in these days. It worked for nearly a minute, then the fear set in. What were they going to do to her?

She told herself that torture was unlikely. Either they wanted money or something they thought they could only get from the president of the United States. Unfortunately that was a big pool of possibilities, everything from sovereignty to nuclear weapons.

Then there was the matter of the no-negotiation policy. The one that told her she could be stuck here for a very long time, and then she could be killed.

Darcy might not love everything about her life at this moment in time, but she wasn't ready for it to be over. Terror tightened her throat and made it impossible to breathe.

She had the sudden thought that she was going to throw up.

Stay calm, she told herself. If she vomited, she could drown in a really gross way. She had to find her Zen center. Not that she'd ever studied Zen, but she could imagine what it was like. A tranquil place. A place where reality was an illusion and all that mattered was the slow, steady beating of her heart.

Deep breaths, she told herself. In and out. No hurry in the air department. Just nice slow —

"Did you hurt her?"

The question came from somewhere behind her as she heard several people approaching. Panic joined fear as she tried to figure out if, in this man's opinion, hurting her would be a plus or not.

"She got banged up in the back of the van," Bill said. "But that's all."

She looked around for some kind of escape. But the huge, empty warehouse didn't offer any places to hide, and being tied to a large, heavy chair limited her options. She tried to scoot and only succeeded in wrenching her back.

"Good. We don't want any unnecessary bloodshed."

Darcy exhaled in relief. Speaking as the

kidnappee, she was delighted to know that bloodshed was to be avoided until necessary. Not that she wanted to know what would be considered necessary.

Their footsteps got closer, then three men were standing in front of her. She recognized her two kidnappers, who stood with a new guy, also in a demon mask. He was taller than the other two, and stronger. Something he proved when he turned on the non-Bill one and grabbed him by the throat.

"What the hell were you thinking?" he demanded, shaking the smaller man like a dog shakes something tasty just before he kills it.

Bill danced from foot to foot, although he didn't rush in to help his friend. "We got her, boss. Just like you said. The president's daughter. This is her."

The leader released non-Bill and curled his hands into fists. He stared at Darcy through the slits of the mask and growled.

"Not *this* one, you idiot. The other one. Lauren. No one cares about this one."

Less than thirty minutes later the van came to a stop. Darcy was still too stunned to react, even as the rear doors opened and the two men reached in to pull her out. One of them cut the bindings on her wrists while the other collected her purse and tossed it on the ground next to her. The broken sandal followed. Then they ran back to the front of the van, jumped inside, and sped away.

She had enough functioning brain left to look for a license plate — there wasn't one — and to note the color and make of the van. Then she sank down on the curb of the deserted loading area at the rear of the mall and rested her filthy arms on her scraped and bloodied knees and her head on her arms.

This hadn't happened, she told herself, even as the truth of it settled around her like a hot, sticky fog. She'd been rejected by kidnappers, which made the event a new high in a lifetime of lows.

Talk about a photo opportunity, she thought grimly. Here she was, battered, bruised, cut up, scraped. Her clothes were dirty and torn, her shoes broken, and she'd just been tossed aside like a used tissue.

Darcy straightened, pulled the tape off her mouth, then gasped as skin tore with the adhesive. That wasn't going to be pretty as it healed. She felt around on the cement until she found her purse and pulled out the panic button. Better late than never, she thought as she pressed down on the bright red button and waited for the cavalry.

Lieutenant Commander Joe Larson had always considered the admiral a reasonable, if distant, commanding officer. All that had changed at 9:18 the previous evening. The admiral wanted someone's head on a stick, and he was gunning for Joe's.

"What kind of half-assed, goddamn asshole . . ."

The tirade continued, but Joe didn't bother listening as his captain got reamed. He could figure out the highlights without hearing them. Besides, the captain would be passing them along personally to Joe soon enough.

Such was the chain of command. The admiral chewed out the captain, the captain chewed out him, and he, well, Joe hadn't decided what he was going to do. Like they said — shit rolled downhill.

He crossed to the window of the office foyer and stared at the activity below. There was plenty of it at the Naval Amphibious Base. And just beyond the building, the Pacific Ocean sparkled in the bright summer morning. Other careers might offer better pay, but none could beat the location on Coronado Island.

Given the admiral's temper, there was

every chance Joe could soon be exploring those other careers. Or stationed on a naval base in Greenland. Screwups came in all shapes and sizes. This one had all the potential firepower of an aircraft carrier. Explaining to the captain that it hadn't been his fault wasn't going to change a damn thing.

Fifteen minutes later, the door to the captain's office opened and the admiral stormed out. Joe stood at attention as the angry man stalked by, then he looked at his commanding officer.

"Come on in, Joe," the other man said in a weary voice.

Joe entered then closed the door behind him. "Sir."

Captain Phillips waved to the empty chair in front of his desk. "You hear all that?"

"Yes, sir."

Phillips, a tall man in his early forties, sighed. "He loved that boat."

Joe didn't respond. The information wasn't news. The admiral had been restoring his nearly eighty-year-old boat for the past five years. The engine was new, and the electronics state-of-the-art, but the rest of it was original, lovingly sanded and varnished by the admiral's own hand.

The man's wife had left him, claiming she

refused to come in second to a floating hunk of wood, and his children rarely visited, knowing they would be put to work on the boat. Six months ago the admiral had decided to live aboard.

Then, last night, at 9:18, the admiral's pride and joy had been accidentally blown up by men under Joe's command. They were lucky the admiral hadn't been on board at the time.

"Want to tell me what happened?" the captain asked.

Joe shrugged. "The team was celebrating being back," he said. The Navy SEAL team in question had just returned from six months of hazardous duty out of the country. "They'd all made it out alive. Even Grayson."

"How's he doing?" the captain asked.

"Lieutenant Grayson is still in the hospital, sir. He's recovering from his injuries."

Grayson had been shot on their last op. His men had brought him back and kept him alive until he'd been evacuated to the hospital ship, then brought back home.

Joe remained perfectly still as he continued. "I spoke with the men on the team yesterday afternoon. They'd had six missions back to back, with minimal downtime in between. I suggested they burn off some steam."

Phillips nodded. "They decided on boat races."

"Yes, sir." Made sense. To a SEAL, the water was a second home. "They used small boats and kept within the marina speed limit." Sort of. "Unfortunately their racing course took them over a BUDS training exercise."

The future SEALs had been in their second round of training, learning to dive and work with explosives underwater.

"Last night the explosives were live. Apparently the movement of the boats racing overhead confused a few of the trainees. They're not allowed to surface to get their bearings. Instead of putting their explosives on the target, they placed them on the admiral's boat."

Talk about plain bad luck, Joe thought grimly. "The explosives were small and shouldn't have caused much damage. Unfortunately the admiral had recently refueled his craft. There was a small leak in the engine. When the explosive went off, it triggered a chain reaction that turned the admiral's pride and joy into kindling. At least that's the preliminary report."

Captain Phillips didn't speak for several

seconds. "Aren't you going to tell me that the admiral tied up in a restricted area? That he shouldn't have been there in the first place?"

"No, sir." What was the point? Joe had been in the navy long enough to know excuses only made the situation worse. Besides, who would have told an admiral to move his boat?

"You have a great career," his captain told him. "You've worked hard, moved up the ranks. I was confident you'd make it to admiral yourself, before you retired."

Joe had walked into some of the most dangerous situations in the world and lived to tell the tale, but nothing he'd experienced prepared him for the sense of fury that gripped him as he sat there and heard his career talked about in the past tense. The navy was all he knew, all he'd ever wanted.

He'd told the men to go have fun. It was *his* responsibility. Technically, he could pass the punishment on down, but next in line was Lieutenant Grayson, currently missing most of his right leg and facing a long road to recovery.

No. This time the chain of command stopped here. With Joe.

Phillips flipped open a file. "You've been with the SEALs nearly ten years, Joe. You're a fine officer and one of the best men I've ever worked with. The admiral wants you punished, and I want to save your career if I can."

"Thank you, sir," Joe said, feeling the first hint of relief.

The captain smiled. "You might want to hold off on your thanks. The best way I know to punish you is to temporarily re-assign you to a special project that has nothing to do with the SEALs. The best way I know to save your ass is to get you the hell out of here for a few weeks and let the admiral cool down. As an interesting point of fact, my brother-in-law is fairly high up the chain of command in the Secret Service. I don't think you knew that."

"No, sir," Joe said, not sure what the information had to do with anything.

"You've mentioned you have family here in California," Phillips said. "The Marcellis. They own a winery just north of Santa Barbara?"

"Yes, sir." Joe had no idea what was going on, but he didn't like it. Technically he was related to the Marcelli clan, but they weren't his family.

"What you don't know," the captain said, "is that the president's daughter was kidnapped yesterday."

Joe stiffened as he pictured the attractive, curvy blonde who frequently served as the president's hostess. "Lauren?"

"No. The other one. Darcy. Apparently they grabbed her by mistake — Lauren was their actual target."

"How could they screw that up?" Joe asked. Darcy was nothing like her sister in looks or temperament.

"No one knows. The point is, both women are being taken out of Washington and sent to different locations. Safe houses, if you will. They'll have their usual Secret Service protection, but until the kidnappers are caught, they need to lay low. This is all confidential, Joe. You aren't to discuss this information with anyone."

"Of course not, sir." Joe had no problem keeping quiet. What he didn't understand was what any of it had to do with him.

Captain Phillips leaned forward. "There is some concern about Darcy. She's not generally cooperative, and frankly no one wants to be locked up in a safe house with her. The thought is if she can be kept safe but still have a semblance of a life, it will be easier for all concerned. Basically a place that is isolated but not solitary. I thought of what you've told me about your family's winery. There's a large house, plenty of room for the team and Darcy. I wasn't sure how I was going to convince you to take this assignment. After last night, I don't have to."

Joe put the rest of the pieces together and didn't like the finished picture. That was to be his punishment. To babysit the president's daughter *and* spend time with the Marcellis.

"I have a SEAL team heading out in two months," he said. "There's important work to be done."

"Someone else can take care of that, Joe. Right now the president's daughter is your responsibility."

"Sir, sending her to the hacienda is an interesting solution," he said, "but the winery is not easily guarded. There are hundreds of acres, employees, staff. Plus my relatives would have to be cleared for security purposes."

"Already done. You're right about the winery being an open space, but who would think to look for her there? The navy is cooperating with the president at his request," Phillips told him. "Unless you want to call the president and explain why you're unwilling to protect his daughter?"

Joe felt the doors of the prison swing closed. "What is my assignment, sir?"

"Coordinate with the Secret Service. Their job is to protect Darcy, but you are to facilitate what they need. Be another pair of eyes. Use your tactical skills to their advantage. When the kidnappers are caught, you'll return here and we'll see if the admiral has cooled off enough for you to resume your duties. In the meantime, do what you can to keep Darcy Jensen happy."

Joe rose and saluted. "Yes, sir," he said and left.

He was completely and totally screwed, sent away in disgrace, his career in jeopardy. He would be lucky to come back as an ensign.

As for keeping Darcy Jensen happy — from what he'd heard, that was a task even a SEAL couldn't pull off.

## 2

Darcy heard the murmurings of her temporary Secret Service team before she heard the knock on the door. The whispered "Swan is here" warned her of her sister's approach.

She stayed in her apartment bedroom, one of the guys in suits would get the door, and continued her packing. In less than four hours she would be whisked away to an undisclosed location for however long it took to find the crazies after her sister. Based on the Secret Service's current level of competency, she could be gone for months.

Not knowing where she was headed made packing a problem. All she knew was she was staying in the continental United States and that she was expected to stay very low-key when she arrived.

News flash — she didn't want to walk around flaunting herself. One kidnapping in a lifetime was more than enough.

She grabbed a handful of shorts, some T-shirts and jeans, and tossed them on the bed.

The bedroom door opened and Lauren entered. The two Secret Service agents with her hovered in the hall then nodded at the single agent standing in the corner of Darcy's bedroom.

Lauren crossed to Darcy, grabbed her upper arms, and stared into her eyes.

"Are you okay?" she asked, sounding near tears. "Did they hurt you?"

Darcy had a few bruises from her ride in the back of the van, some sore muscles, and several raw spots around her wrists from the ropes. She hadn't slept at all the previous night and couldn't imagine ever not feeling afraid again. But the agent in the room kept her from saying all that.

"I'm fine," she said.

Lauren didn't release her. "Are you sure? I was so worried."

A change, Darcy thought. In the past year, *she'd* been the one worried about Lauren.

"If anything had happened to you . . . ," Lauren said, those threatening tears finally making an appearance. "I couldn't stand to lose one more person I love."

Darcy appreciated the sentiment, knew it

was true, and told herself neither of them had time for a breakdown. Lauren had finally surfaced from the emotional devastation of the shocking death of her young husband, and Darcy refused to let her sink back into despair over a botched kidnapping. Darcy might be hearing things go bump in the night, but she refused to let her sister be afraid.

She drew in a deep breath as she took in Lauren's outfit. The aqua and pink sundress just grazed generous curves in unwrinkled perfection. Delicate pearls graced her sister's tiny ears. Her sling backs matched her purse, and a narrow woven silver and pearl bracelet completed the ensemble. She wore her long, wavy blond hair pulled back in an elegant clasp. She would fit in equally well having lunch at the club or hosting an afternoon charity event.

"Why do you always have to dress like an Easter egg?" Darcy asked. "Do you own anything in a primary color? I know you could never wear black. How scandalous. The heavens would open and weep."

Lauren's intense gaze never wavered. "At least I don't dress like a former rock groupie in mourning. Does every single outfit have to be tone-on-tone black? It's summer, for heaven's sake. Lighten up and wear a color."

Darcy felt the corners of her mouth turn up slightly. Lauren began to giggle. Laughter escaped, and then they were hugging each other tight. Darcy hung on tighter than usual.

"When they told me what happened, I nearly died," Lauren whispered in her ear. "I'm so sorry. I wish it had been me."

Darcy straightened. "No, you don't. Trust me on that."

"But they wanted me instead of you."

"Don't they all. That's the world in which we live. I've gotten used to it."

"Darcy, don't." Lauren sighed. "I feel horrible."

"Don't. Do you know where they're taking you?" she asked.

"No. You?"

"I want to be safe. Something I'm not sure the moron brigade can do."

Lauren shot the agent in the room an apologetic glance then turned on her sister. "Darcy, no. You can't be mad at your team."

"Why not? If they'd been doing their job, I wouldn't have been taken." From the corner of her eye she saw the agent flinch. Well, too bad. If they'd been doing their job, she would never have realized that she was at risk.

She'd had Secret Service protection for

years and had never considered it more than an annoyance. She'd always known that she and Lauren were technically possible targets, but she'd felt safe surrounded by the grim-faced agents. Not anymore.

"It's not completely their fault," Lauren said. "No one was expecting you to be kidnapped."

Darcy snorted. "It's their job to expect the unexpected. They're professionals."

"I know, but they didn't mean for anything bad to happen to you."

"Oh. They didn't *mean* it. Then that makes it all right."

Lauren might technically be the firstborn, but she had the personality of a middle child — always seeing the other person's side of things. It was a trait Darcy found annoying on occasion, even as she admired it.

"Darcy . . . ," her sister began.

Darcy waved her off. "Don't sweat it. They'll be on their toes now. That's what matters. So we'll head off to our separate but equal locations and wait for the crazies to be caught."

And then what? She'd tried to live a normal life, but it was impossible while her father was in office.

"There was so much to cancel," Lauren

said. "I had two benefits, and I was going to be at a state dinner." She frowned. "Weren't you flying to New York?"

"Yeah." Darcy didn't want to think about that either.

Lauren groaned. "Your interview. When is it?"

"Monday."

Being the president's daughter put her in the unique position of being unemployable in her chosen field. She was a graphic artist with a master's in marketing. But, as the dozens of companies she'd applied to over the past couple of years had told her, no client wanted to turn down a presentation by someone so close to the president. It could be very bad for business. Rather than put their clients in such an awkward position, she'd been passed over time and again.

A small firm in New York *had* been willing to take a chance on her. Now she was unlikely to make her second interview, and telling them why wasn't going to make them want to hire her.

"Maybe if you explained," Lauren said, looking so earnest Darcy actually laughed.

"What? That I was recently kidnapped and have to lay low until the culprits are found? I don't think that will win me employee of the month."

Lauren sighed. "I know this life is hard for you."

"And I know you love it," Darcy said without rancor. It was true — public life suited her sister. Lauren was never happier than when she was cutting a ribbon at some hospital wing opening, or serving as their father's hostess for a formal dinner for three hundred. Darcy would rather be staked naked in the desert on top of a nest of fire ants.

"I'll be fine," she said before tender-hearted Lauren started to cry again. "Don't worry about it. Have you met your new security team?" she asked, to change the subject to something more neutral.

"No. Have you?"

"Just one of them. Alex Vanmeter. He's downstairs. He looks competent, but I'll be grilling him later to make sure he knows what he's doing."

Lauren stared at her. "The incredibly hunky guy who looks like a street fighter? I'm sure he'll keep you safe."

"I wish I was sure." Darcy shook her head. "You know, I'm actually *not* interested in his looks right now. He could be a troll, as long as he's a troll who knows what he's doing."

She crossed to her dresser and pulled out

bras and panties, then tucked them into the suitcase. She'd already packed up her art supplies and her laptop.

Lauren walked to the window and stared down at the Secret Service team below. "What happened to the two guys assigned to you?" she asked.

"I don't have a clue." Darcy didn't think they were in a good place for having lost her. "Don't worry. I doubt they were taken out back and shot." Although in her mind, they more than deserved a good beating. Or maybe a kidnapping. Let them feel what she'd experienced. Toss them in the back of a filthy van driven by demon-headed guys named Bill and force them to open a purse with their teeth.

"Don't even joke about that," Lauren said. "I feel bad for them. And you, of course."

"Of course. Doesn't seeing both sides ever make you tired?"

Lauren rolled her eyes. "Desperately. I mostly do it to make you crazy."

Darcy grinned. "You usually succeed."

"I'm glad." Lauren turned serious. "You'll be all right, won't you?"

Darcy figured that in time she would be able to sleep and the flashes of terror would recede. Until then, she would simply fake her way through it. That had always worked for her before. "I promise."

"I guess we'll be able to talk by phone on secure lines. I want to hear about everything."

"Me, too."

Lauren moved close, and they hugged again. "I love you," her sister whispered.

"I love you, too. Be good."

"That's my line," Lauren said as she stepped back and waved.

Darcy watched her go then turned back to her packing. For the moment, the fear was gone, but in its place was a dark and lonely space.

Joe arrived at the Marcelli winery shortly after four in the afternoon. He'd put off leaving as long as he could, which had meant all of the morning, but he'd known better than to linger much past noon. He might be entering hell on earth, but he was still a naval officer. His job was to follow orders.

As he turned onto the road that led to the three-story hacienda, he studied the pale yellow stucco structure as he might an enemy target, or a place he would have to defend.

Too many windows and exits, he thought grimly as he took in the French doors leading to balconies and the decorative wrought iron that would allow someone in reasonable shape to climb from flower beds to the tile roof. Trees that others would think provided comfortable shade in the August heat showed him places snipers could hide.

Beyond the house was a multicar garage that could conceal at least fifty armed men, and less than a quarter mile beyond that were the various buildings of the winery.

Perfect, he thought grimly as he pulled his truck up behind the house and turned off the engine. Maybe someone could call in one of those entertainment networks to announce Darcy Jensen's location to add to the challenge.

The rear door of the house opened, and a man stepped onto the porch. Joe recognized Marco Marcelli, his biological father.

"Joe! You're here."

Marco hurried to the truck and met Joe as he closed the driver's door behind him.

Marco studied him for a second before wrapping both arms around Joe in a welcoming hug. Joe accepted the embrace — to do otherwise would invite conversations he didn't want to have, then when he was free, he stepped back and glanced around.

"A lot of grapes," he said, motioning to the vines heavy with fruit.

"A good year," Marco said. "Brenna and Grandpa Lorenzo are excited about the harvest. More wine means more excuses for Colleen and me to travel as we sell the wine. I'm not complaining."

Joe nodded, as if the information had meaning. The Marcellis *were* wine. Marco's children were the fourth generation to grow grapes on this stretch of land. He and his wife, Colleen, were responsible for sales.

Marco patted the side of the truck. "You usually travel light."

"I don't know how long I'm going to be here," Joe said, wishing that wasn't the case. "I couldn't fit everything on my motorcycle, so I rented the truck."

"They haven't told us much," Marco told him. "But several people from the government have been all over the property and have spoken with everyone in the family. They picked you to help."

Joe heard the pride in Marco's voice and thought about telling him that the only reason any of this was happening was because Joe's men had screwed up.

"I thought I'd brief everyone at once," Joe said. "I guess we should do that first, before I unpack."

Marco patted his shoulder. "It's good that you're staying here for a while, Joe. We want

. . .” The older man hesitated. “We're help-ing because of you.”

Joe knew what he was trying to do — show that the family would be there for him. Marco, like every other Marcelli, had spent the past three years doing his best to con-vince Joe he was one of them.

Joe knew different. He might share blood-lines, but they had nothing else in common, and they would never be his family.

“Tessa made up your room,” Marco said.

“I appreciate that.” He looked at the man who thought of himself as Joe's father. “You know this is temporary. I'm only staying until the job is done.”

Marco nodded. “Of course. You're still a navy man.”

The back door opened again. A small, elderly woman with gray hair piled on her head walked onto the porch. “Joseph? Is that you? So that's what they're teaching of-ficers these days? That it's polite to keep an old woman waiting?”

Despite his dislike of the assignment and the pressure he felt being back at the winery, Joe couldn't help smiling as he crossed to the house and climbed the three back stairs.

“No, Tessa, that's not what they teach me,” he said as he bent down to gather her close. Too late he remembered her need to pinch every cheek in range. Her forefinger and thumb closed over his skin with enough strength to snap steel. He might have survived a gunshot wound and a couple of knife fights, but man, could she make him wince.

"Let me look at you," she said, grabbing him by the hand and dragging him into the kitchen. "The government has sent people here. They talk to us and ask questions. They say we need clearance, but they won't say for what." She humphed. "As if we would be a danger to anyone. Now."

She stopped in the center of the kitchen and studied him from head to toe. Her dark eyes missed nothing as she frowned and poked him in the stomach. "You're not eating enough. You look skinny."

"I weigh exactly the same as I did the last time I was here," he told her.

"You were too skinny then, too. All that exercise. It's not good for you. I'm going to feed you while you're here. You'll eat good food. What do you have at the place you live? Junk food? A man your age on his own. It's not a good thing." Her expression softened as she took his hand in hers and rubbed his fingers. "Joseph, you need to be married, eh? A wife would know how to take care of you."

It was a familiar conversation, one he refused to participate in. "Who else is at the hacienda?" he asked.

Grandma Tessa narrowed her gaze. "Your mother and Lorenzo. They'll be here in a few minutes. So what is this all about?"

Just then Colleen Marcelli walked into the kitchen. She was a well-dressed, petite woman a year or so shy of fifty. Her stylish clothes and unlined face made her look much younger, but Joe could do the math. He'd just turned thirty-three, which meant Colleen had had him when she was still in high school.

"Joe," she breathed when she saw him. Her expression blended hope and longing in a painful combination. He could deal with the rest of them, but seeing Colleen always made him feel guilty. He couldn't shake the sense of being a real bastard every time he held her at arm's length. He knew what she wanted — what they all wanted.

Rather than deal with the guilt, he stepped forward and hugged her. Before he straightened, Lorenzo Marcelli, the aging patriarch, strolled into the kitchen.

"So, you're back," the elder Marcelli growled. "They're snooping around here like we're a bunch of terrorists. Send them away."

"Not in my job description," Joe said as he released his mother and shook hands with Marco's father. "You're looking well."

"I'm old," Lorenzo said. "This is all a bunch of nonsense."

"Pop, it's not so bad," Marco said.

"You don't even know what's going on," Lorenzo complained. "None of us do. If those agents trample even one grape, there will be hell to pay."

"Lorenzo!" Tessa reached into her apron pocket and pulled out a rosary. "Don't say that."

"It's true." Lorenzo thumped the cane he'd started using about a year ago and made his way to the large kitchen table in the center of the room. "Well, get on with it. Tell us why we've been taken over like an enemy country."

Joe nodded at Marco, who led Colleen and Tessa to chairs by Lorenzo's. When they were seated, he began.

"What I'm about to tell you is classified information. You are not to discuss it with anyone outside of the immediate family."

Tessa reached for Lorenzo's hand, and Colleen shivered. "That sounds so serious," she said nervously.

"It is," he told her. "Two days ago the president's daughter was kidnapped. She got away, but the kidnappers are still out there."

Tessa gasped and clutched her beads tighter. "Who would do that? She's a lovely girl. So pretty and always helping with those little children."

Colleen nodded. "It was so sad when she lost her husband. Their wedding was so beautiful. They'd barely been married a year when he was killed in that car accident. She got so sad afterward." She reached for Marco. "I can't imagine what she must have gone through, missing him so much."

Lorenzo frowned. "What does this have to do with us? What do we care about his daughter?"

"Lorenzo!" Tessa glared at him. "We care. Lauren Jensen-Smith is a lovely girl." She turned her attention to Joe. "How can we help?" Even as she asked the question, her breath caught. "Oh! Is she coming here?"

"Not exactly," Joe said, wondering why they'd done the same thing he had — jumped to the conclusion that it was Lauren who was in trouble and not Darcy.

"You'll have the president's daughter here, but it won't be Lauren," he said. "It will be the other one. Darcy."

There was a moment of silence. Colleen released her husband's arm and smoothed down her skirt. "I'm sure she's very nice, too."

"That other one?" Lorenzo asked. "I don't know anything about her. Except she never bothered to get married and have babies to make her family proud."

With that he pushed to his feet and used his cane to help him turn. "This is all a waste of time if you ask me," he grumbled as he slowly limped out of the room.

Tessa rose as well. "Are you sure they're not sending Lauren? A nice, pretty girl like that needs to be married." She smiled at him. "Maybe to an officer."

Joe held in a groan. Right. Because his life wasn't hellish enough already. Fortunately a knock on the back door prevented him from responding. He crossed the kitchen and opened it.

"Lieutenant Commander Joseph Larson?" the woman on the other side asked.

He nodded.

"I'm Special Agent Paige Newberry. I saw you arrive and thought I would introduce myself to you and meet the family."

She stepped inside and shook his hand. Paige was tall, only a couple of inches shorter than his own six feet. She wore a dark pants suit and a concealed sidearm. Short hair framed attractive features.

He was used to judging people in a matter of seconds. Joe's first impression of Special Agent Newberry was that she was intelligent, competent, and ready to play on a team. Thank God he wasn't in this alone.

Joe had been briefed early that morning. While the Secret Service was in charge of Darcy and her protection, Joe was there to act as liaison with the family and to offer any expertise the Secret Service might require. As he doubted they wanted or needed his help, he was little more than a glorified babysitter. None of which was the agent's fault.

Joe led her into the kitchen.

"This is Special Agent Paige Newberry," he said. "She's in charge of Darcy Jensen's personal security."

"Actually Special Agent Alex Vanmeter is in charge of this operation," Paige said with a smile. "He's with Darcy right now. They'll be arriving in the morning. I am, however, one of the agents who will be in close contact with Darcy at all times."

Tessa nodded. "You call her by her first name?"

"Yes, ma'am. At her request."

"This is Tessa Marcelli," Joe said by way

of introduction. "Marco Marcelli and his wife, Colleen."

Paige shook hands with all of them. Colleen moved to the ever-present coffeepot and began to pour. "This is really difficult to take in. The president's daughter. Here. What are we supposed to do? How do we act? What do *we* call her?"

Paige smiled. "I think she'd like Darcy best. In fact I would prefer that you use first names with all of us. That way we don't call attention to ourselves."

Colleen looked at her dark suit. "I don't mean to be rude, but you're not exactly fitting in with the locals."

"I know. I brought more casual clothes with me. I thought I'd wait until Special Agent Vanmeter arrives before changing."

Joe stared at Paige. There was something about the way she said "Special Agent Vanmeter." He couldn't put his finger on the inflection, but he would bet it meant something.

"You've worked with him before?" he asked.

Paige nodded. "He's excellent. Very thorough. Darcy will be safe, as will your family, Lieutenant Commander."

"We agreed on first names," Joe said.

"Of course."

Tessa began pulling food out of the refrigerator. "Sit. Sit. You need to eat. Marco, bring Paige some wine."

"Oh, no thanks. I can't drink on duty."

Tessa waved away her words. "You said Darcy won't arrive until the morning. Be on duty then."

Joe led her to the table and sat across from her. In a matter of seconds, seemingly from nowhere, food appeared. Salads, fixings for sandwiches, three kinds of cookies, bread, cheese, and of course pasta. He was used to the quantity of the spread, but Paige looked stunned.

Joe grinned. "You'd better eat, or they'll get surly."

"Of course you'll eat," Tessa said as she set wineglasses in front of them. "So, Paige, are you married?"

Thirty minutes later, Paige and Joe escaped the clutches of Grandma Tessa, as she'd insisted on being called, and stepped out in the sunset. Paige had enjoyed the home-cooked food, even if it came with a pretty big side of matchmaking.

"Interesting family," she said.

"She's determined to get me married," Joe said flatly.

"Yet you've stood strong against her all

these years. Impressive."

He shrugged then glanced around at the vineyards, which stretched for miles.

"Do you really think you can protect Darcy Jensen here?" he asked.

Paige wasn't sure if his question was simple conversation or a genuine concern. "The location is a compromise, but I think it's a good one. Who knows how long it will take to track down the kidnappers? I understand Darcy's need to be in a place where she won't get claustrophobic."

"Better claustrophobic than dead."

"Agreed, but we're going to keep her alive." She walked toward the guesthouse, which would serve as both her sleeping quarters and temporary headquarters. "Darcy will be kept close to the house for the first few days. We'll have agents in the tasting rooms and other tourist areas to keep them from getting anywhere near the hacienda. I've already spoken with Brenna Marcelli about that. She was more than cooperative." She glanced at the naval officer at her side. "Your sister?"

"One of four," Joe said. "She runs this winery, along with a smaller one. Her husband owns Wild Sea."

"Right." Paige remembered her briefing notes and the interview she'd had the previous day. "Nic Giovanni. He's cooperating as well. In fact everyone has been more than helpful."

"Lucky us."

She turned to Joe. He was tall, good-looking, and had a service record that would make anyone proud. But she would bet her next three paychecks he didn't want to be here.

"You're acting as our liaison with the family," she said. "We appreciate that."

"I live to serve."

The fine hairs on the back of her neck rose. She felt like an angry cat trying to puff up to look more intimidating. She might be a hell of an agent, but Joe Marcelli had been a SEAL. In a one-on-one situation, she didn't stand a chance. Still, that wouldn't stop her from taking him on.

"Lieutenant Commander Larson," she said, keeping her voice steady and firm, "I cannot stress the importance of this assignment enough. We are protecting the life of the daughter of the president of the United States. Two days ago someone got close enough to abduct her. She was forcibly taken, tied up, and threatened. Do you think there was even one moment in her life that prepared her for that kind of terror?"

Joe didn't look much more than bored

with the conversation. "I'm a naval officer, Special Agent Newberry. I'll do my job."

"Not good enough. I'm willing to take a bullet for her. If you can't offer that same level of commitment, I don't want you here."

"You don't have the authority to get rid of me."

She leaned in slightly. "Want to test that theory? Nothing is going to happen to Darcy Jensen on my watch. I don't care what I have to do or who I have to offend to keep her safe. If you're not fully on this team, then you're in my way. Do I make myself clear?"

His expression didn't change, but she saw something flash in his eyes. Respect, maybe. However grudgingly given, she would accept it.

"You like her," he said, sounding surprised.

"I do. I've worked with Darcy before. She's funny, smart, and not interested in being the center of attention. That makes my job easier, and I appreciate that. So are you on board?"

He nodded. "A hundred percent."

Paige accepted his word because she had to, but she vowed to keep an eye on him. SEAL or not — if he got in her way, she was taking him down.

Darcy had spent the previous night in a small house on the edge of Baltimore. This morning, after a short flight to Florida, she'd been delivered to another nondescript location on the edge of what looked like a massive swamp. She'd been warned not to leave the house, not to make phone calls, and not to answer the door under any circumstances.

Oh, right. Because she *wanted* to make a general statement, announcing her location to the world.

Someone knocked on the bedroom door. Darcy refused to be seen as a coward, so she uncurled on the bed and sat up.

"Come in," she said, expecting Alex Vanmeter, the special agent in charge of her security and Drew's replacement.

Alex stepped in and nodded at her. "Your father will be here in fifteen minutes."

Darcy blinked at him. "My father? He's in Chicago."

"He's flying back to D.C. tonight and is stopping by to see you."

Before Darcy could say anything, Alex touched the ever-present earpiece and then nodded. "Falcon is on the ground."

Meaning her father had landed and was

being driven to the safe house.

She stood. As Alex excused himself, she entered the bathroom attached to the bedroom and ran a brush through her short, dark hair. She looked tired and either sick or shell-shocked. Makeup could help, but there wasn't much time.

Exactly fourteen minutes later, President Ryan Jensen walked into her temporary bedroom.

"Darcy," he said when his assigned agent had swept the room then left them alone. "How are you feeling?"

"I'm sure the doctors faxed you a medical report. You tell me."

Ryan Jensen had served as vice president for four years before running for the head job. He was eighteen months into his first term. The stresses of the office aged some men, but not her father. Oh, there were a few more gray hairs at his temples, but that only made him more attractive. Last year he'd had to deal with the embarrassing reality of being named the country's most eligible bachelor.

Right now, though, the leader of the free world looked annoyed and frustrated. "Darcy, I'm on a very tight schedule. I changed my flight plan to come by and see you. That has to mean something."

"It does, Dad. Really. I hope you're not keeping anyone important waiting. I mean it's been nearly forty-eight hours since the kidnapping. I wouldn't have wanted you to rush to my side or anything."

His gaze narrowed. "I phoned when I was informed about the kidnapping."

"You did, and it was a very touching call. Did I thank you for it? I meant to."

"You're impossible," he muttered. "Fine. Be angry with me or whomever you'd like. Regardless, I'm glad you're all right and I want you to stay safe. For once, listen to what the agents tell you to do, will you?"

The unfairness of the request took her breath away. She'd *always* listened. They were the ones who had let *her* down.

But what was the point in trying to explain anything? Ryan Jensen had stopped hearing her years ago.

"Be grateful you got away without getting hurt," he added.

Darcy thought about the still-healing scratches on her legs, the rope burns on her wrists, and the pain in her heart. There had been plenty of wounding, but it wasn't the kind he meant.

Someone knocked on the closed door. Ryan Jensen glanced toward it, then back at her. "I need to get to Washington. You'll have a secure line up and running at your safe house in a day or so. Check in and let me know how you are."

"It's what I live for," she told him.

"Dammit, Darcy." He looked at her, started to speak, then caught himself. He turned away and was gone.

When she was alone again, Darcy crawled back onto the bed and pulled her knees to her chest. He was a busy man. She should be grateful he'd diverted to Florida to see her. It could almost mean something.

But instead of convincing herself, she remembered a dark night ten years before. When he'd glared at her and yelled that she wasn't his daughter. She never had been.

Later, he'd apologized. He'd spoken in anger and grief. He hadn't meant it.

Regardless of his contrition, he'd spoken the truth. Ryan Jensen *wasn't* her father. That long-ago night the lies fell away, and his words had changed her forever.

# 3

The plane left Florida shortly after day-break, which, with the time difference, meant an early arrival in California. Darcy hadn't known their destination until an hour into the flight, when Alex Vanmeter had informed her they would be landing at a naval base north of Los Angeles.

As she stepped off the plane usually used to transport the vice president, she saw three black SUVs parked on the tarmac. Secret Service agents flanked her, making it difficult to get down the steep flight of stairs. The second her feet touched the ground, Alex moved in, took her arm, and hustled her to the middle SUV. He opened the door and slid in beside her.

"Pigeon is safe," he said into the microphone at the inside of his left wrist. "Move out."

Seconds later, all three vehicles drove away from the plane.

"At least you're taking my security seriously," she said as she gazed out the window.

"We always have."

"Really? I have a kidnapping that says, not so much."

"The other team screwed up. That won't happen on my watch."

"I really want to believe you, but you're going to have to earn my trust. If that sort of thing matters."

"It does. A comfortable subject is more likely to cooperate."

She glanced at the man sitting next to her. Late thirties, she would guess. About five ten and strong. She could see the ripple of muscles through the suit jacket he wore. There was something about him. Something not quite civilized. As if he hadn't grown up in the company of polite society.

Bad boy turned good guy? She wouldn't want to bet against him in a street fight, a thought she found comforting.

"Do you really think after what happened I'm going to be difficult?" she asked.

"You have a reputation for being a pain in the ass."

Darcy knew all about that. The press wasn't fond of her because when her father had been running for vice president, she'd traveled in the press bus as part of an internship project for one of her college classes. Instead of reporting on the campaign, she'd written an exposé on several members of the press corps, detailing who had substance-abuse problems, who was having an affair, and who had a thing for underaged campaign workers.

She also didn't play the political game very well. But she'd never screwed with her Secret Service team.

"Get back to me with exactly one time when I ducked out or escaped them," she said, holding her temper in check. "Or when I did something they told me not to do. I might have a reputation for being difficult, Alex, but I'm not stupid."

Darcy turned to look at the SUV in front of theirs. To the casual observer, their little convoy was nothing more than three vehicles on the same road. No one else would know there were a total of seven agents and one relative of the president leaving the navy base that morning.

"Where's Lauren going?" she asked.

Alex glanced at her. His dark blue eyes never wavered. "I'm not at liberty to say."

"Because I'm a security risk?"

"Because the fewer people who know, the better. You don't want anything happening to your sister."

He made it a statement rather than a question, but it was still true.

Darcy leaned back in the leather seat and wondered what would happen now. How long would she be kept isolated for her own good, and when could she get back to her regular life, such as it was? She'd already called and canceled her interview in New York. There was no way she could make it, and she wasn't allowed to explain the reason why. Normal was something the rest of the world took for granted. What she wouldn't give to be one of them, even for a little while.

Alex glanced at her. "Have you slept since the kidnapping?"

"Of course," she lied, not wanting to talk to him about it. Alex Vanmeter might be exactly the right person to keep her safe, but he wasn't the warm and friendly type. Besides, she didn't generally confide in people she'd just met. With enough concealer and the right light, she could keep her lack of sleep a secret until she was able to close her eyes without feeling the fear.

The lead SUV signaled a turn. Darcy glanced out the window and realized they were leaving the freeway and heading into what looked like a very picturesque part of Tuscany.

"They grow grapes here?" she asked as she stared at acres and acres of vineyards.

"Yes. The Marcelli family has owned this land over eighty years. Four generations of winemakers."

"Marcelli." The name was vaguely familiar. "As in Marcelli Wines?"

He nodded.

"This is where I'll be staying?" she asked.

"Yes. The family was pleased to cooperate. You should be safe here."

Darcy looked at the heavy, lush grapevines, the tall trees lining the road, and the vineyard sparkling in the distance.

"Not bad duty," she said, picturing an old-style bed-and-breakfast with a view of the ocean. No doubt she and her Secret Service team would take over a wing of the building. There wouldn't be much to do, but she could catch up on her reading. Lying low had never looked so good.

Fifteen minutes later they turned off the road and onto a long driveway. Darcy didn't see any signs for a hotel or a bed-and-breakfast. Instead she saw what looked like a large, pale yellow, three-story house decorated with wrought iron balconies. There were several outbuildings, plenty of trees, and a colorful garden complete with a path and small benches.

"What's with the house?" she asked as the SUV pulled to a stop.

"The Marcelli family has lived here since it was built in the late twenties," Alex said.

They must own the B and B, too. Made sense.

Alex stepped out of the SUV and waited for her to do the same. Darcy climbed out and looked around. The air was still and warm, scented with fruit. Make that grapes, she thought as the back door opened and several people hurried down the stairs to the driveway.

There was an older couple, a not so old couple, an amazingly good-looking guy, some Secret Service agents — easily recognizable by the sunglasses and the dark suits — and Special Agent Paige Newberry.

"Paige," Darcy said, grateful to see at least one familiar face. "At least one person here knows what she's doing."

"Hi, Darcy." Paige stepped forward and smiled. "How was your trip?"

"Good. Long."

Darcy was conscious of everyone watching her. She smoothed the front of her casual black and white sundress. Aware that first impressions mattered, she'd dressed carefully, using makeup, putting on sandals, and digging out another of her bargain handbags that matched.

She knew her sister would have had something disarming to say, and that in a matter of minutes the entire cast of the Make Room for Lauren ensemble would have been delighted to be a part of her life. Darcy hadn't received the gift of small talk. Still, she would play the professional political family member, even if she wasn't that good at it.

"Good morning," she said, telling herself to smile to cover her nervousness as she spoke. "I'm Darcy Jensen."

"Of course you are," the older man said as he thumped his cane on the ground. "This is all a bunch of nonsense if you ask me. She's here. We're here. Now let's get inside before someone gets sunstroke."

"Lorenzo!" The elderly woman at his side scolded him. "She's the president's daughter. Show a little respect."

Paige stepped between them. "Darcy, allow me to present Mr. and Mrs. Lorenzo Marcelli. They own the winery and all the property here." Paige pointed to the slightly younger couple. "This is their son, Marco, and his wife, Colleen. And Lieutenant Commander Joe Larson." Paige hesitated. "He's a former SEAL and our naval liaison with the family."

"Because I'm in danger of being kidnapped and taken out to sea?" Darcy asked. "That's comforting. Be sure someone stocks me up with Dramamine. Any other surprises?"

"That's not why I'm here —" the lieutenant commander said, but he was interrupted when Mrs. Marcelli senior stepped forward.

"I'm Tessa," she said with a smile. "You should call me Grandma Tessa. Everyone does." She grabbed Darcy's upper arms as she studied her. "You're much prettier in person than in the pictures. You should smile more. Welcome. It's good to have you here."

Then, before Darcy could react to the comment or the advice, the small, elderly woman reached up and pinched her cheek. The squeeze sent pain shooting through her entire face and made her eyes water.

"Mama, not so hard," Marco said, putting his arm around his mother and pulling her back. "Don't scare our guest off." He smiled. "Paige said we were to call you by your first name. Are you comfortable with that?"

Darcy nodded, still caught up in the pain in her cheek. That little old lady could twist wood with that grip.

Darcy shook hands with Marco, his wife,

and most of the Secret Service team. Last up was Joe Larson.

He was tall — maybe six feet — and muscled. Not as big, pound for pound, as Alex, but still a lot of man. He might be navy, but she would bet he could give any member of her team a run for his, or her, money.

A former SEAL was good, she thought. He'd probably killed bad guys before. She would have to remember to stick close to him.

"Lieutenant Commander," she said as she stared into eyes as dark as a storm. They shook hands.

"We should probably get inside," Paige said.

The elder Marcelli led the way, followed by his wife. Darcy motioned for Marco and Colleen to follow.

Darcy paused at the bottom of the steps. "I don't get it. Are we staying here?"

"Yes," Paige told her. "You'll be in the main house with the family. Alex and I are in the guesthouse."

Darcy couldn't believe it. "Here? Have you looked around? Open fields. How are you going to keep me safe? There have to be a thousand places for people to hide."

"They're not open fields, they're vineyards," Alex said.

She glared at him. "Thanks for the clarification. I'll be doing a crossword puzzle later. You can stop by and help."

Paige touched her arm. "Darcy, this is a good location for you. There's plenty of protection, but you won't feel trapped or isolated. Plus the family is pretty cool."

She wasn't interested in the family or anything but not feeling afraid.

"I don't like it," she said.

"Tough. Until I hear otherwise from the president, this is where you're staying," Alex said sharply.

"Alex, no." Paige turned to Darcy. "Let's give it a couple of days. I think you'll like it here."

Darcy ignored her. "You're the agent in charge?" she asked Alex.

"Yes."

"Then you better do your job. Because I will take this up with my father."

A bluff, but Alex didn't know that.

Alex shook his head. "Take care of her," he told Paige, then stalked away.

Paige looked at Darcy. "You're in a mood. What's going on?"

Darcy grimaced. "I know. I'm sorry. I'm tired, I'm scared. My team let me be kidnapped. I'm a little wary of that happening again."

"Alex is the best," Paige told her. "We're all here to keep you safe."

"The words sound good, but I'm not much of a believer."

The back door opened, and Joe Larson stuck out his head. "You two coming?"

"Right away," Paige said easily. "I was explaining to Darcy that there are even more Marcellis in her future."

"How many more?" Darcy asked.

"Dozens," Joe said as he stepped out onto the porch. "Four sisters, three spouses, three and a half kids. More grandparents, too. Or at least one more. Mary-Margaret O'Shea, better known as Grammy M."

Darcy didn't know what to do with all that information. There was no way she could keep that many people straight.

"Have they all been checked out?" she asked Paige.

The Secret Service agent smiled. "Yes, and they're all cleared. I've met most of them, but not Grammy M a.k.a. Mary-Margaret O'Shea." She pulled a small notebook out of her jacket pocket and flipped through the pages. "She's living just south of Santa Barbara with Gabriel Reese. He's the grandfather of one of the Marcelli granddaughters' husbands."

Darcy blinked. "I'll never keep this straight."

Paige grinned. "You'll have time to study before the quiz."

Joe held open the back door. "Food's waiting."

Darcy hesitated, then stepped past him and entered a massive kitchen and was confronted by what had to be three tons of food.

Grandma Tessa and Colleen carried trays to a huge kitchen table by a row of windows. There were platters of meats, bowls of pastas, mounds of salads, along with at least three different kinds of bread. The scent of simmering sauces competed with the fragrance of cinnamon and fruit.

The elderly Marcelli walked into the kitchen. "It's ten-thirty in the morning," he grumbled. "Only a fool would eat now."

"Lorenzo, stop. We have company. Darcy, come." Grandma Tessa took her arm. "You must be hungry. All that travel."

As tempting as it all looked, Darcy couldn't imagine keeping down food. She felt too unsettled. But before she could say anything, Lorenzo limped over to stand in front of her.

"How old are you?" he demanded.

"Twenty-six."

"Ha." He grabbed her left hand and looked at her bare fingers. "No ring. No husband, no babies. What is it with you women today? Listen to your parents and grandparents. Get married and have babies." He dropped her hand and poked her in the stomach. "You need babies."

Darcy took a step back. "I'll get right on that."

Colleen sighed heavily. "Lorenzo, please. Stop torturing Darcy. At least let her get settled." She looked around the kitchen and waved at Joe. "Would you take her upstairs and show her around? We've put her in Katie's old bedroom. Brenna and Francesca's is just too frightening." Colleen smiled at her. "You can unpack, then come back down and have something to eat. How does that sound?"

For once Darcy didn't have a snappy comeback. Not knowing what else to do, she smiled and said, "That would be very nice. Thank you."

She followed the naval officer out of the kitchen and down the hall.

"This way," Joe said as he headed for a flight of stairs.

The house was large and well kept. She liked the blend of colors, the earth tones that offered welcome. Although a hotel would have made her feel more safe, she could see the charm of the Marcelli home.

He led the way down a long hallway and stopped at the end. "You have your own room," he said. "It hasn't been decorated since Katie was in high school, but it's comfortable enough. You also have your own bathroom."

She stepped into a large and airy room decorated in shades of lavender. Before she could take in much more than the white eyelet bedspread and the striped wallpaper, a Secret Service agent entered her room, carrying a large suitcase. Three more followed, each with at least one bag. Paige came last. She handed Darcy a wristband.

"Automatic transmitter," she said. "So we know where you are at all times."

"I live to be a blip on a monitor." Darcy took it and snapped it into place. The cold metal was comforting. At least if someone tried to take her away, her team would be instantly alerted.

When Paige had left, Joe glanced at Darcy. "So much for being a regular person."

Surrounded by luggage, security, and wearing the human version of a homing beacon, she wasn't in a position to argue.

"Why on earth would I want to be?" she

asked. "Talk about boring. So how exactly does a naval liaison know so much about the Marcelli family?"

"Colleen and Marco are my parents."

If he'd meant to surprise her, he'd succeeded. "But you have a different last name."

He shrugged. "True enough. If there's anything you need, just ask. The Marcellis lead with their hearts. The Grands will do their best to feed you to death. Colleen will hover and mother you, and the sisters will seduce you with wine, chocolate, and girls' night out."

All of which sounded like fun, but she knew better than to admit that. "Whatever," she said as she picked up one of the smaller bags and put it on the bed. "So what are you doing here? Why aren't you on a ship somewhere?"

"I'm part of the team."

"You're not Secret Service."

"I'm the liaison with the family."

But why would they need one? "The navy doesn't get involved with the personal security of the president's family."

"They do now."

She looked at him. "You were a SEAL?"

"Until I got promoted out of active duty and into logistical planning, yes."

"At least you'll know what you're doing if the kidnapper returns."

As the bedrooms in the guesthouse were identical, Paige had figured it was safe to claim one for herself without waiting for the special agent in charge to okay the decision. She'd unpacked the night before and begun to familiarize herself with the area around the house. Now she listed all the sections that would have to be checked on a regular basis, such as outbuildings, tree groves, and storage sheds.

The front door opened. Paige sucked in a breath to brace herself then glanced up as Alex Vanmeter stalked into the small living room.

He'd gotten older, but then they both had. He was still good-looking, in a rugged, street-fighter kind of way. Barely contained energy radiated from him, making her remember how much heat the two of them had once generated.

"She's going to make this a hell of an assignment," he said as he crossed to the refrigerator, pulled open the door, and checked the contents. "I heard she's a bitch on wheels, but I thought the other agents were lying. Obviously not."

"Yes, they were," Paige said. "Darcy isn't

difficult at all." Or she hadn't been until today.

Alex grabbed a bottle of iced tea. "So you think this attitude of hers is temporary?"

Paige leaned back in her chair. "She's scared, Alex. She was just kidnapped because our department failed to keep her safe. You might want to cut her a break."

She used his first name deliberately. He might be in charge and able to pull rank, but she'd seen him naked, and she wasn't about to let him forget it.

"You've worked with her before," he said. "What do you know about her?"

"That her reputation is a lot more about the press wanting a story than about Darcy herself. She'll cooperate."

"She's not going to have a choice. Nothing is going to happen to her on my watch. I want to meet with the team in two hours. We'll review the location, set up a schedule. I want you working the house. I'll be here, mostly, coordinating everyone. The team will work in eight-hour shifts."

Paige made notes as he spoke. "Anything else?"

"Just one more thing." He moved close to the table and loomed over her. "Are you going to have a problem with me being in charge?"

"We've worked together before," she said.

"Not in quarters as close as these, and not with me running the op."

She stood, dropping her pen on the table. "I asked to be assigned to this team," she said slowly and deliberately. "I care about Darcy and I want to be a part of keeping her safe. As long as you do your job, I don't give a rat's ass who's in charge. You might be a good agent, Alex, but in private, you're not all that."

# 4

Darcy unpacked three pairs of linen slacks, jeans, several shirts, and five pairs of shoes, all black. As she held up her third black T-shirt, she felt her lips twitch. Dear God, she really *did* dress like a rock star groupie in mourning.

Not the best time in the world to notice, she thought as she carried her clothes to the closet. What with her being abducted the last time she'd gone to the mall, she had a feeling she would be doing all her future purchases online. But maybe she could try a color other than black. Maybe —

A knock on the door interrupted her mental list. "Come in," she called.

The door opened and a very pretty, very pregnant woman entered. She had long, dark wavy hair, olive skin, and huge brown eyes. She held a bottle of wine in one hand and a glass in the other.

"Hi, I'm Brenna," the woman said. "I

can't have wine, but I figured you'd need some."

Darcy glanced at the bedside clock. "It's barely eleven in the morning."

"Sure, but you're still on East Coast time." Brenna grinned. "Trust me. With my family, you need all the help you can get. Drink early and often." She set the bottle and glass on the dresser. "Wow. You have a lot of clothes. And they're gorgeous. I'm currently shopping in the tent department of the sporting goods store. What a nightmare. Nic and I both really want kids, but I have to tell you, unless he plans to carry the next one, this is the end of the line for me."

Brenna lowered herself into the room's only chair, then sighed. "Better. Now, you look confused. What didn't I explain?"

Darcy sank down on the edge of the bed. "Who the hell *are* you?"

Brenna grinned, then started to laugh. "Sorry. Brenna Marcelli. Well, technically Brenna Giovanni. I live in the next house over, which is about two miles away. I'm one of Marco and Colleen's daughters. I run Marcelli Wines. I have my own winery, too. Four Sisters. It's doing great, but that's another story."

Darcy felt as if she'd been caught up in a tornado. "Okay. Am I in your room?"

"Nope. You're in Katie's. She has much better taste. I shared a room with my twin, Francesca, and let me tell you, you don't want to stay there. Very scary wallpaper."

"You're one of four sisters?"

Brenna nodded. "Katie's the oldest. She's married to Zach, and they have one daughter, Valerie. Francesca is my fraternal twin. She's married to Sam. They have a fifteen-year-old, his from a previous marriage, and twins who are nearly two and a half. Mia, the youngest of us, has just graduated from Georgetown with a master's in world domination. She starts her job with the State Department in September. Currently, she's traveling with friends, enjoying her last summer of leisure. And you've already met Joe."

"Yes." The good-looking naval officer. "I thought being in a political family was complicated, but we're easy compared to your relatives."

Brenna rested her right hand on her swollen belly. "Don't worry. They won't quiz you on the various relationships for at least a week. But this can't be tough duty. You're used to hanging out at state dinners. I could never do that. I'm way too opinionated."

"I avoid state dinners. That's more my sister's idea of a good time."

"Still, I can't imagine what it must be like

to be the president's daughter. Everything would be so public. I mess up enough in my life that I really appreciate being anonymous."

"There are advantages to no one knowing who you are," Darcy said lightly.

Brenna's expression turned sympathetic. "They told us about the kidnapping. How terrifying. Are you doing okay?"

"I'm fine," Darcy said. "They didn't hurt me."

Brenna glanced at the marks on her wrists. "I would think they did. But you'll be safe here. There are tons of us to protect you. Not that I could really do much. Except maybe sit on the guy until he screamed for mercy. But Joe's burly. All that SEAL training. Just toss him a Q-Tip and he'll take on any enemy."

"A Q-Tip, huh? What could he do with an actual weapon?"

"Conquer the known civilized world. Oh!" She pressed down on her belly. "Someone's awake. It's time for soccer practice." She felt around on both sides of her stomach. "Just the two feet, I think. There can only be two. I couldn't take more."

"Are you expecting more?"

"I'm terrified I'm having twins. The doctor swears there's just the one heartbeat, but they've been wrong before. I'm a twin, my twin had twins, and I firmly believe God has a sense of humor. Plus, I'm huge. Francesca didn't even show until fifteen minutes before she gave birth, and Katie gained exactly twenty-seven pounds. I am a freak of nature."

Darcy wanted to be sympathetic, but she couldn't help laughing. If Brenna was an example of the Marcelli sisters, she couldn't wait to meet them all.

She heard footsteps in the hallway. Grandma Tessa appeared. "Brenna, there you are. How are you feeling? Are your feet swollen?"

Brenna raised a foot. "Pretty much all the time since late June."

"When are you due?" Darcy asked.

"The end of September. Another seven weeks. I don't think I can stand it. Can someone just knock me out until after the delivery?"

Grandma Tessa reached in the pocket of her dress and pulled out a rosary. "Don't talk like that. Babies are a blessing."

Brenna leaned toward Darcy. "It's never good when Grandma Tessa takes a trip around the beads. Just so you know."

Darcy grinned. "Thanks."

Tessa sniffed. "You're already teaching our

guest to be disrespectful. What will your mother think? What will the president think?"

"You don't have to worry about him," Darcy said. "I won't tell."

Grandma Tessa returned her rosary to her pocket. "Lunch is at twelve-thirty. Brenna, you're staying. I called Nic, and he's joining us. Darcy." The old woman reached for her hand. "We're so happy to have you here with us. I'm going to put you across from Joseph. A pretty face like yours will help his appetite. He doesn't eat enough. Plus, an officer, eh? Think how nice everyone would look at the wedding." She winked, released Darcy, and left.

Darcy stared after her. "Am I being set up?"

Brenna chuckled. "Oh, yeah. Big time. Get used to it. Grandma Tessa's been trying to marry Joe off for the past three years. Matchmaking is a way of life in this family. As the president's daughter, you're something of a catch."

She wasn't sure about that. "If Joe's your brother, why does he have a different last name?"

"Ah, that's one of our more interesting stories." Brenna tucked her hair behind her ears. "My parents met and fell in love in high school. Neither set of their parents approved — young love never lasts and all that. So when my mom turned up pregnant, the families pressured her to give up the baby for adoption. Which she did."

Darcy had expected to hear about a child from a previous marriage. "So he was raised by someone else?"

Brenna nodded. "It's really sad. His adoptive parents were great, but they were killed when he was pretty young. He went into foster care. My sisters and I never knew about him. My parents married right out of high school and are obviously really happy together, but they were crushed to find out what Joe went through. But we found him, and now he's one of us." Her smile faded. "At least that's the goal."

Darcy shifted on the bed. "I didn't mean to pry, I just wondered."

"Makes sense. Grandpa Lorenzo gets on him to change his name to Marcelli, but Joe resists. He's still holding back, not ready to be one of us. Which is probably more than you wanted to know, huh?" Brenna slowly pushed to her feet. "I'm going to leave you to unpack. I have some wine I need to check on. See you at lunch."

"Okay. Thanks for the information on the family."

Brenna smiled. "There's so much more, but I don't want to scare you off on your first day. But I'm sure Katie, Mia, and Francesca will be visiting before long. Brace yourself. Remember what I said about drinking wine. It really helps."

Joe did his best to duck out of lunch. The last thing he wanted was a big family meal and a lot of questions about his career — as in why wasn't he leaving the navy to move to the winery — and his love life — had he met someone, when was he getting married and having babies? But when he opened the back door to make his escape, he saw Grammy M and Gabriel arriving, and he could no more run out on her than he could back a car over a puppy. Tessa might perform the strongest cheek pinch on three continents, but Grammy M's warm smile and lilting Irish voice got him every time.

"Joe," she said warmly as she climbed out of the large yellow Cadillac. "I'd heard you'd come home. It's been far too long since we've set eyes on you."

He walked down to hug the tiny, old woman. "I've been busy."

"Too busy for those who love you most?" she asked gently. " 'Tis a sad thing when a grandson stays away."

"I'm here now," he told her.

"So I see. Along with the president's daughter. Who would have thought. Is she pretty?"

Joe didn't want to think about Darcy Jensen or the fact that he'd been *aware* of her from the first second he'd seen her. "She's okay."

Gabriel got out of the car and reached for his cane. "That Lauren's a real looker. I can't say much about her sister. Still, a kidnapping had to take some of the starch out of her sails."

He limped up to join Grammy M, then took her arm. "Step aside, sonny," he snapped. "I'll be escorting my woman to lunch if you don't mind."

Grammy M giggled. "Oh, Gabriel. Don't talk like that in front of the young people. You know it makes them uncomfortable."

"My grandson doesn't mind," Gabriel said with a cackle. "He likes knowing the family plumbing still works at my age."

Joe winced. He was with Grammy M on this particular topic.

He followed the older couple into the kitchen, where he found it in the usual Marcelli chaos. Tessa and Colleen carried huge bowls and platters of food to the dining room. Nic had arrived. He managed to call out a greeting to Joe as he helped a very pregnant Brenna out of a chair. Marco carried in several bottles of wine, then paused to kiss his mother-in-law on the cheek. The action caused Tessa to notice that Grammy M had arrived.

"So you're here," Tessa said in a chilly voice.

"I wanted to meet Darcy," Grammy M told her serenely. "So she could see we weren't all rigid and judgmental."

Tessa bristled. "I'm not sure you should be around a young woman like that. You could send her down the dark path to hell."

Marco headed for his mother while Joe took Grammy M by the arm.

"Let's get you and Gabriel seated," he said, leading her into the dining room.

"Nowhere near the likes of her," Grammy M said. "She's turned cruel and difficult. It's amazing what old age will do to a body."

Gabriel leaned close. "She's jealous."

Grammy M smiled and patted his hand. "Perhaps. I just . . ." Her voice trailed off. "No use crying over spilled milk, as my nana used to say. 'Tis her loss."

Brenna waddled into the room. "You're both stubborn," she said as Nic wrapped his arm around her thick waist. "You two have been friends for what, thirty-plus years? Why let things get in the way now?"

Grammy M picked up her napkin. "Ask Tessa. She started it. Tellin' me I had to choose between her and Gabriel. As if she resented my happiness. That's not friendship."

Nic patted Brenna's shoulder. "Did I tell you not to get involved? Did you listen?"

"I hate that they don't talk. It's not right."

Tessa bustled into the room. "Sit everyone. The food's all ready. Brenna, you're there, with Nic beside you. No, save that seat. It's for Darcy. She'll be across from Joe."

Everyone turned to look at him as he held in a groan. Shit. He'd been home less than twenty-four hours and this was Tessa's second attempt at matchmaking.

Marco came in with a tray of pasta. Colleen followed with baskets of bread. Joe retreated to the kitchen, thinking if he helped carry things maybe he could escape being the center of attention for once.

An unnecessary plan, he realized when he returned and found everyone focused on Darcy Jensen as she entered the dining room.

She still wore the fitted sundress she'd had on when she'd arrived. The black and white fabric hugged slender curves. He preferred women on the lush side of the scale, but she wasn't bad-looking. And she smelled good. He'd always been a sucker for that.

"If this is lunch, I'm not sure I can face dinner," Darcy said into the silence. "It, um, looks delicious."

"It is," Brenna told her. "And you're probably one of those disgusting women who can eat what she wants without gaining a pound. It makes me want to hate you, but I won't." She waved toward Grammy M. "Darcy, I don't believe you've met my maternal grandmother and Gabriel. We call her Grammy M, short for Mary-Margaret O'Shea. Gabriel Reese is her —"

"Paramour in sin," Tessa snapped. "That's right. They're living together without the benefit of marriage." She made a quick sign of the cross. "So have a seat."

Marco jumped to pull out Darcy's chair. Brenna introduced Nic while Colleen hustled her mother-in-law into the kitchen, no doubt to warn her to back off. Joe made himself busy at the buffet, opening bottles of wine.

Lorenzo walked into the dining room and took his place at the head of the table.

"Damn fool idea to have a big meal in the middle of the day," he snapped. "No one will want to work later."

"I was planning to take a nap anyway," Brenna said cheerfully. "I have to, what with not sleeping at night. Here's my question. Why nine months? Why can't pregnancy last three months, or four? Isn't that enough? I know *I'm* ready."

"Your time will come," Grammy M promised. She turned her attention to Darcy. "Welcome, child. How was your journey?"

"Good. I came here via Florida. Traveling in secret takes longer than regular travel." Darcy hesitated, as if not sure what to say. "I, um, appreciate your family taking me in. You've all been very kind."

"We're happy to have you," Colleen said as she walked back into the dining room with another tray. This one contained a roast and potatoes. After setting everything on the table, she motioned for Joe to take his seat. She did the same, with Tessa following close behind.

Lorenzo make a great show of tasting his glass of wine, then nodding. "Brenna, this is one of yours."

"That merlot-cab blend you didn't want me to bother with," she said smugly. "It's perfect, isn't it? I told you it would be." She gazed longingly at the bottle. "I swear the first thing I'm doing after I'm done breast-feeding is getting drunk. I miss wine. I can give up caffeine and processed foods and other alcohol, but I really, really miss wine."

"You'll get there," Nic said as he kissed the top of her head.

"Easy for you to say," she complained. "You get to drink what you want."

Lorenzo waited until everyone had a glass, then raised his. "Welcome, Darcy Jensen. Welcome to the family."

Brenna raised her water, everyone else picked up their wineglass. "Welcome."

Joe looked across the table at Darcy. She looked startled by both the words and the gesture, although she raised her glass and smiled.

He remembered his first reaction to the Marcelli family and had an idea of what she was feeling. Overwhelmed didn't cover it. The Marcellis tended to suck people up and make them their own. Once branded, it was difficult to escape.

As the platters and bowls were passed around, he glanced at her. She listened to the conversation around her but didn't speak much. He would have expected her to claim all the attention, but she seemed content to observe. She took small portions and didn't finish them. He could see her collarbone and the hint of ribs where her dress dipped between her breasts. Did she avoid food because of fashion or something else?

Too skinny. Not his type. And yet . . . He felt it — the subtle tension between them. A precursor to attraction.

Not to worry, he told himself. What he felt didn't matter. As long as he didn't act on it, he was fine. No woman was worth his career, certainly not this one.

"Brenna," Lorenzo said loudly. "You ordered too many barrels. We have no use for them."

"Oh, they're not all for us," she told him. "The extras are for Nic."

Nic looked at his wife with an expression of long-suffering. "I have more than enough barrels."

"No, you don't. You need to age more of your chardonnay in wood, not stainless steel. Then you blend the two together."

"Brenna, Wild Sea is my winery."

"Yes, my love, but that doesn't seem to prevent you from doing it all wrong. Take the extra barrels and use them. You'll see a big increase in the quality of the reserve chardonnay."

Darcy leaned toward him. "Why does it matter what they're stored in?" she asked.

Joe shrugged. "I haven't a clue."

As soon as he spoke, he knew he should

have kept his mouth shut. But it was too late. Lorenzo set down his fork.

"You should know," he growled. "You are the firstborn grandchild. The only boy. This could have all been yours. But no. You resist. Why? So you can play soldier?"

"Pop, stop it," Marco said.

"Don't worry about it," Joe told him. He was used to the old man's complaints. They didn't bother him.

"If he would just try. Give it a chance."

"Not interested," Joe told him.

"I don't know anything about wine," Darcy said. "Except that you're supposed to have red with beef. How big is the Marcelli winery?"

Joe narrowed his gaze. Had she stepped in to deflect the attention from him? Why the hell would she bother?

"More acres than you'd want to walk. I can take you on a tour," Brenna said. "In a manner of speaking. We'll have to use carts, what with me being unable to waddle very far, but there's still a lot to see."

"Sounds like fun," Darcy said. "If it's not too much trouble."

Brenna grinned. "Are you kidding? I love the chance to show off everything I know about wine." She patted Nic's hand. "I'll explain the difference between the quality we shoot for here at Marcelli Wines and the volume they're so proud of at Wild Sea."

"Bite me," Nic said with a grin.

"I believe that's what got us into trouble in the first place," his wife told him. She turned back to Darcy. "Does tomorrow morning work for you?"

"I'm not exactly filling my social calendar these days," Darcy told her. "Name the time."

That evening, Alex walked into the small guesthouse. He'd been avoiding it for the past couple of hours, but he'd run out of work and been forced to return.

The space itself wasn't too bad. He'd turned the dining room into a command center. Computers and monitors covered the table and spilled onto the chairs. A large map of the Marcelli and Wild Sea property covered most of one wall. That left the living room as the only place to sit outside of the two bedrooms.

The rest of the team would be housed at a nearby hotel, but he and Paige would share the house and the single bathroom. He'd suffered through worse, of course. He'd slept in tents, cars, and out in the open, all in the name of getting the job done. The difference was he hadn't done it in such close quarters with Paige.

The bathroom door opened and she walked out. Her hair was damp, and she'd traded in her dark suit for a loose pair of pajama bottoms and a tank top. No bra. Her nipples were clearly visible through the thin, ribbed fabric.

It had been a long time since they'd shared a roof, and he expected her to run for cover when she saw him. When she didn't do anything but nod, he was determined to show he didn't care, either.

"They're in for the night at the house," he said. "Richards had the first shift. He'll let us know if he spots anything."

"I don't think there's going to be trouble, but it's best to be sure," she said as she walked into the kitchen and opened the refrigerator. "Did you taste the pasta Grandma Tessa sent over? It's spectacular. I'm going to have to add a couple of miles to my run every morning or I won't fit into my clothes."

As she spoke, she bent over and pulled out a covered bowl. He wasn't so much interested in the food as in the way the pajama fabric stretched over her ass. He couldn't figure out if she was just being herself or if this was all a carefully constructed plan to drive him insane.

"We need to clear the air," he said, hating how stiff he sounded.

She straightened and faced him. "Is there a problem?"

"You tell me. We started out in the same training class."

"Ah." She reached for a bowl and scooped pasta into it. "You're worried that I'm bitter. Don't sweat it, Alex. You had a couple of lucky breaks, where you got to strut your stuff. You're good, and I'm okay with that."

He hated her causal acceptance. "You used to be driven. You used to want it all." He remembered it had been a mutual decision for them to end things. They'd both been more interested in their careers than in each other.

"Not anymore." She put the small bowl in the microwave and punched in a time. "I guess I've mellowed with age. These days I'm looking for more balance in my life."

She was saying all the right things, and he hated that. "You get that from your husband?"

Her green eyes narrowed. "Yes. Not so much from his life as from his death."

Alex instantly felt like a jerk. "I'm sorry," he said.

"Thanks, but I'm okay with it now. I still

miss him, but I mostly remember the good times."

With that she took her pasta from the microwave and walked to her room.

He watched her go and wondered what she remembered from their time together.

# 5

Darcy had been on plenty of tours in her time. There had been the factory that made shipping boxes — a thrilling journey into the world of cardboard — and a company devoted to the production of thread. She'd seen cheese being made, tractors, tires, microchips, and miniblinds. But never wine. Wine seemed a whole lot more interesting.

She dressed in black cargo pants and a black tank top, then carefully slathered on sunscreen. Somehow over the past couple of years she'd gotten incredibly pale. Unfortunately the lack of color only emphasized the dark circles under her eyes. Another couple of nights without sleep and even her concealer wouldn't work.

It wasn't that she didn't want to sleep, it's that the second she closed her eyes, she felt them grabbing her again. Her wrists throbbed as she remembered the rope. Fear tightened her throat and left her unable to breathe. Far better to give up sleep than face the demons in the dark.

After slipping on sandals, she hurried downstairs where she found Joe waiting in the kitchen. There were no other Marcellis around. Just Joe sitting at the kitchen table and a tempting pot of coffee on the counter.

He glanced up from the paper. "Morning."

He looked neither friendly nor happy to see her, so she nodded a greeting and beelined for her morning jolt of caffeine. After adding the right amount of milk and sweetener, she joined him at the table and gingerly took the entertainment section of the paper.

"Not interested in what's going on in the world?" he asked from behind the paper.

"I already did a half hour of CNN while I was getting ready," she said. "That's about as much current events as I can stand. Besides, if it's really important, the White House sends me a briefing."

He set down the paper and raised his eyebrows. He'd showered and shaved. His hair was military short, his skin tanned, and his shoulders broad enough to carry the weight of the world on them. He looked good. Capable.

A plate of Danish sat between them. Joe

pushed it toward her. "You should eat something."

The dull ache of acid in her stomach told her she should eat a lot, but she couldn't. "I don't remember hiring you as my personal nutritionist. Did we sign a contract?"

"You're too skinny." He reached for his mug. "It's not healthy."

"I'm not sure I care about your opinion. Let me think." She sipped her coffee. "Nope. Don't care."

"Is this a chick thing? Do you want to look like a supermodel or something?"

"Why does it matter?"

"I'm curious."

"And that impacts me how?"

He leaned back in his chair. "Is it because it's morning, or are you naturally unpleasant all the time?"

"I'm naturally unpleasant."

One corner of his mouth twitched in an almost smile. "Good to know. Why aren't you eating?"

"Are you going to dog on me all day until you get an answer?" she asked, more intrigued than frustrated.

"Probably. I don't have a lot to keep me busy. I could use the distraction."

"Fine. I'm not a good stress eater. I wish I were. I understand it's very comforting. But when I'm tense or upset, I can't stand the thought of food."

His gaze slipped to her too-skinny arms. "Been upset a lot lately?"

Darcy shrugged. She knew she'd lost weight in the past year or so. Too much weight. "I've had stuff on my mind."

He returned his attention to the paper. "Brenna should be here in half an hour. Your Secret Service agents want me to come along on the tour, too."

His flat tone told her all she had to know about *his* enthusiasm level. It annoyed her that once he'd gotten his answer, he'd dismissed her.

"Let me guess. You're not dying with excitement at the thought of the winery tour."

He raised his head. "Something like that. But it doesn't matter. I'm here and I'm going to do my job. Never question the chain of command." He pushed the plate of Danish toward her. "Eat one."

"I'm not hun—"

His gaze narrowed. "Try."

She sighed heavily, then picked up a cheese Danish. "Fine. I'll try. Although Yoda said there is no try. There is do, or do not. Or was it do or not do? I can never remember."

Joe's expression didn't change. Nor did he offer an opinion.

*"Star Wars,"* she mumbled as she took a bite and chewed. After swallowing she said, "The second one. *The Empire Strikes Back.* My personal favorite of the first three."

He returned his attention to the paper.

"You're not very friendly," she said.

"Do you need me to be?"

"It wouldn't kill you to make an attempt. Or should I apologize? Oh, Joe, I'm terribly sorry my kidnapping is interfering with your regular life. Silly me. I should have arranged it for a different month."

"I heard you were a pain in the ass," he said.

The words meant nothing, she told herself, even as she felt their sting.

"But you're not a victim," he added. "Good for you."

Not sure what to say to that, she reached for another Danish and tore it in half.

"Did you fight them?" he asked.

It took her a second to figure out he meant the kidnappers. "Yes, but there were four of them, and I'm not exactly buff. I did get in a good head butt though." And she hadn't allowed the fear to control her. When it got bad at night, she reminded herself of that.

"You're tougher than you look," he said.

She wasn't sure what that meant, or what it had to do with him being friendly.

"How was it?" he asked.

She glanced down and realized that she'd finished the second Danish. She pressed one hand to her stomach. The acid burn was gone.

"Delicious," she said.

"Have another."

"Don't push me, sailor. I have connections."

He chuckled. "I bet you do."

A car pulled up out front.

"Brenna," Joe said as he stood. "I'll alert the security team."

Darcy finished her cup of coffee and carried it to the sink. She rinsed it and set it in the dishwasher as the back door burst open and Brenna stepped inside.

"Oh my God, I've gained three pounds in the past *week*," she announced as she entered. "Is that fair? Is it right? I hate being pregnant more than I can tell you. It seriously sucks. I'm huge. Oh, no. Danish. No, no. I can't. The sugar will give me heartburn." She turned to Darcy. "Did you eat one? Was it fabulous? Let me live vicariously through you, I beg you."

Darcy laughed. "It wasn't bad."

"I knew it. And you're so damn skinny.

Look at you." She stopped and covered her mouth with her finger. "Oh, can I say *damn* in front of you? Have I broken the law?"

"You can say anything you want. I'll say *damn,* too, if it makes you feel better."

"It does. Okay, let's go. I hear the Danish calling my name, and if I stay here, I'll give in."

Darcy followed her outside, where she was greeted by a large golden retriever.

"This is Max," Brenna said as the huge dog sniffed and licked and wagged his tail so hard his whole back end shook. "He likes everybody."

"I guess." Darcy bent down to hug him and received a quick doggie kiss for her efforts. "Are you a handsome boy?"

Max yelped in agreement.

"This is going to be a modified tour," Brenna said as she patted her belly. "We'll take carts, which limits where we can go. But you'll get a feel for things. Plus, if you're interested, you can go exploring on your own."

Just then two golf carts came around the house. Joe drove one, while Alex piloted the other. Paige sat beside him.

"Or not," Brenna said. "Will they let you go out on your own?"

"Not anytime soon." Darcy hated that

protection was necessary, and even worse, that she wanted it. She hated being afraid.

"Ready?" Joe asked as he stopped beside Brenna.

"Yes, but I'm driving," she said. "If you argue, I'll take you down."

He grinned. "You can drive."

"Men like it when we take charge," Brenna said. "I don't know why, but I accept it as a secret of the universe."

Darcy appreciated the advice, but she was more intrigued by her Secret Service agents. She'd only ever seen them in suits — black, navy, dark gray. But today both Paige and Alex were in jeans and T-shirts. Paige looked great, but Alex seemed awkward, as if he wasn't comfortable in his own skin.

"Wow, casual," she said, strolling over to their cart. "What gives?"

"We're blending in," Paige said.

Darcy turned to Alex. "You need to relax a little. You're not blending."

"We haven't completed our reconnaissance of the property. There are areas that aren't secured."

"Don't worry," Brenna said as she slid behind the wheel of the other cart. "We won't go anywhere unsecured."

"You don't know where that is," Alex said

between clenched teeth. "I haven't told you."

Brenna patted the seat next to her. "Come on, Darcy. Let's get a move on."

Five minutes later they were bouncing along the edge of a massive vineyard. Max trotted ahead, then turned back and barked, as if urging them to keep up. Joe sat in the rear of their cart, while Paige and Alex came up behind.

"So these are chardonnay grapes," Brenna said. "Note the pale color. They're nearly ripe and will be picked first. The cabs are last to ripen."

"Cabs?"

"Cabernet sauvignon. Our pride and joy. Red wines are the gift of the gods. Whites are nice, too, but honestly, not my favorite."

"Katie only drinks white wine," Joe said.

Brenna glared at him. "He's making trouble. Can you believe it? He disappears for weeks at a time, and when he returns, he makes trouble."

"Just sharing. You women like that."

"Slap him for me," Brenna said. "Slap him really, really hard."

Darcy laughed. The morning was perfect — the coolness of the night had faded, but it wasn't hot yet. The sky was clear, the company enjoyable.

"We grow different kinds of grapes here," Brenna said. "Chardonnay, merlot, cabs, some voigner for blending. We also have vineyards up in Northern California. The grapes are brought down here, and everything is blended together. I hope you're here when we start picking. It's very exciting. The grapes are pressed on the property and put into huge barrels for fermenting."

"I'd like to see that," Darcy said.

Brenna continued to talk about grapes and winemaking, but Darcy found herself focusing more on the family than their wine.

What a wonderful place to grow up, she thought. So much space, so much love and acceptance. Except Joe hadn't known about any of this. What would it be like to find out he had this whole other family who wanted nothing more than to make him one of them? Was he angry about what he'd missed? Hurt his parents had given him up?

They turned around and headed for the barrel rooms.

"Running two different wineries is tough," Brenna was saying. "Mine — Four Sisters — is pretty small, but it still takes a lot of time. Plus, working here has the added thrill of dealing with my grandfather. In theory, I'm in charge. In reality, he argues with me about everything. What wine should be used for the reserve and what should be blended. How long to ferment, whether or not to use oak barrels or stainless steel. Don't even get me started on labels. I've been trying to get him to approve new ones for over three years. But does he? No. We're using the same old crappy labels. He makes me insane. Truly he does."

Lorenzo might annoy his granddaughter, but Darcy heard the love in her voice, too.

They left the carts and walked into the main buildings of the winery. Brenna showed her the pressing room, the fermenting room, and the equipment that delivered ready wine into bottles. Paige hovered by the main entrance while Alex stalked from room to room, checking for terrorists in all the shadows.

"I need to talk to my manager," Brenna said. "I'll just be a second."

Darcy nodded and crouched down to pat Max as she examined the bottling equipment more closely.

"This is interesting," she said. "My peak tour experience had been watching them manufacture M&M's, but this is just as good." She stood. "You must love being a part of it."

Joe shrugged, as if it didn't matter.

She faced him. "You don't care about this?"

"No."

"But they're an amazing family."

"We're related. That doesn't make us family."

She couldn't have been more surprised if he'd morphed into a giant moose.

"But that's crazy," she told him. "Why on earth would you walk away from all this? It's your heritage, it's who you are."

"I'm not interested in their money."

"I'm not talking about money. I'm talking about belonging to something bigger than just you. There's history here, and love. People who care about you."

He turned away. "I'm here because of my job. Nothing else."

She could hear Lauren's voice in her head telling her this was a really good time to change the subject. She didn't want to alienate someone on her security team on her first day. There were probably at least fourteen different, polite ways to handle the situation. Darcy ignored them all.

"I thought you had to be smart to be a SEAL. I guess not."

Brenna returned, and they completed the tour. Joe stayed in the background, watching Darcy as she interacted with everyone she met.

He hadn't thought about her as a person before. To him she'd been little more than the slightly attractive reason he was stuck here instead of back on base. Not that there was any guarantee that he would have been allowed to stay on base after the incident with the admiral's boat.

Now he saw her as an individual — one with a temper. She liked dogs, had a smart mouth, and was shy with strangers, although she forced herself to act otherwise. She was also afraid.

Brenna opened her car door and Max jumped inside. She turned to Darcy.

"I had fun," she said.

"Me, too." Darcy smiled, then leaned in to hug her. Brenna's large stomach got in the way.

"I'm huge," Brenna said with a sigh.

Darcy touched her belly. "You're lucky."

Her voice had a wistful quality that made Joe feel as if he'd stumbled onto something personal. Before he could turn away, Brenna reached for him.

"All right, big guy. I'm outta here. Take care of our guest." She lowered her voice. "I like her. Based on what I read in the paper, I thought I'd hate her, but I don't. So be nice to her."

"You're not the boss of me."

"So you like to think."

Brenna moved to the car and climbed in. Darcy stood there and waved until she disappeared around the corner.

"That was fun," she said when they were alone. "Your sister's great. I really like how she bullies you."

"I let her think she bullies me."

"Oh. Right. That's how it is."

Her eyes were bright with humor, her mouth smiling. She was pretty, he thought, as heat tumbled in his gut and moved south. And as much as he hated to side with Brenna — if she found out she would never let him forget — he agreed with her assessment of Darcy. From what he'd read in the paper, she was supposed to be a class A bitch. So far, no real sign of that.

Paige strolled up. "Hey, Darcy. What's up for the rest of the day?"

"I'm not sure. I'd like to head out and sketch the vineyards."

"Sure. Give us about a thirty-minute heads-up. We'll send you out with a team of three."

Darcy's smile faded. "Sure. Thanks."

Paige wandered back to the guesthouse. Joe turned to Darcy.

"Not in the mood for an entourage?" he asked.

"I don't mind that. Sometimes I forget why I need them. I'm not excited to be reminded."

"You were kidnapped. They want to be careful."

"And I want them to be careful."

She turned toward the house, but he grabbed her arm to stop her. Her skin was soft against his fingers.

"What?" she demanded. "Did I disobey? Do I have to get down and give you twenty?"

He studied her face. The shadows were darker today. "You're not sleeping."

Instantly her expression closed, and she jerked free of his hold. "I'm fine."

"You should talk about it to someone."

"Are you volunteering?"

"Maybe Paige could help."

"Don't worry about me."

He knew what she was going through — not the particulars but what it was like to be unable to come down after an assignment. "There are ways to handle post-traumatic stress —"

"Don't you dare psychoanalyze me," she told him. "You don't know what the hell you're talking about."

"Actually I do. And while you're already pissed off at me, I'm going to tell you to start eating better. And exercising. It will help you sleep."

She headed for the house. "Go away," she called over her shoulder as she ran up the stairs and ducked inside.

He wanted to, but there was nowhere to go. Like her, he was trapped here for the duration. Also like her, he had ghosts haunting his sleep and things he didn't want to remember.

# 6

Two days later Joe heard a commotion in the driveway. As Darcy had stuck close to the house, he'd been trapped inside as well, and he was happy for an excuse to get outdoors. As he stepped outside, a familiar battered Jeep pulled up. Instantly several Secret Service agents appeared and surrounded the vehicle.

"Don't shoot," Mia said as she got out of the driver's side and held up both hands. "We're unarmed."

Joe felt himself smile. When Mia was around, life was never boring.

She spotted him and squealed. "Joe! You're here! Did you know about the Secret Service? They stopped us at the turn-off to the driveway and searched the car. Now I think they're going to take Ian out back and shoot him."

As she spoke a tall, lanky blond guy

climbed out of the Jeep and also held up his hands.

"I don't get it," the kid said, looking both confused and scared. "What did I do?"

Paige took Mia's friend by the arm. "If you'll come this way," she said as she steered him toward the guesthouse.

Mia waited until the agents had walked away before lowering her arms and racing toward Joe.

"What gives?" she demanded as she launched herself toward him. He grabbed her and pulled her against him, then hugged her close.

"All these questions," he said, putting her down. "How about starting with a greeting?"

She grinned up at him. Mia was barely five foot three, with big brown eyes and brown hair she always had streaked blond. Too much makeup stained her face, and she insisted on wearing trashy cropped shirts and too-short shorts. But she was pure energy, and she adored him with a devotion that never wavered.

Her full mouth swelled into a pout. "You should be greeting *me*. You never answer my e-mails. Why is that? I'm very faithful about writing."

He patted her on the head, deliberately

mussing her hair. "I don't consider 'hey, get any lately' correspondence I want to respond to."

"You're such a stick-in-the-mud." She glanced toward the guesthouse and then back at him. "What's up with the police brutality?"

"They're being careful."

"Who's they?"

Joe wasn't sure what to say. Of all his family members, Mia was the biggest risk to blab. "You didn't tell anyone you were coming to visit."

"This is my home, Joseph," Mia told him sternly. "I don't need permission to show up. So what did I interrupt? An alien landing? Secret nuclear experiments? Although Brenna won't like anything that messes with her precious wine. Why don't you —"

The back door opened. Joe heard it, and he knew who had appeared by the expression of total stunned disbelief on Mia's face.

"Holy shit," she breathed. "That's the president's daughter."

Joe glanced back at Darcy. "Meet Mia Marcelli, the youngest and least mannered of the four sisters."

Mia slugged him in the arm, then walked over to Darcy. "Wow. What on earth are you doing here? Are you lost?"

Darcy smiled. "No. I'm hiding out for a few weeks."

Mia turned on him. "That's why those government types came and asked all those questions. I thought it was about something else. This is so incredibly cool." She looked at the guesthouse and gasped. "Oh, no. Ian wasn't cleared, was he? That's the big deal. I brought an unknown enemy into sacred territory. Jeez. What will they do to him?"

Joe didn't have the answer, so he shrugged.

"You're no help," Mia said as she took off at a run toward the guesthouse. "Wait!" she yelled. "He's not a terrorist. We're just sleeping together. Don't hurt him!"

Joe watched her for a second, then turned to Darcy. "We're all so proud."

Darcy continued to watch as Mia entered the Secret Service headquarters. "She's great. I can't wait to meet your other two sisters."

"They're both a little more low-key. Although Francesca has a master's in psychology, which makes her think she knows more than she does."

"Then she must have a field day with you."

Joe hadn't seen much of Darcy in the past couple of days. He knew he'd pissed her off, and he'd half expected her to report him to Paige or Alex, complaining that he'd crossed the line between the hired help and those who were part of the inner circle. But neither of them had said anything to him.

Now he took in the shadows under her eyes — they were darker than before. There was a wariness in her expression, as if she expected him to attack.

He told himself he didn't care if she never slept again, that his entire focus was on getting through this assignment and getting back to the base. Nothing else mattered. Not her, not his family, and especially not the awareness he felt whenever she was around.

"You're looking fierce about something," Darcy said. "I was teasing about your sister. You don't have to be so sensitive."

He stiffened as if she'd shot him. "I'm *not* sensitive."

Darcy held in a smile. Men were so predictable. Violate their sense of manliness and they got all prickly and defensive.

"Of course not. How could I have thought such a thing?" He glared at her but didn't speak. No doubt he wasn't sure if she was kidding. The last time they'd been together, he'd pissed her off, and she'd reacted. Maybe overreacted. She suspected Joe had only been trying to help.

"I like your family," she said as a change

of subject. "Mia reminds me a lot of Brenna."

"They're alike," he admitted. "Katie and Francesca are similar, too. Less volatile."

She smiled. "Less interested in making you crazy?"

"Sometimes."

"You're a lucky man, Joe Larson," she said. "You have a family most people would envy."

His expression turned from wary to trapped. She sensed he did *not* want to be having this conversation with her. She also knew that he wasn't comfortable walking away from her. After all, she was the person they were all trying to keep safe.

"Oh, I have to admit I like that," she murmured.

His dark gaze lasered in on her face. "Like what?"

"Having power over an ex-SEAL."

One eyebrow rose. "Not in this lifetime or the next."

"Uh-huh. The thing is, you can't go anywhere, can you?"

She moved closer, then circled around him. Was it possible to make him do tricks? She grinned. His eyes narrowed.

"Ever married?" she asked.

"Once. You?"

She laughed. "You hardly have to ask. Nearly every detail of my life has been played out in the press. No engagements, no serious boyfriends. At least not in a while. Dating the president's daughter comes with restrictions most guys aren't willing to take on. Now back to you. What happened to the little woman?"

"I used to ship out for six, eight months at a time. Kind of makes it hard to keep the home fires burning."

Yet other men managed to do it. Why not Joe? He was good-looking enough. He had a body that was near godlike in its perfection. When he forgot to act as though he had a stick up his ass, he was okay to talk to. So why no entourage of women hanging on him? Why did he always act as if he would rather be somewhere else?

"You do like women, right?" she asked, pretending a seriousness she didn't feel.

Fury erupted in him. She felt both the energy and the heat, but his control was impressive. Not by a flicker of a lash did he react to the insult. "What do you think?"

"I think your past could make for a very interesting story. But don't worry. I won't ask you. There are plenty of folks around here who would like nothing more than to tell me all they know about you."

He groaned.

"Oh, yeah," she said with a laugh. "The hell of family. Why is it so hard for you to be with them?"

"This isn't a conversation we're going to have."

"Why not?"

"The subject doesn't interest me."

But it interested her. Why did he resist such a wonderful group of people? From what she'd seen in the past two days, all that the Marcellis wanted was the freedom to love him. What wouldn't she give to have a piece of that for herself.

"I can help you with this," she said.

"No, thanks."

"Oh, but you don't have a choice. We're trapped here, and I could use a distraction." She didn't mean any of it, but threatening him was fun.

"When did you get to be an expert?" he asked.

"I'm not. Those who can, do. Those who can't, teach. That's me. Your new instructor on getting along with your family. We'll have classes and everything. You can thank me later."

"Not likely." His gaze narrowed. "This is a joke, right?"

She arched her eyebrows. "Maybe. Maybe not."

The man actually growled. She had a feeling he was thinking that he would rather have an arm cut off than deal with her *and* the Marcellis. Not that he had a choice. Neither of them were going anywhere, and she was in a position to force her will on him.

For once being the president's daughter didn't seem like such a bad thing.

Mia Marcelli didn't sit still, Paige noted. She squirmed, hunched over, straightened, then bounced to her feet.

"I didn't know what those agents wanted when they came to see me last week," Mia said as she took the mug of coffee Paige offered. "I thought it was about the spy stuff."

"What spy stuff?"

Mia rolled her eyes. "They keep asking me to be a spy. Is that crazy or what? I mean look at me. Do I blend in?"

"Why you?" Paige asked. "Do you know?"

Mia shrugged. "I do languages. Give me a good instructor and a few weeks and I can function using that language. Give me three months and I can talk like a native. It's my brain. I'm really smart about other stuff, too, but languages are my thang. I try to pick up a couple every year, you know, just for fun."

As Paige had struggled with high school Spanish and barely passed, she didn't know what to say. "Good for you. Did you accept any of the offers?"

Mia wrinkled her nose. "No. I just graduated from Georgetown, and I'm starting with the State Department in September. This is my last summer of freedom, and I was going to spend it traveling with Ian. Are you guys going to kill him?"

Paige laughed. "No. We want to find out more about him, though."

"Because of Darcy." Mia's eyes got wide. "Why is she here?"

"There was a kidnapping attempt on Lauren. They took Darcy by mistake."

"Whoa — that's scary. I wonder how you guys picked this place to hide her. But it's good. I mean, the Grands will love her to death. I know they always make me feel better when I've had a bad day or something."

Alex walked into the kitchen. "We're nearly done," he told Paige, then he turned to Mia. "Your friend will be free to go in about an hour."

"So he's not dangerous?" Mia asked. "I could have told you that. Ian's fun, but not the least bit deep, and isn't depth of character required for true commitment to a cause?"

Alex stared at her without speaking. Paige was careful to hide her amusement.

Mia rose and walked over to Alex. "You obviously work out. Talk about muscles. So who are you?"

"Special Agent Alex Vanmeter. I'm in charge of this operation."

"Ooh, our fearless leader." She glanced at Paige and grinned. "I just love military types. And guys into security. There's that whole 'take a bullet' mentality. The ultimate sacrifice. Of course it doesn't measure up against Kyle Reese in *Terminator*. He traveled across time, but death is a close second."

Alex sighed heavily. "Ms. Marcelli," he began.

Mia moved in close and rubbed her palm against his upper arm. "Mia. Call me Mia. And I'll call you Alex." She stared into his eyes. "Ian's just a summer fling. It's not serious at all. I mean, he's fun, but I can't imagine living with him for the next sixty years. He talks too much, and I'd be forced to kill him. Then I'd need to be punished. Would you want to be the one to punish me, Special Agent in Charge Vanmeter?"

Paige had a feeling that if Alex had been

drinking, he would have spit. Color darkened his cheeks as he jerked free of her touch and stepped back.

"Perhaps you would like to return to the house until we're finished questioning your friend," he said firmly.

Mia sighed. "All right. But if you change your mind, let me know."

She waggled her fingers at Paige and sauntered out of the guesthouse.

Paige began to chuckle as soon as Mia left.

Alex glared at her. "You think that's funny?"

"That you have a groupie? Absolutely. She's just playing with you, Alex. She doesn't mean it."

He grabbed a bottle of iced tea from the refrigerator. "If she gets in the way of my job, I want you to talk to her."

"Oh, no. If you have a problem with Mia, you take it up with her. She's not a threat, and if you can't handle a little flirting from a twenty-one-year-old grad student, then you're not the man I thought you were."

Alex's glare deepened. "You *like* her."

"Of course. She's fabulous."

"Then she's your problem."

"Sorry, no. I'm busy with Darcy." She moved close and batted her eyes. "But I'm sure a big, bad agent like you can handle little Mia."

Alex set the bottle on the counter and grabbed her upper arms. There was nothing challenging about his hold, or threatening. But the second he touched her, everything changed.

For a moment, time shifted and Paige found herself slipping back to her weeks in training. When Alex had been so much more than a fellow recruit. The heat of his hand burned through to memories she'd thought she had forgotten. The scent of his body reminded her of being naked and in bed and never ever having enough of him.

Wanting slammed into her like a shot from a .45. Need joined it, making her hungry and weak and suddenly afraid.

Then time righted itself and she was back in the kitchen, a very different person than she'd been before.

"This isn't a game, Paige. This is deadly serious."

She nodded, not sure if he meant the situation with Darcy, the trouble with Mia, or what was happening between him and her.

He dropped his hand, grabbed his iced tea, and walked away. She was left alone in the kitchen, shaken, aroused, and confused as hell.

■ ■ ■ ■

Darcy sat in front of the window, doing her best to draw the vineyard. The problem was her view was limited by a couple of large trees. As much as she would like to walk outside and find the perfect spot for an afternoon of drawing, she wasn't sure she was willing to put up with the security entourage that would accompany her. Their silent but very real presence wouldn't do much for her creativity.

Before she could decide if the pain was worth the price, someone knocked on the door. Before she could say anything, it burst open and Mia bounced into the room.

"I can't believe you're here," the younger Marcelli said as she jumped onto the bed and stretched out. "It's very exciting. I'm the youngest. You knew that, right? Mom made one last attempt to have a son, and I came along. They've hidden their disappointment pretty well. And now they adore me, so they're stuck, right? Plus they have Joe. So, you're here. Wow. How are you adjusting? Was it too horrible being kidnapped? I'll bet you were brave. You look like the brave type. I would have screamed and begged and really embarrassed myself,

I just know it. Do you like having Secret Service agents all around? I met Alex. He's hunky." She glanced around, as if checking that they were alone, then lowered her voice. "Do you, like, get to have sex with the agents? Is that too personal? Should I wait a couple of days before asking that?"

Darcy put down her pencil and stared at her visitor. "Honest to God, I have no idea what to say to you."

Mia tucked her hands behind her head and beamed. "I know. I often have that effect on people, but they love me anyway."

"I can only imagine."

Mia sat up. "They searched the car. I turned into the driveway, and these men appeared from nowhere. They had guns and ordered me to stop. I had to show them ID, then they searched the car. I think they were looking for a bomb or something. Then they said we could drive up to the house but not to get out of the Jeep until we were instructed to. It's like being in a spy movie. And the worst part is I can't tell anyone. That seriously sucks."

Darcy felt as if she could barely catch her breath. She'd thought that Brenna was high energy, but Brenna had nothing on Mia.

"I guess I can talk about it with Ian," Mia continued. "Of course I can't talk to him about Alex." She grinned. "You didn't answer my question about sex with the agents, did you?"

"No. And that's my answer. No. Haven't, wouldn't, don't want to."

"But he's very hunky."

"Maybe. I can't imagine him naked, though. He's too uptight."

Mia sighed and flopped back on the bed. "Oh, I can clearly see him naked, and it's a very nice picture, let me tell you. Yum." She raised her head. "You know I'm just playing, right? I say a lot of stuff to make people nervous, but I don't really mean it. Ian and I are together — at least for now. I wouldn't cheat on him or anything."

"I'm sure Alex will be relieved to hear that."

Mia grinned. "You're not going to tell him are you?"

"Nope. Let him suffer."

"Good. So what do you think of us?"

"I like the family," Darcy said and meant it. "Everyone has made me feel really welcome."

"We're like that. The Grands are so cool, and my folks are, too. Are Grammy M and Grandma Tessa still not talking?"

"They don't seem to get along."

"I hate that." Mia scooted around so her

head was at the foot of the bed, then she flopped over onto her stomach. "I wish they'd make up. But they're both so stubborn. Maybe having Joe here will help. They adore him. We all do. Not that he's so crazy about us."

The bright light in her eyes faded. "Have you heard how he came to be here?"

"I know that he was given up for adoption and then found years later."

"Yeah. It's totally horrible that my mom had to do that. Now Joe's here, but he's not a part of us, you know. He won't let anyone get close. I make him crazy, which is fun, but it's not the same as being, you know, emotionally intimate. Brenna's the one he gets along with the best, but he holds back from everyone. He doesn't have a girlfriend."

She paused expectantly.

Darcy did her best to look innocent. "Oh. Should I be taking notes?"

Mia giggled. "No, but are you interested?"

"I barely know the man."

"What does that matter?"

"Amazingly enough, it matters to me."

"Oh, well. Maybe next time. You should think about it, though. I'll bet he's great in bed." Mia wrinkled her nose. "You know, I don't think I can talk about Joe's sex life.

As intriguing as it would be, he's my brother, and there's a serious ick factor."

"I'm sure your family will be delighted to know you have limits."

Mia sat up. "I don't want limits. But there it is. The thought of my brother having sex is gross. So if you guys do it, I don't want to know."

Darcy made an X over her heart. "My lips will be sealed."

"He's probably gorgeous," Mia added thoughtfully. "Joe naked. I wonder if he has any scars, you know, from wounds and stuff."

There was a noise in the hall. Both Darcy and Mia turned toward the open door. Joe stood there. Darcy couldn't read the expression on his face, but it seemed to be an intriguing combination of horror and fear.

Mia sighed. "He heard the naked part," she said in a mock whisper.

Darcy did her best not to laugh. "Possibly even the sex part." She cleared her throat. "Hi, Joe. We were just talking about you."

Joe's dark gaze locked with her own. For a second, she would have sworn he'd vowed payback. Then he turned on his heel and left.

Mia started to laugh. Darcy joined in. She laughed until tears filled her eyes and she could barely breathe. Until that minute she would have said getting kidnapped was one of the worst things that had ever happened to her, but suddenly, she wondered if maybe it hadn't been so bad after all.

# 7

Darcy was up early because, well, not sleeping had a way of making a person face the dawn. She stood at her bedroom window, watching pale light creep across the vineyards. Suddenly her fingers itched for a pencil. She wanted to capture the moment, the changing light, the way the dew sparkled on the leaves.

She would never make it as an artist, she acknowledged, pulling on jeans and a T-shirt, then quickly brushing her hair. It was the reason she'd studied graphic arts and advertising in college. But not having an abundance of talent didn't stop her from wanting to capture the world with a quick sketch on a perfect morning.

She collected her supplies, then quietly made her way downstairs. The house was still. Reasonable, normal people wouldn't be up for at least another hour. Which meant she could sneak outside and enjoy the morning in solitude.

As the thought formed, she felt a tendril of fear snake along her spine. Did she *want* to be alone? Was it safe?

"Not going there," Darcy muttered. She pushed the questions away, along with the chill, and focused on the chance to just *be* for an hour or so.

But when she stepped outside, she saw an unfamiliar Secret Service agent in a car by the back door. He got out of the car as soon as he saw her.

"Morning, Ms. Jensen."

"Morning. And it's Darcy."

He nodded. "How can I help you?"

Part of her wanted to forget it. To just go back into the house and wait until all this was over. But a stronger voice in her head told her that she couldn't wait much longer without going crazy. She had to start doing something.

"I want to draw the vineyard this morning," she said, holding up her sketch pad. "I'm guessing it will take about an hour."

"Okay. Give me a second." He picked up a walkie-talkie and spoke into it.

No doubt getting permission, she thought glumly. What if they said no?

Before she could decide on a course of action, she felt a slight prickling between her shoulder blades. She turned and saw Joe coming out of the house.

Contradictory emotions warred within her. Part of her wondered why she couldn't spend five minutes alone outside of her bedroom. Another part of her acknowledged that if someone had to disturb the quiet, she wouldn't mind if it was Joe.

"You're up early," she said.

"Old habits," he told her.

She waited for him to comment on her being awake as well, but he didn't. Instead he nodded at the pad and pencils.

"Hoping for inspiration?" he asked.

"I was, but it's turning out to be a big deal."

The Secret Service agent put down the walkie-talkie. "Okay, I'm ready," he said, then spoke into his everpresent wrist communicator. "Pigeon is leaving. Repeat, Pigeon is leaving."

Joe raised his eyebrows.

"Don't say it," Darcy told him. "My father is Falcon, my sister is Swan, and I'm Pigeon. Does the Secret Service have a sense of humor or what?"

Joe stepped toward the other man. "Why don't you stay here," he told him. "I'll go with our bird friend while she draws."

The agent frowned. "I'm supposed to be

with Ms. Jensen, ah, Darcy, as protection."

"Check with Paige," Joe said. "She'll clear it." Then, without waiting for approval, he returned to Darcy's side and pointed toward the vineyard. "Let's go."

"Pretty smooth," she said when they were out of earshot and walking through vines heavy with grapes. "You said to contact Paige, not Alex, knowing she's the softer touch."

"Uh-huh."

"What makes you think it's easier for me to have you along than the other agent?"

"I don't call you Ms. Jensen."

She smiled. "Good point." And in truth, she didn't mind having Joe around.

"Where are we going?" he asked.

"Not a clue. We'll walk until I find inspiration."

They continued walking, she in front, he right behind. Dew spattered her arms and soaked her jeans. There was a peacefulness to the quiet, and a sense of safety. As if nothing bad could ever happen here.

At the other end of that plot of grapes they found a narrow dirt track. Darcy paused to survey the miles of grapes and a cluster of trees to the west.

"That way," she said, pointing. As they followed the path, they were able to walk side by side.

"I talked to my sister last night," she said. "They're holding her on some farm in the Midwest. She's surrounded by cornfields. When I told her about the wine, she was very jealous."

Joe looked at her. "You shouldn't discuss your location, even on a secure line."

Darcy grinned. She liked messing with him — it was a little like pulling a tiger's tail — dangerous but very exhilarating.

"You think?" she asked with a grin. "Don't worry, my little SEAL friend. I told her I was in Washington state. They make wine there, too. But as you're a part of all this, I'm guessing you already know that."

He shrugged.

She studied him. "How much, exactly, do you know about wine?"

"I'm a beer drinker myself."

She winced. "That can't be good. Aren't you interested in wine?"

"No."

"But it's your heritage. It's in your blood."

"I want salt water in my blood."

The man was nothing if not consistent, she thought. Still, to have so much right there for the taking. "I envy you," she said quietly. "It's just my father, my sister, and me. And I don't get along all that well with

Mr. President." For reasons she had never discussed with anyone. "Which means it's pretty much Lauren and me. We're close, although we're not that much alike. She's perfect and I'm —"

As she spoke, she stumbled on a loose rock in the road. Before she could catch her balance on her own, Joe grabbed her arm and pulled her upright.

They stood there, in the center of the road, his hand on her arm, his fingers touching bare skin. They were close enough for her to feel the heat from his body and his slow, steady breathing. She could see the various colors of brown that colored his irises and the faint scar on the edge of his jaw.

Her stomach clenched in anticipation, which was crazy. Nothing was going to happen.

But for the moment, that single heartbeat of time, she wanted it to. She wanted him to . . . oh, who knew. Kiss her? Say something sweet? She wasn't particularly picky, as long as he acknowledged the connection between them.

But he didn't, and she started to feel awkward. She pulled free of his grasp.

"Obviously Lauren is the perfect one," she said with a laugh that didn't exactly sound real. "I'm the clumsy one."

"You're still not sleeping."

"I know. Some. A little."

"Hardly at all."

Annoyance replaced her awareness of him. "Haven't we already had this particular conversation? If you recall, it didn't end well."

"If the objective isn't achieved on the first mission, the team doesn't give up."

She glared at him. "There are so many things wrong with that statement, I don't know where to begin. For one thing, you're not a team, and I'm sure as hell not a mission."

He shifted uncomfortably. "You know what I mean."

"I do, and it's insulting."

"Darcy, you can't avoid what happened forever. It's not going away until you deal with it. The longer you wait the harder it gets."

She didn't want to hear that. She wanted to continue to think that the fear would one day just be gone.

"Go away," she said, turning her back on him.

He put his hand on her shoulder and moved her until they were facing each other again. "No can do. Look, I understand. You think I don't, but you're wrong. I've been scared and alone and bad things have happened to me, too. I can help."

She refused to cooperate. Instead of speaking, she pressed her lips together.

He looked at her. "You're stubborn."

"It's one of my best qualities."

"Want to take a poll on that?" He lowered his hand from her shoulder and sighed heavily. "Here's the thing," he said. "I've had years of training and experience. You didn't have any. When I walk into a dangerous situation I expect trouble, but you were just minding your own business at the mall. Those bastards grabbed you with no warning, and the people whose job it is to protect you screwed up. They weren't there and they didn't notice. You were totally and completely alone."

She honestly hadn't believed anyone could understand what it had been like, but with a few words, he showed her that he got it.

"Tell me what happened," he said gently.

She hesitated, then the words came tumbling out. "I w-was in the back of the store and walking to the dressing rooms. They grabbed me. I didn't have time to scream. They put tape on my mouth and tied my hands behind me, then threw me in the back of a van."

She didn't want to talk about it, she told herself, but she couldn't stop the words from spilling out. Somehow she was walking and telling him everything. About the van and how dirty it was, how she'd tried to get to her panic button but couldn't. About the warehouse and being tied to the chair and scared, so scared, they were going to kill her.

"I tried to get away," she said. "But there was nowhere to go, and the chair didn't make things easy. Then I tried to stay calm. I was afraid I was going to throw up, and I didn't want that. Then the guy in charge showed up. He looked at me and he said —"

She stopped in the middle of the path. Suddenly it was too hard to hold on to her pencils and sketch pad. They dropped to the ground. She rubbed at her still-healing wrists and wished away the rest of the pain.

"What?" Joe asked, his voice more gentle than she'd ever heard it before. "What did he say?"

Oh, God. Tears burned. Weak, stupid tears. She would *not* give in. Not now.

"I — He said that I wasn't the one they wanted." She summoned anger and glared at him. "There. Are you happy? He said not this one. No one cares about this one. I was a mistake. Then they took me back to the mall, dumped me on the loading dock, and drove away."

Jesus. Joe didn't know what to say to that. What could anyone say? Darcy stared at him, her expression defiant. She was angry, but it was a thin veneer that could crack at any time, and he sure didn't want to be around when it did.

Before he could figure out how to respond, she started talking again.

"I love my sister," she said, her voice shaking. "Lauren is my best friend. She understands me and loves me. I admire her so much. But the thing is . . . the very worst thing is, sometimes I hate her." More tears filled Darcy's eyes. "I hate her because I'm weak and small and jealous. And then I feel so horrible, because I want to be like her and I don't know how and everyone loves her best. I'm jealous of my own sister. What does that say about me? What?"

The last word came on a sob. Joe felt both trapped and deeply inadequate to the task. What was it about a crying woman that reduced most men to cowards? He wanted to bolt, but he couldn't, so he did the only thing that made sense to him. He pulled her close and kissed her.

The shock of Joe's lips on hers was enough

to stop Darcy's tears. One second she'd been in an uncontrolled free fall of self-loathing, and the next she was pressed against a man made entirely of rock, his arms around her body and his mouth very much on hers.

She couldn't think, couldn't speak; she could only react, tilting her head slightly so he could kiss her more. Because it felt good. *Better* than good.

His lips were an impossible combination of yielding and firm. He held her with just the right amount of possession. Heat surrounded her, melting all the hard edges and drying her tears. She raised her hands to his shoulders and allowed herself to be swept away by the soft pressure.

He didn't deepen the kiss, but she was okay with that. It had been a long time since she'd wanted a man, so long she'd almost forgotten what it felt like to feel the first fluttering of desire low in her belly. Her breasts went from simply a sticky-out part of her body to exquisitely sensitive, and her legs actually got weak.

When he stepped back, she didn't know what to say. Embarrassment battled with self-preservation. When in doubt, be a bitch. But before she could say anything to shatter the moment, she caught a glimpse of something dark and powerful in his eyes.

Need.

He hadn't just kissed her to stop her crying. He'd kissed her because he'd wanted to. The revelation kept her mouth shut and opened her mind to a thousand amazing possibilities.

"Hell," he muttered.

She nodded in agreement. Talk about a complication.

"I'm —" He shook his head, as if not sure what to say. Then he turned on his heel and walked away.

Darcy watched him go. When he had disappeared into the grove of trees they'd been heading for in the first place, she picked up her sketch book and pencils and started for the house. Around her, the morning stirred to life. She heard birds and someone driving up to the winery.

What on earth had just happened? She'd spilled her guts to Joe, and then he'd kissed her. Even more amazing, she'd felt it. She couldn't remember the last time she'd allowed herself to engage sexually. The few physical relationships she'd had in her past had all ended badly. It had seemed smarter to not go there again.

But now, with Joe, she found herself anticipating the next time she would see him. Oh, sure, it would be awkward, but they'd get over it. Besides, she would have the thrill of knowing he'd *wanted* to kiss her. Which made for a very good day.

Joe avoided the house for the next couple of hours, but he knew he couldn't stay away forever. What the hell had he been thinking? Talk about letting the little head run his life. Darcy was supposed to be under his protection, not in his arms. Was he looking for ways to screw up his career more? Because if he was, he'd found a hell of a good way to do it.

Angry with himself for being an ass, her for being so damn tempting, and the world in general because he was stuck here, he stalked into the house and found Brenna sitting in the kitchen. She had a plate of pasta in front of her and several slices of bread next to her glass of milk.

"Morning," she said cheerfully when she saw him.

He glanced at the clock. It was barely ten-thirty.

She followed his gaze. "Hey, I'm eating for the team. Don't you dare get coffee," she ordered when he started toward the pot.

"What? If you can't have any, no one else

gets to?" he asked as he poured himself a mug.

"Exactly. Oh, man. It's great, isn't it?"

He took a long, slow drink. "Not bad."

She groaned. "Pig." Then she stabbed several pieces of penne and chewed on them.

"You'll be able to drink coffee soon," he told her.

"Not if I'm breast-feeding. And I plan to, for at least a while. I mean I think I can have a little, but it won't be the same. I miss my pot of coffee. And wine. And pretty much everything else I had to give up. This had better be an amazing baby, because if it's not, I'm writing a letter of complaint."

"I can't wait to see who you mail it to."

She grinned. "I'm Catholic, big guy. I have access to spiritual management you can only dream about."

"So I've heard."

He pulled out a chair and settled across from her. "Is this a late breakfast or an early lunch?"

"It's my meal in between. I've been starving for days. Not sure why. Maybe the baby's having a growth spurt. Do they do that?"

"Do I look like I know?"

"Not especially. I brought you something."

She pointed to the stack of books on the table. "Since you're stuck here for a while I thought you'd like a chance to find enlightenment."

He glanced at the books and saw several of them were textbooks on wine making and grape growing.

This was Brenna — subtle as an explosion. Too bad he wasn't interested in playing the game.

"Not for me," he said.

"Oh, come on, Joe. You could look them over. Read a few pages. You might find yourself fascinated."

"Brenna, don't push me on this."

"Why not? I'm pregnant. It's not as if you can threaten me physically. Besides, it's time you accepted who you are — a Marcelli. Wine is cool."

He swore under his breath, then pushed to his feet. "I'm *not* interested and I'm never going to be interested. Not in this place, the land, or the wine. Just so we're all clear on the subject. This isn't my home, and you're not my family."

A flick of movement caught his attention. He turned and saw Grandma Tessa standing in the doorway that led to the dining room. Her eyes were wide and filled with pain.

Perfect, Joe thought grimly. The day was going just perfect.

He hesitated, not sure what to say, then he figured there weren't any words and he stalked out of the house.

Darcy wandered through the various rooms of the winery. Although Brenna had given a very detailed tour, she couldn't remember what all the equipment was for. The various barrels were marked, but not in any language she recognized. She supposed there was a code that explained what was inside, when it had been put in the barrel, and maybe even when it was supposed to come out.

All so interesting, she thought, breathing in the thick scent of grapes and wine and something yeasty — almost like bread. She found herself wanting to know more about the process and how the decisions were made.

"So you're intrigued."

She turned and found Grandpa Lorenzo standing behind her. "I'll admit it," she told him with a smile. "I didn't realize how much I didn't know about wine until I got here. I don't drink it much at home, and when I go out, someone else usually picks."

"Without wine, there can't be life," the

elderly man told her. "Come. I will show you."

He leaned heavily on his cane as he led the way into another room filled with large, stainless steel vats.

"The white wines," he said. "Chardonnays and blends. Different kinds of barrels give a different taste."

"But how can metal give a taste at all?" she asked.

"You are right. The wine is different because it doesn't have the flavors of the wood. We play tricks with the grapes. We tease them and coax them. Sometimes they listen, sometimes they do not. Like children. We know what is best, but there are times everyone has to learn on his own."

He led her into a room filled with all kinds of equipment and a narrow conveyor belt that looked like a snake. "We bottle here. You will come and watch. It's very interesting. Brenna can't stand to be here. She says the treatment is too hard on the wine and it makes her sad to see it battered."

He pointed out where the barrels were emptied and how the liquid flowed into the bottles. Labels were applied, corks pushed in, then sealed with foil coverings.

"So many things can go wrong," Lorenzo told her. "The bottles don't move, the wine doesn't pour, the labels are crooked. But we persevere and then we have this. . . ."

He opened a door, and she saw cases of wine nearly stacked to the ceiling. They were everywhere, leaving only enough space for a small table, a phone, and an intercom.

"My retreat," he said. "When I want to be alone. I like the room when it's like this — crowded before the trucks come to take the wine away. In a few days it will be empty. I spend my afternoons out here. Tessa worries about me. I'm too old to be alone." He touched the intercom. "I call her from here. It buzzes in the kitchen. But still she worries. An old woman."

Darcy heard the love in his voice, and it made her feel warm inside. They had to have been married fifty or sixty years, yet there was still caring, still affection.

"You're very lucky," she said.

"You would think so, eh, but look at this." He opened one of the cases and pulled out a bottle of chardonnay. He pointed at the label. "The same one for too many years. But can we get a new one? No. Brenna brings me designs. They're so bad. Animals and flowers. We are Marcelli Wines. We have a proud tradition."

His voice lowered and his expression softened. "Now she has a baby of her own to keep her busy. So the labels will stay, and we will go on."

"I can't believe she runs two wineries," Darcy said. "That's pretty amazing."

"Yes. Too much, sometimes, but she's stubborn. When I wouldn't let her run Marcelli, she started her own label. Foolish girl. But the first releases are out. She scored high and sold everything within a week."

There was pride in his voice. Darcy understood that Grandpa Lorenzo would be an exacting boss, but she wouldn't mind dealing with the old man. For him, family was everything.

"You have a sister?" he asked.

"Yes. Lauren."

Lorenzo nodded. "And your mother?"

"She died when I was sixteen. My father never remarried. In politics it's difficult to find the time to have a personal life."

"Still, a man shouldn't be alone. It's not right. Look at my Joe. Alone for too many years."

Darcy laughed. "You're not subtle, are you?"

"I'm an old man who wants to see his only grandson married. He's a handsome fellow. Strong. He would be a good provider."

Darcy grinned. "Yes, and he seems to have

very nice teeth. I'm sure he'll be a good breeder."

Lorenzo smiled. "You tease me."

"A little. I don't think Joe is interested in me that way." Although he had just kissed her. Hmm, the lip-pressing did sort of make things more intriguing.

"You could make him interested," Lorenzo said. "You have ways."

"Not as many as you'd think."

"Darcy?"

She heard someone calling her name. A familiar someone. Male, tall, and with good teeth.

"We're in here," she yelled.

Joe walked into the storage room. "Paige and Alex were going crazy. You disappeared."

"Oh, sorry. Your grandfather and I were just talking."

"About you," Lorenzo said. "About your heritage."

Joe shook his head. "Not now, old man. Let me get Darcy back to her Secret Service team."

"What about this family?" Lorenzo demanded, banging his cane on the wooden floor. "What about your duty to it? You should be married and having babies."

"Okay, gotta go," Darcy said, taking that

as her cue to leave. She waved and hurried out of the room. Oh, yeah. Hanging with Alex and Paige was much less pressure than dealing with Joe's inability to get along with his family.

Joe watched Darcy duck out. Lucky her. She could simply walk away.

"I'm not interested in getting married," he said calmly.

"So we all know. And what will happen when you are? What will you call her?"

Joe frowned. "My wife?"

"Will she be a Larson? That is not your real name. You are a Marcelli. You should take back the family name. Be proud you are one of us."

"Not in this lifetime," Joe growled as he turned on his heel and walked out of the room. Change his name? He was Joe Larson, always had been. It was bad enough the old man pressured him about getting married, and now Brenna expected him to learn more about the winery.

The need to run, to bolt for freedom, quickened his step, but there wasn't anywhere to go. As long as Darcy Jensen was in residence, he was trapped.

He'd barely made it to the barrel room of the winery when he ran into Alex Vanmeter. The head of security didn't look happy as he glared at Joe and announced, "We have to talk."

# 8

Alex led Joe around to the back of the winery and checked to make sure they were alone. Then he turned on Joe and let loose.

"What were you thinking?" the agent demanded. Fury tightened his features and sharpened his voice. "You are our liaison with the family. You're a goddamn trained SEAL. You're supposed to be protecting Darcy, not putting her in danger. You have no right to prance around here, sucking face with the president's daughter."

Joe groaned. Between his family and Darcy, he was in the seventh level of hell and sinking fast.

He didn't have to ask how Alex knew about the kiss. No doubt the agent on duty had followed them and seen the whole thing.

"Do you know what we're up against?" Alex demanded. "This is not an easy location to keep secure."

"Then you shouldn't have picked it," Joe told him. "I'm doing my job, and that's all you get from me. Darcy can kiss who she wants. It's not putting her at risk, so you can stop the lecture."

Alex's expression hardened. "You're right, Lieutenant Commander. Kissing her didn't put her at risk, but walking off and leaving her alone sure did."

Joe stiffened. Alex was right. Joe had reacted in the moment, both by kissing her and then by stalking off. He'd needed to get away, to figure out what he thought he was doing. In that moment he hadn't considered who Darcy was or why she was here. If that other agent hadn't been there . . .

He swore long and loudly.

"My thoughts exactly," Alex said. "I'll be e-mailing a report to your commanding officer. I don't imagine you'll be with us much longer."

Joe knew he'd more than earned the action. He heard a flushing sound, followed by the visual of his career slipping down the toilet. The hell of it was, this time he had no one to blame but himself.

"In your position, I would do exactly the same," he said quietly. "You're right. I left the subject unprotected. If your man hadn't been there, she would have been completely exposed and vulnerable. It won't happen again."

Alex didn't look convinced. "Why should I believe you?"

"Because I don't make the same mistake twice. Because I know my job."

Alex shook his head. "Fine. Then remember to do it the next time you're alone with Darcy."

He turned and walked away.

Joe stared after him. What was wrong with him? He *knew* better. Why had he reacted to Darcy? Why had he kissed her?

It wasn't just because she was a woman. He'd worked with women before. Dozens of times. A lot of them had been prettier, smarter, or sexier, and he'd never once lost sight of his objective. Enemy operatives had attempted to seduce him with some highly erotic practices, and he'd ignored them all.

So why Darcy?

"Joe! There you are."

Mia rounded the corner of the building with Ian in tow. Joe's bad mood worsened when he saw the tall, thin young man. There was something about Ian that got on his nerves. Reason number one surfaced the second the lanky blond caught sight of him.

"Hey, Joe," Ian said cheerfully. "How's it going? We've been walking around the winery. It's so great here. I've never been to a winery before." He chuckled. "I've never been much of a wine drinker. But yesterday afternoon Mia took me over to the tasting room. It's really nice there. I like the garden and all the grass around it. She said you guys have weddings there. It would be beautiful for a wedding. Anyway, we had lots of different wines. We tried all the merlots and had a couple of the Four Sisters pinots. Those were really great. Mia told me all about Brenna starting her own winery. That's really cool. That she would do that. You're in the navy, right? A SEAL? I saw that movie. Navy SEALs. It was great. Macho. Didn't that one guy get shot? Huh. I guess if they'd had you along, that wouldn't have happened? Oh, the Secret Service cleared me. But I guess you knew that. I'm still here."

When he paused for breath, Mia jumped in. "So how are things?"

Joe shrugged. "Fine." He stared at Ian. What did she see in the guy? Mia caught his gaze and grinned, as if she could read his mind. She mouthed something that looked very much like "he's really good in bed," which he didn't want to know.

"I haven't had a chance to talk to Darcy," Ian said. "What's she like? She's prettier in person, don't you think? Of course I really like Lauren. She's always helping with those sick kids and it was really sad when her husband died. It was in that ice storm, wasn't it? When D.C. was shut down and his car went off the road. I saw their whole wedding. I was in high school and my mom had this big party and all her friends came over and watched. She made these funny sandwiches and a little wedding cake. It was really good, with a chocolate filling."

Joe started backing away. "I, ah, gotta write a report," he said, interrupting Ian's flow of conversation. "See you guys around."

With that, he ducked into a rear door of the winery and wandered the halls as he headed toward the front of the building. As he rounded a corner, he saw Marco sitting in an office and knocked on the open door.

"Joe! Come in. What are you doing here?"

"Escaping Ian. Mia's had some interesting guys before but never anyone like him," he said, taking a seat.

"I know." Marco leaned back in his chair. "I'm never fond of anyone my youngest daughter is sleeping with, but Ian is worse than most. I try to tell myself that he's basically a nice guy, even though he never stops talking. Besides, your mother likes him, as does mine."

Joe didn't react to Colleen being called his mother, or the guilt he felt over what had happened with Tessa. Instead he focused on the topic at hand. "Then they're too easy."

Marco nodded at the sales report posted on the wall by the door. "We're having a good year. My father has done a great job with the winery for many years, but Brenna brings a touch of magic to the wines. She knows what our customers want."

"She's working hard," Joe acknowledged, wondering if he was about to get nailed again.

Marco struck immediately. "She could use some help."

Joe regretted sitting down. "I'm sure she can hire a good manager to help after the baby's born."

"It's more than that," Marco told him. "Joe, I know you love what you do with the navy, but in time that will end. You'll put in your twenty and retire. Then what? Where will you go? We would like you to come here. You're a Marcelli, Joe. You belong here."

Joe stood. "Look, Marco, I know what you want, what the whole family wants. It's not going to happen. I appreciate that you're trying. It's great. You guys are terrific, but this isn't my world and you're not. . . ." He hesitated, not sure he could say they weren't his family again. Hadn't he hurt enough people already that morning?

"This isn't for me," he finished lamely.

Marco nodded without speaking, but Joe saw the pain in his eyes. Whoever thought families were a good idea, he wondered as he excused himself and escaped into the quiet of the hallway. Give him a nice armed insurgence any day. At least there he would know what to do.

Paige faced the special agent in charge and prepared to do battle. "You're not reporting Joe to his superior officer," she said, going for a calm, but forceful, tone.

"I am," Alex said flatly. "What he did is inexcusable."

"I agree he screwed up, but that's no reason to serve him up on a platter. I'm sure he was shocked by what happened." She'd been shocked. It had been a long time since the president's daughter had gotten involved with anyone, and if Paige were offering opinions, she would bet Joe was one of the good guys, but Joe and Darcy? It didn't seem very likely.

"He left her *alone*," Alex reminded her.

"No, he didn't. Agent Briggs was with them."

"He didn't know that. It's my decision, and I'm not changing my mind."

He turned to leave, but Paige grabbed his arm to hold him in place. Temper flared in his dark blue eyes, but she had a feeling he wouldn't shake her off.

"It's not about Joe," she told him. "If you report him, you'll have to explain the circumstances. You'll have to talk about the fact that they kissed. Darcy will be humiliated. Give the girl a break."

"There are rules to follow," Alex began.

"Oh, and you've never once bent them?"

"No."

Figures. "Try being human," she said. "Just this once. You've already lectured Joe. He's not going to screw up again."

"He shouldn't have screwed up at all. He knows better. He can't walk around thinking with his dick. He needs his brain engaged."

She looked at him and sighed. "I don't remember you being this much of a bastard before."

"My only concern is Darcy's safety."

"What about her happiness?"

"She won't be very happy when she's dead."

He was right, Paige realized. They were talking about Darcy's life, and there was no room for error. She released him.

"Giving up?" he asked.

She nodded. "Darcy is my primary concern. I want her alive *and* happy, but if I only have one choice, I'll pick alive."

Darcy curled up in the library. It was a quiet spot in the Marcelli house, and she liked the view she had of the vineyards out the east-facing window. She also liked that she was completely and totally alone, and not scared about it. When she'd returned from her visit with Grandpa Lorenzo, she'd informed Paige she would stay in for the rest of the afternoon, which meant she didn't have to deal with any security.

Now, as she leaned back in the big leather chair, she breathed in a sense of peace. Maybe it was knowing there were so many people around to keep her safe. Maybe it was because her brain still buzzed with the memory of Joe's kiss. Maybe her astrological moon was rising into a better house. Whatever the reason, she didn't care. Feeling good was fabulous.

She picked up her book, then set it down again. She'd loved the feel of his body against hers. It had been a long time since a man had held her as if he meant it. She wouldn't mind a repeat of the kiss and maybe a little bit of time spent playing the bases with Joe. Not that he was likely to offer, but a girl could dream.

The door to the library opened and the star of her sexual fantasies walked in. He glanced around, then spotted her.

"Oh. You're here."

She smiled, not the least bit put out by his sullenness. From what she could tell, Joe hated everyone. His attitude wasn't personal. "I've always admired a man who handled his abundance of charm with such grace. It's so elegant."

"I'm having a bad day."

"Should I take that comment personally?"

"What?" He closed the door behind him then crossed to the window. "No. It's not about, you know."

You know? How interesting. The big, bad Navy SEAL couldn't say *kiss?* He prowled the room like a tiger, and she had the urge to tweak his tail.

"I don't know, actually. What are you talking about?"

He glared at her. "Our kiss."

"Oh. That."

His eyebrows drew together, and she had a feeling he was going to start yelling at her.

All that energy, she thought, more intrigued than afraid. He must have been one fine soldier.

"I hate Ian," he grumbled.

The change of subject caught her off guard for a second. "He's not so bad."

"He's not sleeping with your sister."

"That's true." She tilted her head. "You've never claimed one of the Marcellis as family before."

"Don't read anything into it. It's just Mia's a baby. She thinks she's wild and tough, but she's not."

"And you worry about her."

He stopped in midstride and glared.

"Don't worry," she said. "My lips are sealed. Besides, even if I wasn't interested in keeping your secrets, I don't want to mess up a good thing. I like it here."

"Don't sound so surprised."

"I am. I didn't think I would. There are too many people and it's so wide open here. But I like the whole family. You should try to appreciate what you have."

"Look, I've heard enough of that to last a lifetime."

"If you were smarter, you'd realize how lucky you are to have found the Marcellis."

"They found me."

"And you've been fighting them ever since."

He returned to the window. "Can we change the subject?"

"We can, but I don't want to. Besides, if you hate what we're talking about, you could leave."

His silence told her he couldn't. But why?

"Are you hiding out here?" she asked.

"I'm running out of places to go."

A feeling she understood. She uncoiled her legs and rested her feet on the floor. "Okay. I'll stop torturing you for sport, but I won't change the subject. You have a terrific family. You're crazy if you don't appreciate that."

He looked at her. "Why does it matter so much to you?"

Because he had everything she'd ever wanted. "My family is small, and we're not so close," she said instead.

"Then you take 'em. I want to get back to base."

"So the navy is your real home?" she asked.

"Yeah."

"It must be nice to spend your day saving the world."

His gaze narrowed, as if he thought she might be teasing him. Darcy did her best to look innocent, although the excessive blinking might have given her away. But before Joe could get all macho on her again, the door opened and Grandma Tessa stepped inside.

"Joseph," she said tentatively, her expression fearful. "I thought you'd come inside." She nodded at Darcy. "I made sandwiches. You didn't come to lunch."

He looked at her, then back out the window. "I'm not hungry."

Darcy winced as the old woman seemed to shrink two inches. "All right, Joseph."

Tessa turned and left.

Darcy stood, walked over to Joe, and socked him in the arm as hard as she could. He looked at her.

"What was that for?"

"It's for whatever you did to Grandma Tessa."

Joe stared hard at the view. "Get off of me."

She socked him again. He didn't budge, but she really hurt her hand. "What did you do?" she demanded.

"Nothing."

"Tell me or I'll start talking about girl stuff."

He winced. "I can handle it."

Oh, no he couldn't. She searched her

memories for something that would bring him to his knees.

"I was twelve when I got my first period," she began.

He swore. "Fine. I had a fight with Brenna. I told her the Marcellis weren't my family. Tessa walked in and heard me."

She sucked in a breath. "That bites. How could you do that to her? She's an old woman who loves you."

"I didn't do it on purpose," he yelled as he turned toward her. "Okay? I'm sorry. I shouldn't have said it."

She leaned toward him. "Well, don't apologize to me. And don't yell. Besides if you were really sorry, you would have taken her sandwich."

He opened his mouth, then closed it. "What?"

"The sandwich. *The sandwich.* Man, you might know a whole bunch about guns and rescuing people but you don't know anything about women, do you? Ever hear the expression 'food is love'? Tessa is old-world Italian. She shows her affection by feeding her family. Every time she offers you food, she's offering you love. When you reject the meal, you reject her."

"That's stupid."

She really wanted to hit him again, but

her knuckles still hurt. "No, it's not. Just eat the food."

"I don't want to," he said as he walked out of the library. "This is all bullshit."

# 9

Life got ugly for Darcy when her favorite black cotton pants wouldn't zip up without her performing an inelegant shimmy on her back, on the bed. Once she sat up, breathing became impossible.

While she knew she had to put on a few pounds, she didn't think gaining them directly in her stomach and hips was anyone's idea of attractive. There was only one thing to do.

After rooting through one of her still-packed suitcases, she came across a pair of bicycle shorts, a black sports bra, and some serious-looking athletic shoes. They'd been designed by NASA or somebody equally scientific. Apparently if she put in some effort while wearing them, she could jump tall buildings and all that.

"Oh, yeah," she muttered as she laced up the shoes. "This is me — working out."

Ten minutes later she'd made her way to

the Marcelli workout room. As all the equipment was relatively new and didn't look very used, she wondered if the space had been created for Joe's infrequent visits home. Somehow she couldn't see Grandma Tessa taking twenty on the treadmill.

She bypassed the running machine and went directly to the elliptical. There she punched in one of the existing programs, set the tension for as easy as possible, and pushed the On button.

Exercising was bad enough, but this room made it worse with four walls of mirrors. She got to watch her face turn bright red, then admire the drops of sweat as they formed and dripped off her nose. Talk about fashion forward.

Oh God, she thought nearly six minutes into her workout. She couldn't breathe. No way she'd gotten this out of shape. She was only twenty-six.

"On the outside," she wheezed. "On the inside, I'm a hundred and nine. Why does healthy have to be so h-hard?"

She sucked in a breath as the machine increased the tension. According to the heart monitor, she'd barely broken triple digits on her heart rate, but her chest felt tight, and her legs were ready to quit in serious protest. Flames licked up her thighs, and not the exciting, sexy kind.

"Lauren does this every day," she gasped. "And she runs. She's sicker than I thought."

At fifteen minutes into her twenty-minute program, she knew she was going to die. The Secret Service would come looking for her and find her sweaty but lifeless body bent over the machine. Paige would be sad, but everyone else would simply move on to the next assignment.

"I can't do this. I ca—"

The workout room door opened and Joe walked in.

Suddenly things like breathing and painful muscles didn't matter. Not when there was an entire buffet of eye candy, not only in person but reflected in the mirrors.

She instantly straightened so he wouldn't know how close she'd come to quitting and sucked in her gut. A deep breath and a lot of effort allowed her to say, "Morning. How's it going," as if she weren't completely winded.

Joe looked at her, then the door. He'd pretty much avoided everyone for the past twenty-four hours. Would he duck out now?

Apparently he needed the workout more than he wanted to be away from her. He grunted a greeting and walked to the treadmill. He, too, punched in a program, but he set his for warp speed. After about thirty seconds of a fast walk, he started jogging, then broke into a run.

Darcy had planned on doing her twenty minutes, then escaping to her room for some serious relaxation. But with Joe running so earnestly and his loose T-shirt flopping over thick, powerful muscles, she thought she might stay long enough to work with the set of free weights in the far corner.

Her machine beeped, freeing her from its torture. She patted her face with the towel she'd brought, then moved to the bench by the weights. It was in the perfect position, allowing her to see Joe from not only the front but also the back, which was reflected in the mirror.

"Missed you at dinner last night," she said as she picked up two ten-pound weights and raised them to shoulder height. "Grammy M stopped by, which meant Grandma Tessa was in a snit. She wasn't talking, but no one could tell because Ian babbled on and on about college and his studies and where he and Mia have been. He made Vegas sound boring, something I didn't think was possible."

Joe picked up the pace on the treadmill, which she took to mean that he was really enjoying their conversation.

"I'm here because of the pasta," she continued. "It's going all to my stomach, which is bad enough, but I know the next stop is my thighs."

"You're lifting wrong."

She paused in midpush, the weights just above her head, her elbows bent.

"What?"

"Start with your palms facing in, then turn them out as you push up."

She dropped the weights to her lap because it was too complicated to change position in midexercise. For a half second she considered ignoring his instructions. If she did it wrong again would he abandon the treadmill to sit next to her and show her how? Would he put his large, masculine hands on her damp, hot body and —

Whoa — stop that fantasy train right there. No more sexy thoughts about Joe, she told herself firmly. He wasn't for her. He didn't even like her. One kiss did not a relationship make.

She did a set of ten presses, then switched to bicep curls. He continued to run at a grueling pace designed to make her hurt just watching him.

"Why are you mad?" he asked.

"I'm not."

"You're scowling."

She glanced in the mirror and realized he was right. She instantly relaxed her face and tried to think happy thoughts.

"Not a morning person?" he asked.

"I'm fine."

"You haven't had coffee yet."

She didn't ask how he knew. "I couldn't fit into my pants. I figured I'd better start working out."

"You need to gain weight."

"Thanks for the news flash, but you've already berated me for that. You don't get to do it again."

He grinned. "It's not like you can stop me."

She felt the scowl reappear.

"Yell at me," he said. "I can take it. Are you sleeping?"

"I'm not talking about that with you."

"But it's an interesting topic."

He was trying to make her mad, and he was succeeding. "Let's talk about you," she snapped. "I may be a skinny insomniac with post-traumatic shock or some such crap, but at least I don't go around hurting my grandmother's feelings."

"Good point."

It didn't feel like a good point. If anything, Darcy would say it felt small and mean-spirited. "I, ah . . ." Apologize, she told herself. The thing was, she didn't do it very often, so she wasn't very good at it. "I shouldn't have said that."

"Why not? It's true."

That stunned her, but the shock was nothing when compared with what he said next. "I've been thinking about what you said. The food-is-love connection. You might be right."

If she'd had any rhythm, she would have stood up and done a little victory dance. Instead she contented herself with a smug smile.

"Gee, thanks for the endorsement. I won't let it go to my head. Besides, the concept is hardly revolutionary. Most mothers show love with food, mine always did. The Marcelli family is Italian, so they have that gene in spades." She considered his past. "Didn't your adoptive mother do the same thing?"

"I don't remember. I was a kid when my parents died. I barely remember what they look like."

The sadness inherent in the statement made her want to walk over and hug him. Both the jogging and her visceral reaction to him made that action impossible. Still, an ache settled in her midsection and made her more determined than ever to help him connect with his family.

"I'm sure she did the same thing," Darcy told him. "I'm not sure we as women can help it."

"Maybe," he admitted, with obvious reluctance. "My ex used to make cookies for her kids when they had a bad day."

"See?" She instantly wanted to ask more questions about his previous marriage but thought her obvious curiosity might destroy the moment.

She set down the weights and stood. "I know you're ambivalent about your family, but what I don't know is why. They only want to love you, Joe. What's so bad about that?"

He hit the Stop button on the treadmill and glared at her. "You're not going to let this go, are you?"

She shook her head as the moment died. "It's too important."

"Why do you care?"

"I'm a compassionate person, and don't you dare laugh. It's true."

Joe didn't doubt it. He might not enjoy his current assignment, but it wasn't because of Darcy. Somehow the press had become convinced she was a prima dona bitch with an attitude, and they slanted all their stories that way. But it wasn't true. Oh, sure, Darcy could use sarcasm like a weapon and she was verbally deadly when she was angry, but at heart, she was a complete pushover.

He wiped his face and neck, then stepped off the treadmill and headed for the mats covering the floor at the rear of the room.

"Come here," he said.

Her expression turned suspicious. "Why?"

He held in a grin. "Don't you trust me?"

"Not as much as you might think."

"I know I can't ask you to change the subject. For some reason you're convinced you can heal me and make me want to bond with my family. So I'm trying to distract you."

"Uh-huh. How?"

He crooked his index finger, beckoning her over. "Come on, Darcy. You know you want to."

"I'm not sure I want to at all," she said, but she began to move toward him. "Are you going to teach me some new exercises?"

"Nope. I'm going to teach you a few moves to ward off would-be attackers. Your Secret Service team should have done it already."

"I've been to a few self-defense classes."

"Not good enough. I'm going to teach you to fight dirty. Stand here." He positioned her in front of him. "I'm going to grab you.

I want you to try and break free."

He leaned forward and wrapped both arms around her. The second he did, he knew he'd made a huge mistake.

She was hot and sweaty from her workout, which should have been a turnoff, but instead it made him think of other kinds of activity that could work up a sweat. He instantly pictured them rolling around together in bed, bodies sliding together, hands reaching, them both straining to —

He shook off the thought and did his best not to react. In nylon shorts there was no way he could hide a hard-on.

Focus, he told himself. He had to remember what was important.

"Elbow me in the midsection," he said. "As hard as you can. And don't worry, you can't hurt me."

She sucked in a breath, then rammed her elbow into his midsection. He barely felt it.

"Harder, Darcy. I'm the bad guy. Do it like you mean it."

She hit him again, but it wasn't much more than a slight blow. Her security wrist band barely moved. He released her. "Are you even trying?"

She huffed. "Yes. And let me say for the record — ouch." She rubbed her arm.

He couldn't help chuckling. "That was it?

That was your big power play?"

Fury darkened her eyes and determination pulled at her mouth. Even all blotchy and damp, she was still pretty, he thought, amused by her temper. The sports bra and shorts left nothing to the imagination. She might be all female, but she was sadly lacking in curves. Still, he wanted her. Funny how it didn't matter that she wasn't his usual type.

"I want to do it again," she said, turning her back to him.

He obliged her by stepping close and grabbing her. One of his hands was right below her left breast. He felt the heat of the modest swell, and it was all he could do not to reach up and cup the feminine flesh. Would her nipple get hard right away? Would it —

Bam! She nailed him hard in the gut, and he'd forgotten to prepare. Her bony elbow connected painfully with a rib. At the same time she stomped down hard on his foot, then turned to face him, both hands raised in fists.

"Better," he said, ignoring the pain. "But don't take on your attacker. Run like hell. My point is, you can't use conventional methods to hurt a man who's bigger and

stronger. That's what I wanted to demon-
strate."

She looked disappointed. "I didn't hurt
you?"

He ignored the fading pain in his midsection. "Do I look hurt?"

"I guess not."

He pointed to her face. "Go for the eyes.
Or the base of your palm to the base of the
nose. Push hard, toward the eyes." He
explained a few other vulnerable points.

"What if there's more than one?" she
asked when he'd paused. "What do I do
then?"

He remembered the attack that had
brought her here in the first place. "How
many were there?"

"Four. They grabbed me and tied me up
before I could do anything."

He reached out and put his hand on her
shoulder. "You're not going to win against
four guys, Darcy. There's nothing you could
have done."

"But you could have held off four guys?"

He shrugged. "I have years of training."

"Could I learn?"

Would it help? Would it make her feel
safer? "If you wanted to. First you need to
get some muscle on your body. Those
weights you were working with are fine to

tone up, but you need to be pushing yourself." He glanced over her frame. "You should be able to bench-press a hundred pounds and leg press double that."

Her eyes widened. "Are you crazy? I'll look like some kind of freak."

"You won't bulk up. Women don't. Besides, muscle makes you tight and defined." He shook his head. "What is it about women and looking muscular?"

"It's cultural. As the half of the species rewarded for being bigger, you wouldn't understand."

"But you look fine."

"You said I was too skinny."

"You are."

She sighed. "Let me guess. You like lots of curves on your women."

He sensed this was a dangerous conversation and didn't respond with more than a shrug.

"I knew it."

"You look perfectly okay," he said.

"Oh, wow. I can hardly breathe from the excited beating of my heart. What a compliment. I'll treasure it always."

He didn't think she was upset, but he wasn't sure. "You know you're attractive, right?"

"I guess."

Her unenthusiastic response and the way she averted her gaze made him wonder if she did. He moved a little closer.

"Darcy, you are. You have a pretty face, great eyes, and when you smile, it's like you're sharing a secret with the world."

She ducked her head. "Thanks. I appreciate you saying that, but in my family, Lauren's the pretty one. Not that I mind," she added hastily.

"You need to get over your sister complex."

She looked at him and rolled her eyes. "Gee, Dr. Larson, thanks for the psychological evaluation. But it's not that simple. Life keeps getting in the way. For example, the first guy I ever slept with turned out to not be interested in me at all. He suffered through our relationship simply to get an invitation home for winter break where he hit on my sister. Lauren, being Lauren, refused to have anything to do with him, but that didn't take away the sting."

Why had he started this conversation?

"He's a jerk, and you're better off without him," Joe told her.

"I know that, but it's not the point. And at the time, it really hurt. There I was, heartbroken, and my sister was trying to make it better. She's just a nice person."

"She sounds perfect."

Darcy nodded. "She is. Pretty much in everything she does. Everyone loves her."

"Perfect can get boring."

Darcy glared at him. "Don't you say anything bad about my sister."

He held up both hands and took a step back. "You have a pretty complex relationship with Lauren."

"I know." She sighed. "Sorry for snapping. Sometimes . . ." She smiled. "I'm a multifaceted person."

And charming, he thought as he moved closer. Funny, vulnerable. And the president's daughter. He was just the hired help. Getting involved would be crazy.

"Oh, wow," she breathed as she stared up at him.

"I'm not going to kiss you," he told her.

"I can see that."

Darcy watched desire darken Joe's eyes. He might claim he wasn't going to kiss her, but she would bet a lot of money that he wanted to. She felt all shivery and hot and nervous. But she didn't move away. Not even an inch. If there was the potential for some lip-lock, she wanted to be there for the whole thing.

He reached out and touched her cheek with his fingers. "I could lose my career over this," he said quietly.

"No woman could ever be worth that."

"Agreed."

But he didn't step away, and the thought thrilled her. He wanted her. She could feel it in the tension in his body. He wanted *her*. Not Lauren, he wasn't interested in political favors. He was —

He leaned forward and claimed her mouth with his. There was heat and promise in that first brush of his lips. She relaxed into him, raising her arms to his shoulders, and let her body sag into his hardness. He pulled her close, angled his head, and swept his tongue against her bottom lip.

She parted without thinking. Need overwhelmed her, and the second he eased inside to claim her, she knew it wasn't going to be enough. She wanted more. She wanted all of it.

Hunger swept through her, causing her to run her hands up and down his back, urging him closer. Her breasts flattened against his chest, her thighs nestled with his. She wanted to rub against him like a cat — she wanted him touching her everywhere.

Instead she had to content herself with a deep, sensual, perfect kiss. He claimed her mouth with a mastery that left her breathless. His tongue circled hers, teasing, arousing, delighting. His large hands stroked her back before moving lower to cup her rear. When he squeezed, she arched forward, bringing her belly in contact with his erection.

Her breath caught as she realized he was hard. She'd made him want her. Need swelled as did her nipples. They ached. *She* ached.

Not knowing what else to do, she slid her hands under his T-shirt until she touched bare skin. He was hot and slightly damp, and she found herself wanting to explore him all over. First with her fingers and then with her tongue. She wanted to taste him and consume him.

He pulled back with a suddenness that made her gasp. They stared at each other, both breathing hard. Joe's eyes were dilated.

Silence filled the room. She waited for him to dismiss what had happened between them. Not because she believed he could, but because her luck with men just wasn't that good. He stunned her when he gave her a half-grin, half-grimace and said, "It wasn't supposed to be that great."

"Yeah?" she asked, unable to keep from smiling.

"Yeah. You're big trouble. Your father is my commander in chief."

"Does that really matter?"

"It should."

Which didn't answer her question.

"You go first," he said, motioning to the door.

Right. So they weren't seen together.

"I'll wait here," he continued. "Until it's safe."

"I doubt anyone is lurking in the hallway."

"That's not what I mean." He pointed at his crotch.

"Oh." He was obviously hard, and it was damned impressive. "Right. You don't want to flash that at Grandma Tessa."

He winced. "Talking about her will help solve the problem."

"I live to serve."

Mia caught up with Darcy late that morning. "You have to come right now," Mia said as she burst into Darcy's room. "I'm convinced there's something going on between Paige and Alex."

"What? That's crazy. Agents can't be involved."

"I don't know what the rules are, but they're always giving each other these smoldering looks. I've called a meeting of the Marcelli women and you *have* to be there. I mean, you're one of us, now."

Darcy didn't think that was true, but she was delighted to be asked. "I'm in."

"Cool." Mia grinned. "Francesca is coming, too, so you can meet her and the twins. They're at the insane age. Running around and getting into everything. There's two of them and only seven of us. I'm not sure we'll manage."

Darcy laughed. "I think we can handle it."

Mia shook her head. "Have you ever been around toddler twins? Trust me, every second is an adventure."

It turned out Mia was telling the truth. Eric and Haley were two and a half and too adorable for words. They both had dark hair, and blue, blue eyes. Haley had the kind of curls women sell their souls for. They were also bundles of energy who refused to be contained.

The Marcelli women gathered in the large living room where Darcy met Francesca Reese for the first time. Brenna's fraternal twin was tall and slender, with short, dark hair and beautiful features.

Brenna settled in a corner of the couch, then announced she would need help when it was time for her to stand up.

"Do you like her hair?" Brenna asked, pointing at Francesca.

Darcy nodded. "It's really cute."

"So typical. I cut my hair three years ago and I looked like a yak. She does it right after the twins were born and she's a supermodel." Brenna eyed the twins as they raced around the coffee table. "Please, God, no twins for me. I'd have to kill myself."

Grammy M picked up her cup of tea. "Brenna, darlin', be careful how you're talkin' to the Lord."

"But I'm sincere. I'm really worried about the twin thing. I can't have twins. I just can't. I'll be forced to send them back."

"Good luck," Colleen told her daughter. "They resist the process." She glanced around. "This is nice, having my girls here. Except for Katie. I miss her. If only she lived closer."

Grammy M smiled at Brenna. "See how a mother loves her children? You'll do the same, twins or not."

"I guess." Brenna didn't sound convinced.

Mia flopped down on the second sofa and reached for a cookie on one of the plates of food Grandma Tessa had brought into the room. There'd been a minor scuffle in the kitchen when Grammy M had shown up with brownies, but now Tessa's cookies and Grammy M's brownies sat at separate tables.

"Wouldn't it show up in an ultrasound?"

Mia asked as she munched. "Wouldn't they see four arms or legs?"

"I've only had a couple to make sure things are all right. Nic and I don't want to know the sex of the baby, and if you keep going, someone is bound to slip. It's just that at one of the ultrasounds, the technician said there were two babies, but since then, we've only seen one." Brenna tried to lean forward, then sagged back and held out her hand. "Someone give me a brownie, please. I need chocolate."

Little Haley dove for the brownie Colleen picked up, slipped, and banged her head on the coffee table. She started crying, and Eric joined in, Darcy supposed, to be supportive. Francesca grabbed for one twin, Colleen took the other, and Brenna clutched her brownie.

Mia waited until the sobs had died down, then cleared her throat. "I'm sure you're all wondering why I called this meeting."

"You said it was because you thought Paige and Alex have something going on," Darcy said.

Francesca smiled at her. "They're your Secret Service agents, right?"

"Two of many," Darcy said with a shrug.

Francesca rocked Haley. "You must get tired of having so many people around."

"Yeah," Brenna said. "I had plenty of that when I lived here."

Tessa bustled into the room and scowled at her granddaughter. "We're your family, and you're lucky to have us."

Brenna grinned. "I love you, too, Grandma Tessa."

The old woman's face softened into a smile.

"Hey, back to my agenda," Mia said. "Paige and Alex. I haven't actually seen them doing anything, but there are plenty of longing glances. It makes me wonder what's up. Darcy. You're the person most likely to know."

Everyone looked at her. Darcy held her mug of tea like a shield. "Time out. I don't know anything. I've had Paige on my security team before, but I've only just met Alex. To be honest, he's so by the book, I can't imagine him with a woman."

"Still waters," Colleen said. "Men like that can surprise you."

Brenna, Francesca, and Mia looked at one another, then Mia said, "Mom, if that is *any* reference to your sex life with Dad, I beg you to stop. No one here wants to know. Especially your daughters. Yuck."

Colleen's smile turned smug. "All right, girls, don't freak out."

"I'm totally freaked," Brenna said. "What about you?"

Francesca nodded. "It's an image I never want in my brain."

"Alex and Paige," Mia said. "Stay focused, people."

Darcy looked at her. "I don't understand. Do you want to help them get together?"

"Of course." Mia sat up straighter. "I figure we can trick them into being alone together."

Interesting plan, Darcy thought. "But they're already sharing the guesthouse. Doesn't that mean they're alone together every night?"

"Oh." Mia sank back onto the sofa. "Good point. I guess they don't need our help. So, Darcy, what do you think of Joe?"

Darcy immediately sensed the danger of the situation. Still, she faced the other women bravely and decided the best defense and all that.

"He's great. What can you tell me about his ex-wife?"

She'd expected a few murmurs about how lovely she was or maybe shrugs when they said they'd never met her. She didn't expect stunned silence, followed by forty-seven questions at once.

"Married?" Brenna asked. "When did he

get married?"

"There's an ex-wife?" Francesca asked. "Do we know her?"

"Tell me she's dead," Grandma Tessa said as she pulled her beads out of her pocket. "Better that than a divorce."

"I wonder if she'll tell us what he looked like naked," Mia mused.

Joe wandered into the kitchen in the late afternoon. He crossed to the refrigerator before he realized Tessa was at the stove. She looked up when he entered but didn't say anything. Still, the hurt in her eyes was enough to make him feel like a slug.

Dammit, what was he supposed to say to her? He couldn't give her what she wanted, but that didn't give him the excuse to be cruel.

He crossed to her and gave her a hug. "I'm sorry about what I said."

She held him with a fierceness that surprised him. "It's been three years, Joseph." She stepped back and stared up at him. "How long? When are we family?"

He didn't know how to answer that. He wasn't going to lie, but he didn't want to hurt her again.

She was so small and frail — she didn't even come to his shoulder. Funny how she seemed so much bigger when she was bustling in the kitchen or bringing a grown man to his knees with one of her deadly cheek pinches.

Finally she turned away. "I'll make you some pasta," she said. "You didn't eat lunch. You must be hungry."

His first instinct was to say no, but then he remembered what Darcy had told him. About food being love.

"I'd like that," he said and was rewarded with a glowing smile.

"Sit, sit. You'll have bread, too. And salad. Maybe some wine. You like the red, yes?"

"That would be great. Thanks."

She served the food, poured the wine, then sat down across from him. Later he would swear she waited until he'd taken the first forkful of food and his mouth was full.

"So, Joseph. Tell me about your wife."

# 10

Still feeling the need to hide out after inadvertently dropping a bombshell on the family, Darcy retreated to her room and picked up the secure phone that had been installed the second day of her visit. She dialed a familiar number and was connected with her father's personal assistant.

"It's Darcy," she said. "Is he available?"

"No, honey. He's in a meeting with China. Want me to interrupt?"

Darcy glanced at her watch. It was nearly five here, which made it close to eight in D.C. As per usual, her father was working late.

"No. That's okay. Tell him . . ." What? That she missed him? That would make him laugh. "Tell him I called."

"Will do. Are you okay? Having a good time?"

Darcy looked around the room, at the familiar furnishings and the view of the vineyard just beyond her window.

"I'm having a great time," she said.

Darcy's bedroom door opened without warning and Joe stalked inside. She was about to point out that he should at least pretend to knock — what if she'd been naked — when she saw the slight twitch in his cheek and something that looked amazingly like the need to squash, beat, or maim in his eyes.

She put down the book she'd been reading and held up both hands in a gesture that some might take to be surrender.

"You never said it was a secret," she pointed out, speaking quickly. "It didn't occur to me they didn't know. I mean, come on. It's been three years and you never bothered to mention to your family that you'd been married? That's not my fault."

He closed the door and walked to the bed. She thought about scooting over and patting the mattress in invitation but doubted that was why he was here.

"You're right," he said, his voice tight and clipped, which could be caused by his clenched teeth. "I didn't tell them."

"And you didn't say I shouldn't say anything."

"Right."

"And you really should have mentioned it to them before this."

He crossed to the single chair in the room and sank onto the cushion. "Apparently."

"Are they hysterical?"

"Tessa's done her rosary twice and is begging me to tell her that my ex is dead, because a dead wife is a whole lot better than divorce in her book. Grammy M and Colleen are hurt, and Brenna and Mia are mad. I haven't talked with Marco or Lorenzo yet, but I'm sure they'll give me an earful."

He seemed surprised. Men, she thought. Sometimes they weren't all that bright.

"They're your family. You may not think of them as such, but they think of themselves that way. It's not like you stubbed your toe and forgot to mention it. You were *married.* You had a whole other life."

He shrugged. "I'm not married now. Haven't been in a while."

"What happened?" she asked. "I mean why did you guys split up?"

He stared at her without speaking. Darcy figured he was trying to intimidate her. While it kind of worked, she wanted to know more than she was afraid of him.

"It's a logical question," she told him. "You'd ask me the same thing if our positions were reversed."

"No, I wouldn't."

"Okay. Your loss. So what happened?"

Joe leaned back in the chair and rubbed the bridge of his nose. "She couldn't handle me having to leave without any notice and being gone for months at a time. I'd warned her what it would be like, and she said it was fine. But hearing about it and living it were different. One time I came home and she was gone."

Darcy's heart cracked a little in sympathy. "I'm sorry. That must have been horrible."

"It wasn't one of my best moments." He shrugged. "I got over her quicker than I should have, which says something about the state of our relationship, but I really missed the kids."

"How many?"

"Two. Eight and ten. They were great," he said with a smile that told her he had a lot of good memories. "Later, when I realized who I missed the most, I wondered if they were the real reason I'd wanted to get married. To have an instant family."

As soon as the words were out, he straightened, getting all stiff, as if he regretted the confession.

He'd wanted children in his life? She never would have guessed.

"That's just so sad," she told him.

"Whatever. I got over it." He looked at her. "My family doesn't need to know about the kids."

"Not a problem. I won't say anything. I didn't mean to spill secrets about your divorce."

"I know. I should have told them myself."

But he hadn't. Knowing him as she did, she could guess why. But what didn't make sense was why he'd told her.

Shortly after midnight, Alex found himself walking restlessly through the small guesthouse. He should have been getting some sleep. He wasn't on duty, and come morning there would be plenty to do. But he wasn't sleepy and the light still shining under Paige's door beckoned him like a siren's call.

She'd changed, he acknowledged. Softened, but not in a way that interfered with her doing her job. In that respect, she was as focused as always. She seemed more balanced, more connected with people. The drive had faded, maybe disappeared. He would have bet on her staying as career driven as she'd been when he'd first met her, and it pissed him off that the change was due to another man.

He paused outside of her door and put his hand on the knob. Going in would be stupid and weak. Better to walk away. He'd managed to forget about her once before. In fact, after they'd split up and gone their separate ways, he'd barely thought about her at all. So what was the big deal now? He could —

He knocked on the door and opened it at the same time. Paige sat on her bed, reading. There was a glass of wine on the nightstand and soft music playing in the background.

She raised her eyebrows. "It's a little late for business," she said. "And we're officially off duty."

"I know."

He started to back out of the room, but she gestured to the open bottle of wine on the dresser. "Help yourself," she told him.

There was a second glass on the tray. Had she been expecting company? Expecting him?

After pouring himself a glass of chardonnay, he moved to the overstuffed chair in the corner of the room and sank down.

"The assignment's going well," he said into the silence.

Paige closed her book and set it beside her. She wore the same pajamas he'd seen her in before. A tank top over loose pants. No bra. The curve of her breast was clearly visible, as was the slight pucker of her nipple.

She picked up her wine and took a sip. "I agree. Darcy is relaxing, which is good. I had an interesting talk with Joe today. He thinks Darcy should receive some advanced self-defense training. Maybe get started in some form of martial arts. He also suggested I put together a workout program for her that will get her into some heavy weights."

Alex wasn't sure it would help. "She was taken by four men. Very few women would be able to stop that."

"Agreed, but the training and additional strength would give her more of a sense of control. That might help her sleep at night."

He worried more about the subject's physical safety than her emotional state of mind. Still it couldn't hurt.

"Whatever you want to do with her is fine with me," he said.

"How thrilled I am to have my leader's permission," she said with a grin. "I know Darcy will do the dance of joy."

He felt the teasing more than he should have. "Why were you telling me if not to get permission."

"I was having a conversation, Alex. You might remember them."

She thought he was too into the job. Not interesting enough. The assessment stung. He'd had to work his ass off to get his present assignment. She, of all people, should appreciate that.

"I know how to have a conversation," he said. "Let's have one. Do you miss being married?"

He wasn't sure if the question surprised her, but it shocked the hell out of him. He'd planned on saying something about the winery. Those other words had come from nowhere.

"I miss Ben," she said quietly. Her green eyes seemed to darken with what? Memories? Pain?

"A lot of people were surprised when you got married," he said. Mostly him. "What happened?"

"The usual." She smiled. "I met Ben and fell in love."

She'd claimed to love *him* but there'd been no talk of marriage. No search for a happily ever after. Why? What had that Ben guy had that he, Alex, hadn't?

"It screwed up your career," he said.

"If you mean I didn't get ahead as quickly as I could have, that's true. On the other hand, I actually had a private life, and that was very important to me. Ben taught me life isn't an all-or-nothing sport. There are points of compromise, and sometimes that's even better than winning."

On what planet? Alex drank more wine and wished they were talking about anything else.

"When I met Ben," she continued, "I warned him I would work long hours and have to travel. He said he would rather have me around some of the time than not at all. It was a unique perspective."

Alex didn't know what to do with that information. "So, how did he die?"

"Lymphoma. He had it when we met, but he was in remission. Unfortunately, it came back and then he died."

Alex stared at her. "You knew he was dying when you married him?"

"I knew the disease was likely to reoccur and that the odds of us growing old together were slim."

"Why would you do that?"

Paige smiled. "Because I loved him. Because I would rather have had a short time with him than none at all."

Annoyance flared into something bigger and hotter. "You were willing to give up your career for some guy who was dying, but you broke up with me because your career was all-important?"

"I told you, Ben taught me to compromise. Besides, you never wanted to marry me."

"Oh, yeah? How do *you* know?"

One corner of her mouth turned up. "You never asked."

This was not how he'd wanted the evening to go. He stood and put the glass back on her dresser. "I won't bother you anymore," he said stiffly.

"You're not a bother."

Anger gave energy to his stride as he walked to the door. "I'll see you in the morning. Good night."

"Alex, wait."

But he didn't. Instead he stepped into the hall and closed her door behind him.

He stood there in the darkness, but she didn't come out. She didn't beg him to return. And then he didn't know why he'd left in the first place, but it was too late to change that now.


Joe walked through the winery. Funny how this was the one place he could usually find to be alone. No Grandma Tessa trying to feed him or talk about his ex-wife. No Brenna wanting to talk about grapes or his ex-wife, or Mia wanting to talk about God knows what, including his ex-wife, with Ian offering a hundred different opinions. No Darcy.

He didn't have a specific complaint about her, except he was an idiot where she was concerned. He wasn't supposed to even *like* her. She should be a nonperson. Simply the subject to be kept safe. Nothing more. But she was real and alive, and for some reason he'd yet to figure out, she got to him.

In an effort to distract himself, he walked into Lorenzo's office. The old man wasn't there — a good thing because Joe wasn't interested in going another round on inheritance, his future, or changing his name from Larson to Marcelli.

He glanced at the old ledger books, the charts that detailed production, and the big map on the wall — the one that showed all the Marcelli land, and most of Wild Sea next door. He moved closer and traced the line of the coast, then studied the elegant script that spelled out the family name.

He wasn't one of them, never had been, never would be. But no matter how many times he told them, they ignored him. It was as if they thought they could make him believe by their combined force of will. As if they could force him into what they saw as his destiny.

A familiar slow step caught his attention. He turned to the doorway and saw Lorenzo enter the room. The old man nodded at Joe, then made his way to his desk where he sat down heavily.

"There are too many women in this family," he announced as he rested his cane against the desk. "There always have been. God could have blessed me with five grandsons, but instead he saw fit to surround me with women." He leaned back in his chair and eyed Joe. "You had the right idea. Join the navy and leave the women behind."

Joe grinned. "They're letting women in the navy these days. Even on the ships."

"Fools. It was better before. When a man could be alone with his thoughts. Now — all the talking. If Tessa is awake her lips are moving, and not in prayer."

Joe held in his amusement. "At this point, she's not going to change."

Lorenzo nodded. "I know. She makes me tired. Of course you would know that. A man learns things when he takes a wife."

Joe groaned. "Not you, too."

"Of course me." The old man shook his head. "You didn't tell us."

"It didn't matter. The marriage was long over before I knew about the Marcellis."

Before Joe could respond, Ian popped his head in the office. "Hey. There you are. I thought I'd find you here. Hi. We're going to be heading out. Mia and I want to go down to San Diego for a few days before coming back here. Joe, you think you could get us on base? It would be really cool to see some of the ships and planes and stuff up close. I'd really like to."

Ian stepped into the office and looked around. "Great place. Marcelli is the best. Everything is so interesting here. I really like the wine stuff. Mia doesn't know much, but we've done tasting and watched the guys working. If I wasn't going into government work, I think I'd want to work with wine. But here. Not in Napa or up there. I grew up here." He spotted the map on the wall. "Cool. I know this part of the coast. My grandfather took me fishing out here all the time."

Ian traced a spot on the map and grinned at Joe. "There are some caves here. A few are really deep. You can get a big boat in them. Some fill up with every tide, so you don't want to be there at the wrong time. It could be really bad. But I liked the caves. You probably know all about swimming in caves, from being a SEAL. Right? Maybe you two could go fishing. Or if you wait until Mia and I come back, I could go with you."

Ian actually paused for breath. Lorenzo looked shell-shocked while Joe took advantage of the lull. "Is that Mia calling you?" he asked.

"What? Oh, she doesn't know I came in here. I'd better go find her. Thanks for everything. You guys have been great." He shook hands with Lorenzo, then turned to Joe. "Mia thinks you're terrific. She's always talking about you and —"

Joe pulled his hand free. "Thanks. You'd better go find her. You know how Mia gets."

"What? Oh, right."

Ian disappeared. Joe crossed to the chair opposite Lorenzo's and sank down. "Not my favorite guy."

Lorenzo frowned. "What does she see in him?"

"Nothing."

"Then why is she with him? I want Mia married and having babies, but not with that one."

Joe agreed. "Mia isn't interested in settling down right now. So she picks men who don't challenge her. She could never be with someone she didn't respect. That means she's protected — she won't fall in love with someone like Ian."

Lorenzo stared at him. "You have considered this."

He shrugged. "I've had a lot of free time since I got here."

"You have been around the women too long. They are changing your brain. Come. We'll go taste from the barrels. You can tell me what you think."

Lorenzo slowly rose to his feet. Leaning heavily on the cane, he led the way into the barrel room, where he motioned for one of the workers to come along. Small samples of wine were poured and glasses handed around.

Joe braced himself for a volley of criticism. There was no way he could survive a barrel tasting with his limited knowledge. Despite three years of visits to the Marcellis, he still preferred beer to wine.

"You taste what will be there in the future," Lorenzo said, swirling the liquid in his glass and studying it. "The hints of how the flower will blossom." He inhaled the smell of the wine. "It is still young. Like a child. But when it grows, what will it become?"

Joe took a sip and grimaced. The flavor was too sharp, too thick, too much of everything. Before he could say anything, Lorenzo also tasted the wine.

"You see," he said. "The blending has already begun."

"Uh-huh."

The old man's eyes narrowed. "What do you taste?" he asked sharply.

Joe shrugged and told the truth. "Really bad wine."

Lorenzo muttered something under his breath before saying, "You know nothing of us. Nothing of our wine. You should know. This should be who you are."

Joe was tired of the argument, tired of the criticism. "Who's fault is that?" he asked, allowing his temper to get the best of him. "If I remember correctly, you're the one who made sure I was sent away, so don't go blaming me for what I do and don't know. You're responsible, old man."

"That was a long time ago," Lorenzo snapped. "You know about us now. You should be here, married, having babies. You owe this family."

Joe set down his glass. "I owe you *nothing.* After thirty years I find out about you. So what? I have a whole life that doesn't include you or the Marcellis. You get that? I made my own way in the world. You came looking for me when it was finally convenient. You keep pushing, but I'm not interested."

Lorenzo narrowed his gaze. "So now you say you don't want your family. What kind of man thinks such a thing?"

"I do."

"Because the navy is so wonderful? What happens when you get old, eh? They won't want you anymore. But here, we will always want you."

"That's bullshit," Joe yelled, matching Lorenzo's rising voice. "You don't want me. You want some stud service to continue the family name because you have an outdated concept of a woman's place in the world. Brenna's doing this a whole lot better than I ever could."

"Wow."

Joe turned and saw Darcy standing in the barrel room. She looked more amused than shocked by all the shouting.

"What do you want?" he demanded.

She folded her arms over her chest and leaned against the wall. "If anyone was curious about the two of you being related, this moment would satisfy them. You even yell the same. Anyway, Mia and Ian are packed up and leaving. I thought the two of you might want to say good-bye."

Lorenzo shook his head. "That girl," he said as he limped out of the room.

Darcy stayed where she was, watching Joe.

"I wouldn't have pegged you for a screamer," she said. "But you were matching him, decibel for decibel. It kinda kills my image of the cool, collected SEAL."

"He pisses me off."

"I guess." Her mouth curved into a smile. "Who would have thought Grandpa Lorenzo could take on the big, bad military guy and win."

He moved close and stared down at her. "I know forty-seven ways to kill you with my bare hands."

"Uh-huh." The smile widened. "And I can bring you to your knees with a single sentence."

No way, he told himself, liking how she wasn't intimidated by him or the argument.

"Prove it."

She rested one hand on his chest, drew in a deep breath, and then sighed. "Joe, I think we should talk about our feelings."

# 11

"I don't think my stitches are even," Darcy said as she stared at the ten-inch square of fabric in her hands. "Aren't they supposed to be even?"

Paige leaned over and studied Darcy's work, then glanced at her own. "Hey, you're doing better than me. At this rate, the most they'll let me do is collect leftover scraps and throw them in the trash."

Darcy tugged at the thread, but it wouldn't pull through all the way, which left a little bit sticking up that didn't exactly match the rest of the pattern.

"This is for a good cause," she muttered. "Tell me it is, because I'm so not getting it."

"We're becoming better seamstresses so that when the next Marcelli bride gets her dress made we can help. Not that we'll be here, but it beats weeding the vineyards, right?"

Darcy smiled. "I don't think they'd make us do that."

So far the Marcellis hadn't asked her to do much of anything except show up for meals and be friendly. Grammy M had stopped by with the squares of fabric and had taught them a couple of basic quilting stitches, with the understanding that in time they would put their newfound skills to good use on a wedding gown.

While Darcy loved the idea of a family of women sewing each bride's dress, she had a feeling she wasn't going to be here long enough to see it happen. Although maybe they would invite her back when Mia got married.

"Have you talked to Lauren?" Paige asked, before she tugged too hard, broke her thread, and swore. "I'm not domestic. It's as simple as that."

"You and me both," Darcy said with a laugh. She tossed her square onto the coffee table in front of the sofa. "Yeah, I've talked to Lauren. I feel really guilty. I'm here and she's stuck in some farmhouse in the Midwest. Lately she seems to know way too much about growing corn, which is a little scary. I don't think she has anything else to do with her day but watch it grow and ripen."

Paige grinned. "She's fine. I promise."

"Hope so." Darcy glanced at the agent. "You know, Mia's convinced there's something going on between you and Alex."

Paige paused in the act of threading her needle. She blinked twice. "Really?"

The innocence was too studied, too forced. "Is there?"

"Special Agent Vanmeter and I are working on your security team," Paige said primly.

"And sharing a house. By the way, Mia told the entire family and wants us to help get you together."

Paige sagged against the sofa. "Tell me you're kidding."

"Not even a little. Of course now everyone is distracted by the news Joe was married before, if that helps."

"It doesn't."

Darcy was stunned. "There *is* something going on."

"No, there's not. But . . ." She hesitated. "There was. A lot of years ago. Alex and I met during our initial training and we developed a thing for each other. But when training was over, we both decided our careers were more important than any relationship and we went our separate ways."

Darcy hadn't had a clue. She supposed no one did, except Mia, and that was the point. "And now?" she asked.

"Now we're protecting you."

Darcy didn't think she believed that was the end of it. "Nothing else. No lingering sparks?"

Paige smiled. "Spark is too strong. There might be some heavy smoldering, but it doesn't mean anything."

"Because Alex is such a tight-ass?"

The smile turned into a grin. "You've noticed."

"Hard not to. The guy practically invented the word. He needs to lighten up."

"He wants to keep you safe."

It was a philosophy Darcy could get behind. Except, over the past couple of days, she'd found herself being less afraid. Less wary of every noise and person she met.

"Are you going to pursue it?" Darcy asked.

"Not a clue," Paige admitted. "What about you? Lieutenant Commander Larson looks very hunky."

Darcy leaned forward and grabbed her fabric square. At the mention of Joe her insides got all tight and her face felt hot.

"He's okay," she said quietly.

Paige laughed. "Honey, we all know he

kissed you out in the vineyard. You were observed by an agent."

Darcy looked at her. "You're kidding."

"Sorry. No."

Great. One of the many joys of being related to the president. At least they didn't know about the kiss in the exercise room.

"He's cute and all," she admitted, "but I don't really have great luck with guys." The ones she'd met wanted her either for her sister or for her family connections.

"Are you worried he's only interested because you could help him with his career?" Paige asked.

Darcy hadn't considered that. "Could I?"

Paige looked at her. "Honey, with a couple of phone calls, you could practically get him his own ship. I doubt he'd be interested. Not in any command he didn't earn. He shares that with Alex."

Darcy chuckled. "Are you saying Joe's a tight-ass, too."

"Pretty much."

Darcy hadn't touched that particular body part, but she'd leaned against a lot of him, and he was rock solid everywhere. A quality she'd never considered in a man before but now found very desirable.

Colleen walked into the living room. She carried a tray heavy with sandwiches, cookies, and the inevitable bottle of Marcelli wine. This one was a cab-merlot blend.

"Now what are you two girls talking about?" Colleen asked as she set the tray on the coffee table and sat in the wing chair opposite the sofa.

Paige waved her scrap of fabric. "That I was never very good at the domestic arts. All this lack of success is making me feel inadequate. I'm going to go clean my gun."

Darcy watched her go, then turned to Joe's mother. "I'm afraid I'm not any better at this. My stitches aren't even."

Colleen opened the bottle of wine and poured them each a glass. "I wouldn't worry about it. At the rate we're going, one of my granddaughters will have grown up and gotten engaged before Mia ever considers settling down." She handed Darcy a glass, then relaxed in her chair. "I love Mia so much, but too many days with her around exhausts me."

"She's sure full of energy."

"Among other things. I thought Lorenzo was going to have a heart attack when he realized Ian was sharing Mia's room. We'd given him his own, of course, but young people today. . . ." Colleen stopped and frowned. "My God. Did I actually say that? 'Young people today'?" She closed her eyes.

"I'm turning into my mother, only without the charming accent."

Darcy laughed.

Colleen looked at her and smiled. "I suppose it was bound to happen."

"We're all getting older."

"I'm afraid you won't be able to claim that for some time," Colleen said. "On the one hand Mia wears me out, on the other the house seems quiet without her. I'm glad we have you here with us, Darcy."

The unexpected words surprised Darcy. She tried to be a good houseguest, but she knew she was a relative stranger here. "You've all been very kind."

"Trust me. We're not altruistic enough to be noble. We like having you around," Colleen told her. "Although I'm not sure being an honorary Marcelli is as exciting as the life you're used to. After all, you can go to the White House anytime you'd like."

Darcy nodded because it was expected, but in truth she didn't feel as if she could just drop in. Maybe to see Lauren, but not for any other reason. Certainly not to see her father. Appointments were required.

"It must be hard for the president," Colleen said as she set down her glass of wine. "He's been a widower for a long time, yet it can't be easy for him to date."

"Not really. There's a lot of speculation about his love life, but he has always said he won't get involved with anyone until he's out of office."

"I suppose that makes sense. How would he know if the woman was interested in him or what he could offer? Still, he must be lonely."

Darcy reached for a small sandwich but didn't bite into it. She'd never considered that her father also had to deal with hangers-on. Sure, in his regular life, but not romantically. Of course there would be women who would want to marry the president. A fair number probably wanted to just sleep with him, but she didn't want to think about that. Talk about an ick factor.

"Of course he has his girls," Colleen said. "Children are a blessing. And you're both so close. You in town and Lauren right there in the private quarters." She smiled. "I think you were smart to have your own place so you could keep your privacy."

"It is nice," Darcy said because she knew the truth was far less appealing. A part of her *had* been interested in living in the White House. She'd imagined a room across from her sister and plenty of moments to enjoy the once-in-a-lifetime opportunity. But she'd never been invited.

When rooms had been assigned and living arrangements discussed, the assumption had been she would be staying in her D.C. apartment.

She'd kept her hurt to herself. She hadn't wanted to upset Lauren or put her in the awkward position of having to petition their father on Darcy's behalf.

"Do you go to many dinners and evenings there?" Colleen asked.

"Some. He hasn't really started entertaining much yet. I received invitations when he was vice president, but I was still in graduate school and had to refuse a lot of them."

Lauren had teased her about not wanting to come to anything but being unwilling to flat out say so. Lauren had said —

Darcy picked up her wine and took a sip. Was that what had happened? Had she said no so many times that they'd stopped asking? Did they think she wasn't interested?

No, she told herself. That wasn't possible. They *had* to know the truth. Didn't they?

The days stayed warm and sunny. Joe knew from his nighttime reading that warm sunny days were best right before harvest. That the heat and light brought out the sugar in the grapes. Or did it keep sugar from being in the grapes? Damn. He'd just read about it the other night. Why couldn't he remember?

Because this wasn't his thing, he told himself. He wasn't interested in wine or Marcelli land or grapes.

He rounded the corner of the house and saw Darcy in the shade, leaning against the back of a large jacaranda tree. Her eyes were closed, and her book had fallen off her lap. Just behind her were two agents, playing cards.

Joe nodded at them, then approached her. He crouched down at the edge of the blanket and waited until she opened her eyes and saw him.

"Hey," she murmured, her voice low and her skin slightly flushed.

She wore a loose tank top and shorts, both black. Flip-flops lay beside the blanket. Any makeup she'd applied that morning had faded, leaving her lips bare and only a shade or two darker than her cheeks.

She was gorgeous. Sexy, soft, and a thousand other things he shouldn't think. If he did, the physical manifestation of his thoughts would inform everyone in visual range exactly what he had on his mind.

"Hey, yourself." He sat next to her. "You're still not sleeping."

"Don't go there, big guy. I'm too drowsy

to fight with you today."

"It's not a fight if you do what I say."

Her eyes widened as she laughed. "Do you think there's even the tiniest chance that's going to happen?"

"Not in this lifetime."

"Or on this planet," she told him. "I'm okay. And for your information, I'm sleeping better."

"How much?"

"Maybe fifteen percent."

"Not good enough." Her hand lay beside his. He wanted to pick it up and touch it, maybe lace their fingers together. Which meant his brain had failed and he was in serious need of some combat time.

"You should talk to somebody," he told her. "A professional. Even my SEAL teams need help now and then."

"Okay. Maybe. When this is over and I'm back in D.C."

He thought about pushing back, but if she saw someone sooner it would mean one more body who knew her location. That crowd was already too big for comfort.

"Brenna says the chardonnay grapes will be ready to harvest in a couple of weeks," Darcy said. "I kind of want to be here to see that."

He glanced around to make sure no one

was listening, then lowered his voice. "I've been reading some of the books she left me. Harvest is a lot of work. There are —" He broke off at her smile. "What?" he demanded.

"Oooh, I could really blackmail you with the fact that you're studying up on wine."

"But you won't. We're in this together."

The second the words were out, he wondered what he was talking about. Darcy should have been surprised, too, but instead of calling him on it, she changed the subject.

"I've never spent any time in this part of the country, and I have to say I'm sorry about that. I really love it here. I could get used to this kind of life." She glanced at him. "I mean that at face value, so don't get all weird on me."

"I rarely get weird on anyone. I can see how it could be appealing."

She stretched out her legs, then drew a knee to her chest. "Really? So why are you so determined to get away from here as fast as you can?"

A legitimate question. "I love what I do," he said. "I make a difference every day. I trust my guys with my life, and they do the same with me."

Her dark eyes settled on his face. "And you can't trust the Marcellis?"

"Not the same way."

"That's unfortunate, because they are just as willing to give up their lives for you. They love you, Joe. More than you know and certainly more than you deserve. I wish you could see that."

He shrugged, not sure what to say.

"The good news is they're not going to give up," she told him. "You are so stuck with them."

"I've figured that out already. Brenna and Mia are easy, but I don't know what to do with the rest of them."

"You're letting Grandma Tessa feed you. That's something."

He shrugged. "It's just food."

"Not to her. My next goal is for you to start calling people by their actual names."

He didn't like the sound of that. "What are you talking about?"

"You avoid mentioning anyone by name. Probably because you don't want to call Colleen and Marco Mom and Dad, which makes sense, but what about the Grands. Even I'm calling them Grammy M and Grandma Tessa. It's who they are. The fact that they're related to you is beside the point."

He made a noise low in his throat. She laughed.

"Are you growling at me?" she asked, sounding more delighted than annoyed.

"Yes."

"I've never had a man growl at me before."

"They were probably all too scared of your Secret Service agents."

"And you're not?"

"I could take every one of them."

Darcy stood by the window in her room, but instead of the view, she saw questions. So many opportunities had seemed to slip through her fingers. Times when she could have said something, only to hesitate out of fear or concern or need. What had she missed because of that hesitation? What had been lost?

She crossed to the secure phone on the nightstand in the corner and dialed Lauren's number. Her sister answered in two rings.

"Hi, it's me," Darcy said.

"Hi, you. How's it going? Are you basking in your sunny days and sultry nights?"

Darcy smiled. "There's not much sultry here. Humidity is required for that."

Lauren sighed. "There's plenty here. Near record levels. The corn is growing, though. Growing and moving closer to the house. I'm beginning to feel like a character in a

219

Stephen King novel. Soon I'll be slipping into insanity."

Darcy sat on the edge of the bed and battled guilt. "I'm sorry you're stuck wherever you are."

"Me, too, but I'll survive. The Secret Service guys are nice, and I'm teaching myself to cook. Nothing up to White House standards, of course, but I never really bothered before. Even when I was married . . ." Her voice trailed off.

Darcy knew her sister enough to know she was about to get lost in the past. Given that Lauren was trapped in the middle of nowhere and on her own, she didn't think that was a good idea.

"You should plan your welcome-home party," Darcy said quickly. "Start working on the guest list. You can put me on top."

Lauren laughed. "Hardly. You don't like all those fancy events, but I appreciate you making the effort for me."

"Is that what you think?" Darcy asked lightly. "That I don't like the White House social scene?"

"You don't. When Dad was vice president, he made sure you got invitations to everything, but you never came. I know grad school kept you really busy, but we both figured you were too polite to actually say you hated that kind of stuff."

Darcy wasn't sure what to say. Yes, she had been busy with school, but she'd also been confused and feeling unwelcome.

"I thought the kindest thing was to not ask you anymore," Lauren added. "Was I wrong?"

"No. Of course not." Darcy flopped back on the bed. "Maybe. I mean I know I kept refusing invitations, but I didn't want to be cut off from you two."

Lauren sucked in a breath. "Is that how you feel?"

"Sometimes."

"Oh, Darcy. I'm sorry. You know we don't want that."

Darcy's mouth twisted. "I know *you* don't want that."

"Stop it. Dad loves you. He talks about you and asks about you, which he wouldn't have to do if you called him and came by sometimes. He's busy, but he's still your father and he cares about you."

Darcy wanted to believe that, even though it wasn't true. After her mother had died, she'd been so lost. Finding out the truth about her biological father the same day that her mother died had nearly destroyed her. Worse, the man who was her biological father was already dead, so she'd lost him before she ever found him. She'd been emotionally battered and unable to feel anything for months. Ryan Jensen had reached out to her time and again, only to have her walk away from him. Just about the time she'd been ready to reach back, he'd stopped trying.

"It's complicated," she said.

"It doesn't have to be," Lauren told her. "He wants you in his life."

Darcy wasn't so sure, but maybe she should find out before making any more decisions.

"All right," her sister said. "Change of subject. I'm so bored here. Tell me something exciting that's happening in your life."

Darcy opened her mouth to say there wasn't anything exciting, but what came out instead was, "I've met someone."

Lauren squealed. "You're kidding. That's so great. The petty, bitter side of me is complaining that you get to meet a guy while I'm stuck in a cornfield, but I will squash those evil thoughts and focus only on you. Who is he? What's he like?"

"He's . . ." Darcy curled up on the bed and grinned. "He's gorgeous. A naval officer and a former SEAL. I know nothing will come of it, but still, I really like him."

Lauren sighed. "Sounds fabulous. Okay

start at the beginning and talk slowly. I want to know every detail."

"So you're reading the books," Brenna said. "Learning about the wine. What do you think?"

Joe held in a groan. "I'm sorry I said anything about them."

"I don't doubt that," Brenna said cheerfully, "but you did, and now I get to grill you on them. It's time to give in. Let the wine have its way with you."

They were in the storeroom in the winery. Brenna had gotten even bigger, which didn't seem possible. How far could one body stretch before splitting open?

As uncomfortable as it made him to look at her bulging stomach, his situation was made worse by the fact that he couldn't just walk away. Not from a very pregnant woman who looked as if she could go into labor at any time. No matter how much she bugged him.

"I'm not interested in the wine," he said, facing her and folding his arms over his chest. "I've told you."

"I only listen to about half of what you say. It's not personal — I deal with all men that way." She grinned. "You can't escape us. This is your destiny, Joe."

"Not in this lifetime."

The humor fled her eyes as she grabbed his arm. "I'm serious here. I'm pregnant. I'm going to have a baby. That's bound to cut into my time. Four Sisters is growing. Grandpa Lorenzo won't live forever. I need some help."

The walls instantly began moving in on him. He pulled away from her and moved toward the door. "Marco can take over."

"Whoa. Stop right there. No one is taking over from me. I said help. Like a partner."

"Like I said — Marco."

"Sorry, big brother. You're the one. You're the heir. Not just because you're male, although that's a big part of it, but also because you have the determination to make things happen. You have a lot to learn before you'll be of any help to me. So you need to start now. You have responsibilities."

He wanted to hit something or throw something. The barrels were too large and the desk behind him had been screwed down. He thought about tearing the intercom out of the wall, but what would that accomplish?

He glared at her. "It's not going to happen," he said, speaking slowly. "You can't make me want this. I'm not interested in you, in them, in the winery. In any of it."

"Is this why your marriage failed?" she asked softly. "Because you wouldn't let anyone in?"

"You don't know what you're talking about."

"Don't I?" She rubbed her stomach. "We're not leaving you, Joe. No matter how long you're gone or how much you push us away. It's been three years. What will it take for us to finally earn your trust?"

When he didn't answer, Brenna shook her head and walked out without saying a word. Seconds later Darcy appeared. Her knowing expression only made the need to destroy something even stronger.

"Go away," he growled.

"I wasn't listening in," she said. "You were yelling pretty loud until the end there. I'm guessing the whole back forty knows what you two were fighting about. Don't you ever get tired of having the same argument over and over again?"

"Yes. They need to give it up."

"Or you need to give in."

He threw up his hands. "Perfect. You want to run my life, do you? It's your fault it's screwed up in the first place."

"Oh, right. Because the sole purpose of the kidnapping was to mess up your career plans. I'm trying to help you here, you jackass. But you're too stubborn to see the truth. You keep pushing them away, and they keep coming back."

She moved closer. "You say the navy is your family, your life. But what do they care about you? You're a rank and a number. Someone capable of doing a good job. There are a dozen guys who could take your place. Even now someone else is doing your job, and that's what's killing you. But this is different. This is your family. They love you. It's specific and personal and you're blowing it."

He didn't want to hear any of this. "Don't call me a jackass."

"Why not? You're acting like one. You're such a typical male, wanting to be defined by what you do. But you're more than that."

He moved close and considered shaking her. "You're the most annoying woman I know."

"Maybe, but I'm trying to help you. You should be grateful and offer me a small but tasteful gift. Flowers or chocolate."

He grabbed her and pulled her close. But instead of shaking her, he lowered his head and kissed her.

She let herself sink into him as she wrapped her arms around his neck.

"That works, too," she whispered before kissing him back.

# 12

Man, oh man, did Joe know how to kiss. Darcy closed her eyes and let herself get lost in the sensation of his warm mouth on hers. Despite the fact that they'd kissed before, he didn't attack or assume. Instead he coaxed her into responding. Gentle brushes of flesh against flesh had her wishing for more before he even offered.

He let her get used to the feel of his hard body, his arms around her. He let her inhale the scent of him and melt in his heat. Only then did he lightly nip her lower lip.

He followed the shape of her mouth, tracing the line slowly, so slowly that she finally grabbed him by the back of his head and pulled him close.

Even as he swept inside her mouth, he chuckled. She felt the rumble low in his chest and smiled in return. They were good together, she thought hazily, right before the passion exploded.

The need came without warning. One second she'd been enjoying his kiss, the next she was desperate. Hunger claimed her. Large, powerful, and nearly out of control, it made her cling, reach, seek. She wanted him touching her everywhere, she wanted him naked and ready. Right here, right now.

"Joe," she breathed, not sure what to say.

He raised his head slightly, and she saw the fire in his eyes. They stared at each other for two heartbeats, then fell together in a frenzy of wanting that left them both breathless.

He kissed her again, but this time he wasn't kidding. He claimed her, stroking the inside of her mouth with a fervency that made her shake.

She closed her lips and sucked on his tongue. He groaned, then lowered his hands to her hips, where he pulled her against him. She went willingly, wanting to know he was aroused. Her belly brushed against his erection and her insides clenched.

She clung to him, even as she tried to pull at his T-shirt. Bare skin, she thought frantically. She needed bare skin.

He pulled back enough to press his mouth to her cheek, then her jaw. He moved down the side of her neck until he reached her collarbone. The warm, damp trail of kisses made her tremble. At the same time he reached for the front of her sleeveless blouse and began to work the buttons.

"Yes," she whispered, giving up on his T-shirt and helping him get her undressed.

Even as they fumbled with tiny buttons and impossible fastenings, they kissed, noses bumping, lips missing. In the heat of the moment, perfection didn't matter.

When her blouse was finally open, he reached for the front clasp of her black bra and opened it one-handed. She had a half second to be impressed with his technique before he bent down and claimed her left breast with his mouth.

The combination of hot, wet kisses, a sucking pressure, and her own building need nearly made her scream. She grabbed his head to hold him in place.

"Don't stop," she breathed. "Please, don't stop."

Ribbons of pleasure wove their way through her, circling around her breasts before heading to that growing ache between her legs. She felt herself swell and dampen. She wanted him inside her now. Right this second. She couldn't wait —

He moved to her other breast and flicked his tongue against the tight nipple. She gasped her pleasure. He did it again, then straightened. Before she could protest, he replaced his mouth with his very skilled fingers and kissed her.

Oh, yeah, she thought as she circled his tongue with hers and sank into the pleasure. This was good. Better than good. It was amazing.

He dropped his hands to the waistband of her shorts and unfastened them. Somewhere along the way, she'd already kicked off her sandals.

"I want you," he breathed into her ear. His breath was hot and tickled in the most erotic way possible. "I want you, Darcy. Hot, wet, and screaming when I make you come."

Her eyes widened. No one had ever talked to her during sex before. She'd always found the event to be silent and fairly unsatisfying. It looked as if all that was about to change.

A shiver of anticipation rippled through her.

"I can't promise to scream," she whispered as he pushed down her shorts and panties.

He pulled back a little and stared at her. His eyes were the color of stormy midnight, his expression predatory. He was a man who wanted a woman and meant to have her. Thrill joined anticipation.

"Can you promise to come?" he asked as

he slipped his hand between her thighs.

Someone had given him a schematic, she thought happily as he went directly to her very favorite spot and began to tease it. Electricity shot through her, making her want to get to the finish right away as much as she wanted to make it last forever. He circled and rubbed and then slid his fingers inside of her while his thumb kept up the intimate dance.

"Darcy?"

She forced her eyes open. "What?"

"Can you come?"

The first flicker of promise tightened her muscles. "As long as you keep doing that."

He gave her a slow, sexy smile designed to bring her to her knees. But before she could stumble, he grabbed her by the waist and lifted her onto the desk.

"I'll go you one better," he said and slipped between her thighs.

Even as his arousal filled her, stretching her and touching nerve endings starved for a little attention, he returned his fingers to her most sensitive spot. As if that wasn't enough, he leaned in and kissed her. Talk about multitasking, she thought, as her brain began to shut down in a delicious overload of sensation.

There was heat everywhere. Heat and

hunger and the promise of perfect release. Muscles tensed in anticipation. Her body ached. She parted her legs more, then wrapped them around his hips to bring him in closer still.

In and out, in and out. The friction against her slick, swollen center was exactly right. She could feel his tension and knew he was close, but he held back, waiting on her.

"Almost," she breathed against his mouth. "Joe."

He stared at her, willing her to come for him. Willing her to scream.

Brenna hauled herself up the back stairs and waddled into the kitchen. She wanted to stalk, but it wasn't going to happen. Until she gave birth to the planet-size baby she carried, her stalking days were behind her. Along with her dancing days, her running days, and her sleeping days.

"I hate gestating," she said as she leaned against the counter.

Grandma Tessa smiled in sympathy. "The babies make it worth it."

Brenna glared at her. "There are no babies. Just so we're clear. There's the one baby. Singular."

Her mother crossed to her and touched her forehead. "Are you feeling all right?

You're flushed."

"I'm crabby. It's Joe. He's being stubborn and pigheaded. I know they're the same, but it's annoying. He's annoying. I hate him." She sighed. "Okay, not really."

Her mother offered her a glass of water and she took a sip. Because she *needed* more pressure on her bladder these days.

"We were talking in the storeroom. Arguing. He won't listen."

"He's stubborn," Colleen said.

Brenna looked at her mother. "He told Darcy his wife left because of the time he was gone."

Colleen and Grandma Tessa shared a glance. The older woman reached for her rosary.

"It could be true," Colleen said. "He believes it. I saw it in his eyes when he told us."

"That's not why," Brenna said. "She left because he wouldn't let her in. He wouldn't love her."

Grandma Tessa shook her head. "We don't know that."

"What if that's the way he is? What if he can't change." Her eyes burned with tears. Damn hormones. "I love him. We all do."

"And we're going to keep loving him," Colleen said.

"I know. I wish . . ." Brenna reached for the intercom. She wanted to tell him to get in here so she could sock him in the stomach, then hug him. Schizophrenic love at its best.

She pushed the intercom and heard a curious sound.

It wasn't conversation. Not exactly. It was . . . breathing. Hot, heavy breathing.

She released the intercom and jumped back.

Colleen frowned as Grandma Tessa reached for her beads.

"Dear Lord," her grandmother said. "What was it? Some giant beast in the storeroom?"

It didn't sound like an animal to Brenna. "I don't get it," she said. "I left Joe in there and passed Darcy on the way. . . ." Understanding dawned. But as soon as the thought formed, she pushed it away.

No. It wasn't possible. Her stiff-necked brother would never loosen up enough to —

She pushed the intercom again and heard Lieutenant Commander Joseph Larson say something very dirty.

"Oh my God," Brenna shrieked.

She backed away from the intercom. She looked from her stunned mother to her equally shocked grandmother and began to laugh.

Colleen grinned. "Guess Joe found himself a girl."

"In the storeroom?" Tessa asked, sounding outraged. "It's immoral."

"It's fun," Brenna said. "I always hoped he'd find someone, but the president's daughter? What on earth is he thinking?"

Darcy braced herself on the table and bucked against Joe. So close. So close. He rubbed her center, moving faster and faster until she had no choice but to fly into her release.

She wanted to warn him, to say something, but she couldn't speak. Her muscles convulsed as she came over and over again. Pleasure poured through her, a river of release. It was good. It was better than good — it was damn close to perfect.

Joe straightened and looked at Darcy. Her eyes were wide, and she was still breathing hard. He tucked her hair behind her ears then leaned in and kissed the tip of her nose.

"Not bad for somebody famous," he said.

As he'd expected, she grinned, then swatted his arm.

"Not bad for some macho, paramilitary

type," she told him.

"There's no 'para' about it. I *am* military."

"Yeah, yeah, like that's going to impress me."

He touched her chin so she had to meet his gaze. "You screamed."

Color rose on her cheeks. "Did not."

She was right. She hadn't screamed. But she'd grabbed on to him as if she never wanted to let go, and she'd taken him on the ride of his life.

Reluctantly he stepped back and reached for his jeans.

"Ah, the postcoital cleanup," she said as she lowered herself to the floor, then reached for her panties and shorts.

He supposed he should feel awkward about what they'd just done. It hadn't been planned, and he didn't usually give in to impulses like that. If anyone found out . . .

He didn't want to think about that, even though he was going to have to — eventually. But right now there were other issues.

"You're looking serious." She finished fastening her bra, then started with the buttons on her blouse. "Regrets?"

"No." He pulled her close and lightly kissed her. She held on tight. "Questions."

"Such as?"

"You on any birth control?"

He watched her closely, knowing he would be able to guess by her expression. Instead of panic, he saw something very close to smug victory.

"I'm on the Pill. Aren't you lucky," she said, leaning against him.

"Damn straight." He stroked her short hair. "I usually take precautions. You messed with my mind."

"Little ol' me?"

"No one else here." He felt her tremble. "Darcy? You okay?"

She nodded but wouldn't look at him. He touched his finger to her chin and raised her head.

"What?" he asked.

She looked defiant, shy, and embarrassed. An amazing trick.

"I'm being sophisticated and worldly," she said. "Don't mess that up."

And then he got it. He lashed out when he felt threatened; she used humor. He thought about her life — the public scrutiny, the Secret Service agents.

"Hard to date when you're the president's daughter?" he asked quietly.

"You have no idea."

He kissed her. "The guys in D.C. are idiots. And not just the ones in office."

"Thanks."

"I mean it."

She raised herself on tiptoe and kissed him. "I know." A smile tugged at the corners of her mouth. "You've just had sex with the youngest daughter of your commander in chief. I think you need to propose now. It's really the least you can do."

He wanted to pull her close again, but he respected her need to stay strong.

"Wouldn't you get nervous if I did?" he said. "It's almost worth it to see."

"Almost isn't the same." She stepped back and smoothed down the front of her blouse. "How do I look?"

"Sexy."

She dismissed him with a flick of her hand. "I don't care about that. Do I look normal? I don't want anyone guessing what just happened. We have your family to think of, and my security team. Trust me, none of them need to know."

"Agreed."

He studied her, taking in the swell of her breasts a whole lot more than the straightness of her clothes, then motioned for her to turn around.

When she'd completed a full circle, she held her arms out at her sides and said, "Well?"

"Perfect," he said. He moved in and

claimed her in a hot, deep kiss that soon had his body ready for round two.

She moaned. "Good idea. Bad timing, but a great idea. We got lucky once. Do you realize the odds of someone walking in on us?"

Amazing how he almost didn't care.

"I'll go first," she said as she pushed away and started for the door. "Wait a few seconds before following." Her gaze dropped to his crotch, where he knew she could see he was hard again. "Or longer."

Darcy felt like the beautiful young princess in a classic fairy tale. It was only a matter of time until the birds broke into song and the little woodland creatures gathered supplies to make her a fabulous ball gown.

It was the sex. Parts of her body ached from the physical activities, but it was the kind of ache that made her smile and want to do it again. For that she could thank Joe.

He'd been great. Not just with the mechanics, although he could certainly earn a merit badge in technique and stamina, but with how he'd acted.

He'd made her feel comfortable, both during and after. He'd joked and he'd held her, and best of all, he'd wanted her again. Guys might be able to fake a lot of things, but not an erection that size!

Life was good, she thought as she headed toward the main building of the winery. Who knew getting kidnapped would turn out to be so beneficial for her personal life?

Still smiling, Darcy entered the main building of the winery. She felt more than saw the Secret Service agents behind her, but she ignored them. Today nothing could get in the way of her good mood.

"There you are," Grandpa Lorenzo said as she started down the hallway. He stood at the entrance to his office. "I've been looking for you, Darcy. Come in."

He sounded so stern and disapproving, she instantly felt guilty. It was all she could do to keep from rushing to his side, grabbing his arm, and promising she would always keep her room clean. Instead she followed him into his office and took the chair he pointed at.

He stared at her for a long time. Darcy stared back, noting the gray in his hair and how tired he looked. Then she ran through a list of possible infractions but couldn't come up with a single one.

"So, you like the winery," he said.

She hadn't had a clue as to what he wanted to talk about, but her liking the winery hadn't been on the short list.

"Yes," she said. "Of course. It's beautiful

here, and the process of making wine fascinates me. I know I'm an imposition to your family, but I can't help hoping I'm here through part of the harvest. I'd like to see the picking and the pressing."

Lorenzo smiled. "You have the love in your veins. It's like that for some. You don't always have to be born into it. You're young, there's still time. You could study and be a part of all this."

She wasn't so sure about that. She had a feeling that as nice as the Marcelli family had been to her, they wouldn't be all that sorry to get their lives back. No one enjoyed having Secret Service agents running around on their property.

"Tessa cleaned your room the other day and found this."

He set something on his desk. It took Darcy a second to realize it was her portfolio. Lorenzo withdrew several large sheets from her sketch pad.

At least they were only drawings, she thought, surprised that Tessa had gone through her stuff and embarrassed that something so private had been viewed by others. Note to self — don't start a diary while in the Marcelli home.

She drew in a deep breath, preparing herself to take Lorenzo and his wife on about violating her privacy, when he said, "I like these. This one the most."

He tapped one of the designs, then turned it toward her. "You can make me more like this?"

She stared at the page of wine labels she'd been toying with. There were several incarnations, using the Marcelli name as the centerpiece in some and the house in the others. Lorenzo pointed to the one with the house.

"I like this one. I like the different colors. You've done pale for chardonnay, and darker for merlot. So the labels are all the same, but different, yes?"

She nodded slowly. "You like these?"

"Very much. The work Brenna brings me." He shook his head. "Amateurs. Yes, they draw, they design, but they don't feel the wine in their blood. They don't know the land, the work, the grapes. You, Darcy, you feel it in here." He pounded his chest. "We'll use these for the new Marcelli labels."

"W-what?"

"For the wine. Brenna will like them, too. She's a smart girl. She'll know how you have to draw them so we can turn them into labels. Stand up to her on the price. She'll try to talk you down, but this time, I think, we pay more, eh?"

He wanted her labels? On Marcelli wine bottles? "On all of them?" she asked tentatively.

"Yes. For all. You will be a part of us, then."

Darcy sprang from her seat and raced around the desk. She threw herself at Lorenzo, who gathered her close and hugged her. He was thin and frail under his loose clothes, but he still squeezed her until she couldn't breathe.

It felt good, she thought happily. It felt great.

When he released her, she grinned. "This is my first real design job. I've been trying to find work, but it's hard. No advertising agency wants to hire me. What client is going to be comfortable complaining about a design by the president's daughter? So I went back to college to get my master's degree. I thought that would help, but it hasn't yet. Until now."

Lorenzo squeezed her hand. "This isn't about your education, child. It's about what you feel in your heart. That's what's important. Never forget that."

Joe finished his afternoon briefing with the security team and headed back for the house. Marco joined him a few feet from the back door and asked him to wait.

"We have to talk," Marco told him.

Until that moment, Joe had been having a good day. Making love with Darcy might not have been the smartest thing he'd ever done, but it had been one of the best. He'd enjoyed every second of her company. And he hadn't wanted to go — an unusual situation for a man who generally preferred to be alone.

"What's up?" he asked.

Marco shook his head. "Next time you might want to make sure the intercom is off."

Joe felt sucker punched. "You know?"

"Everybody knows."

# 13

Darcy sat propped up on her bed, several sketches scattered around her. She had a meeting in the morning with Grandpa Lorenzo and Brenna to finalize their choices for the wine labels, and she wanted to be able to offer them a variety of options.

Excitement made it difficult to concentrate on the designs. She wanted to dance around the room and scream her delight. Brenna had called earlier to say she was thrilled to finally have new label designs. Which meant Darcy had her first ever paying job.

Okay — she wasn't going to be able to make a career out of this one client, but at least she finally felt legitimate in her chosen profession.

As she worked, or tried to work, she hummed. She felt good all over. She loved this place, and she loved the Marcellis. Would they be willing to adopt her?

She grinned at the thought. Probably not a good idea, what with her and Joe having had sex. Not that they knew, but if she was adopted it would create, as Mia had said, a pretty serious ick factor.

Someone knocked on her closed bedroom door. Grandma Tessa to do a little more reconnaissance? "Come in."

The door opened, and Joe stepped into her room and closed the door behind him. Darcy instantly straightened. Her stomach tightened, her thighs heated, and she desperately wanted to pat the bed in invitation.

He was so gorgeous, she thought as she took in his tall, muscular build and the faint smile. Good enough to be both main course and dessert.

"Stop it," he said conversationally.

She blinked at him. "Stop what?"

"Whatever it is you're thinking. I can't help wanting you, and you're not making it any easier to say no."

He wanted her! Her emotions did a little soft-shoe. "Maybe you don't have to say no."

He groaned. "Yeah, I do."

"But it was so good." Perfect even.

He narrowed his gaze. "Darcy, I'm not kidding. There's a problem."

She refused to let go of her good mood.

"You're not going to get weird on me, are you?"

"Not in the way you think. They know."

The last two words didn't quite make it to her brain. "They know." Huh. Who knew what? Who could possibly know. . . .

She collapsed onto her pillows. "Oh God. Your family?"

"That would be them."

Panic filled her. "No. They can't. I didn't say anything. I didn't even hint." She stared at him. "I know you didn't say anything. You wouldn't even under threat of torture."

"I wouldn't even with *actual* torture." He crossed to the bed and sat down next to her. "We were in the storage room," he said.

"I actually know that. Did someone see us?"

"No, they heard. There's an intercom system."

She felt herself blush. "Who was it?" she asked, not sure who would be worse.

"Brenna, Grandma Tessa, and my mother."

She opened her mouth, then closed it. What exactly was she supposed to say?

Brenna she could handle, but. . . . "Your mother and Grandma Tessa?" The blush turned fiery.

"They spread the news to the rest of the

family. Marco pulled me aside about an hour ago and tried to have the sex talk with me. It was humiliating."

"I'll bet." She covered her face with her hands. "They know. I can't believe it. I always thought the ongoing humiliation of my life was because I'm in the public eye, but I guess not. Maybe it's just me."

Joe reached for her hands and pulled them away. "Don't worry. No one's going to say anything."

"Not to my face, but they'll be talking about it. They know." She wanted to crawl under the bed and never come out. Then she thought of something. "Did they tell Paige or Alex? Alex really wouldn't like us doing that, and he might try to get you in trouble. You have your career to think about."

"I know. But the Marcellis are good at closing ranks. No one on the Secret Service team knows."

"Are you sure?"

He nodded. "If Alex had a clue, he'd rip me a new one. Trust me." He leaned close and gently kissed her. "Want to take it back?"

She didn't have to think about that. "Not even for a second."

"Me, either."

They stared at each other before Joe straightened and said he should get out of her room before there were even more rumors. Darcy nodded but couldn't speak. She couldn't do anything but stare at him. Because in that short period of time, somewhere between the light kiss and his walking out of her room, she felt a definite sort of tugging in the vicinity of her heart.

She wasn't sure what it meant, but she knew it couldn't be good. Not when her stay here was temporary, her track record with men was worse than dismal, and Joe was the kind of guy who didn't do relationships.

Paige hung up the phone and finished writing her notes. When Alex walked into the kitchen, she pushed the paper toward him.

"They've arrested two of the kidnappers," she said. "They have leads on the rest of them. I'm going to tell Darcy when I see her. She'll be thrilled."

Alex looked over the paper. "At least if the rest of them are on the run, they won't have time to plan another kidnapping."

"That should make our job easier," she said.

"I don't need my job easier."

Of course not, she thought. But he did need a sense of humor.

He walked to the refrigerator, opened it, and stared inside. Then he closed it and turned to her. "Would you have married me?"

Paige stared at him. "Excuse me?"

"If I'd asked. Before. Would you have married me?"

She had no idea what he was thinking or why he'd brought this up now. It didn't make sense.

"Alex, I don't understand why —"

"Yes or no," he said sharply. "It's a simple question."

"Not for me." Nothing about this was simple.

Would she have married him? She stared at his eyes. There'd been a time when she'd wanted to get lost in those eyes. When being with him had been so important.

"I don't know," she said after a while. "I don't believe you would have asked. And if you had and I'd said yes, then one of us would have had to leave the Secret Service. You would have expected me to be the one to leave."

He frowned. "Right."

She smiled. How typical of him. "Then no," she said gently. "I wouldn't have married you."

He folded his arms over his chest. "Why?

Because I wasn't willing to give up my career for you? This is what I've always wanted."

"What about what I wanted? You'd have asked me to give up the one thing you wouldn't. It doesn't seem fair or a very healthy way to start a marriage. One criterion of a successful relationship is love makes each party stronger, giving them more of what they want. Love isn't supposed to take your dreams away."

"There was no way for us to win."

She considered the statement. "I guess not. Some relationships are like that."

"I don't accept that."

What was it about stubborn men? "You not accepting it doesn't change the truth."

He stared at her for another couple of seconds, then turned and walked out of the room.

Paige had no idea what all that had been about. She respected Alex a lot. She thought he was totally hot, and his being in the next room made some nights long and difficult. But there were times when his mind was a complete mystery to her.

She gathered her paperwork, but before she could stand up, he stalked back into the room, walked over to the table, bent down, and kissed her.

He cupped her face in his large hands and pressed his mouth to hers. The action was so unexpected, she didn't know what to think, and then she couldn't think because her brain had shut down in order to let her feel everything.

He held her gently. His lips rediscovered hers in a soft caress that took her breath away. She parted before he even asked, wanting him to claim her the way men had been claiming women since the beginning of time.

He swept into her mouth and circled her tongue with his. Then as quickly as it had begun, the kiss was over. He straightened, then walked away without saying a single word.

"I'll fix you a nice cuppa," Grammy M said to Joe as he walked into the kitchen the next morning.

He squinted at the time and saw it was barely after six. "You're here early."

"I like to start my day with the sun," she said cheerfully.

Tessa walked into the kitchen and scowled. "It's all that sinning. It keeps you from sleeping."

Grammy M glared at her. "You're very concerned about the state of my soul. All this talk of sinning. Could it be because your own man isn't making you happy in the bedroom?"

Joe winced and headed for the door. No way did he want to get in the middle of this.

Tessa might be elderly, but she was fast, spry, and she had that killer grip. She got him by the arm and steered him to the table.

"Sit," she ordered, and he sat.

"I'll make that tea," Grammy M said, smiling at him.

Tessa narrowed her gaze. "Joseph doesn't drink tea. He's a man. He drinks coffee."

Grammy M turned to him. "Didn't you say you'd be wantin' tea?"

"I, ah . . ."

Tessa speared him with a look that could stop a tank. "Joseph, you always have coffee."

"I, ah . . ."

They ignored him as they both raced to the stove. Joe figured he was about to get both and he'd better drink them equally. Maybe they could just pour them into a big mug and he could choke them down together.

"I'll fix you an omelet," Tessa announced.

"I have fresh scones to go with that," Grammy M said.

"Fruit," Tessa added.

Grammy M sniffed. "And some bacon. Maybe sausage."

"I'll be using the stove," Tessa told her.

"Oh, I see. And you'll be needin' all of the burners for your omelet. Last time I made one, I only needed the one pan. But you were never very good in the —"

"Stop," Joe yelled. "I beg you. It's too early for this."

The Grands stared at him, at each other, then turned their backs and went to work.

Coffee arrived first. Joe sipped it until Grammy M plopped a cup of tea in front of him. Then he alternated. The women worked in silence, carefully stepping around each other, not getting too close.

He looked away as he remembered how it had been his first couple of visits. Before Grammy M had moved in with Gabriel and the old ladies had had a falling-out. He remembered their elegant dance in the kitchen, a rhythm honed from years of practice and working together. He'd never heard a harsh word exchanged.

"Will you be seein' Darcy later today?" Grammy M asked.

Joe held in a groan. So the news had been passed on to her, had it? No doubt Colleen had told her. Which meant Mia and the other sisters knew, too.

"She lives here," he said. "Hard to avoid her."

"Not that you want to," Tessa said with a wink. "She's a pretty girl."

"Not my type."

Tessa smacked him on the back of the head. "You say that now?"

Okay, poor strategy, he thought as he rubbed where she'd nailed him. "I mean she's not . . ." He closed his mouth and reached for the coffee. It would be better to endure whatever they had in mind, then make his escape.

"It's past time you were married," Grammy M said as she put bacon into a pan. "You're not getting any younger."

He nodded and reached for the tea.

"A man shouldn't be alone," Tessa said. "It's not good. What will happen when you're old, eh? You'll be living above the garage with a dog. What kind of life is that?"

"Is that my only option?" he asked before he could stop himself.

"What will become of you?" Grammy M wanted to know.

The only bright spot in this conversation was that they were finally on the same side of an argument.

"You need love in your life," Tessa said.

"You need to love a woman and let her love you."

After getting smacked for saying Darcy wasn't his type, he didn't want to think about what would happen if he said he didn't love her.

Grammy M put a plate of scones in front of him. Tessa slid an omelet onto a plate and set it on the table. Bacon and fruit quickly followed.

"The president's daughter, Joseph," Grammy M said, her voice scolding. "You can't have your way with her then turn your back on her. You're a better man than that."

"She's right," Tessa said, looking as if she'd smelled something disgusting.

Joe felt the walls closing in. These were thicker and harder to climb.

"You don't have to live here, in this house," Tessa said. "You could build something else. Close by. On the land."

Joe stared at the food, then at the Grands. He believed what Darcy had told him — that for these old women food was love. But right now he couldn't take any more. He stood, backed away, and when he was clear of the house, he turned and escaped.

# 14

"Did you hear?" Lauren asked eagerly, her voice as clear as if she were in the same room, despite the distance and the secure line. "They've caught a couple of the kidnappers."

"Yes. Isn't it great?" Darcy asked, trying for as much enthusiasm as possible when in truth the news had made her heart sink.

"We'll be able to leave soon," Lauren said. "I can't wait. I'm getting so tired of my own company. The agents are nice, but they're not here to baby-sit me. The good news is I've caught up on my reading."

Darcy felt a twinge of guilt — her stay at the Marcelli house had been so perfect, she never wanted it to end.

"The downside," Lauren said, "is you're going to have to leave Joe. Or will you still be seeing him?"

Despite being upset at the thought of leaving, mention of Joe made her smile. "I don't know. Maybe." She wanted to. But in reality was that possible? Her smile faded. "He lives in San Diego. I'm in D.C. He's a naval officer, and I'm the daughter of the commander in chief. I think that makes us more star-crossed lovers than the happily-ever-after type."

"Lovers, huh?" Lauren teased. "I want to hear all about that."

Darcy wasn't willing to talk about it — not yet. "It's a figure of speech. Don't get too excited. Besides, this isn't going anywhere. He's not the relationship type."

"How do you know?"

"He resists his family."

"You're not trying to be his mother. Romantic love is different."

"He's been married." Darcy filled her in on the generalities, then sighed. "They say people who don't learn from history are destined to repeat it. In my case, that's true. Here I am, falling for a guy as inaccessible as my father."

As soon as the words came out, she wanted to call them back. She clutched the phone tighter and braced herself.

"Dad's not inaccessible," Lauren said softly.

"I know. I didn't mean it that way. I'm

sorry. Please, let's not get into this long-distance."

"Okay." Lauren sighed. "Joe sounds so great, regardless of whatever issues the two of you may have. I want to meet him. I know. When this is all over, you stay there and I'll come by to pick you up. That way I can check out the military cutie and meet the family."

Darcy sat up. Her first thought was to scream out her protest. Not Lauren. Not here. This was the one place on the planet where everyone liked her for herself. There hadn't been any comparing, any disappointing second finishes. No one had rejected her. If Lauren came now, all that would change.

"Your enthusiasm is overwhelming," Lauren said, the hurt clear in her voice.

Darcy flopped back on the bed. "It's not that. Of course I want you to meet Joe and everyone."

"You might try saying that like you mean it. Don't worry. I'm not going to show up."

She felt like a worm. A selfish worm who had been living the good life while her sister had been stuck in a cornfield.

"Lauren, please. I'm sorry. It's just . . ." She drew in a deep breath. "I'm scared, okay? Joe is really special. I like him a lot.

Maybe more than a lot. I haven't felt this way before, and it's scary and exciting and new and I don't want to lose him."

"Why would you?"

Darcy squeezed her eyes shut. "Have you looked in the mirror lately?"

"Oh, please. You're just as pretty and much more exotic looking. I'm just your basic blue-eyed blonde. With very common features. Besides . . ." She lowered her voice. "You have to know I'd never do anything to take Joe away. I'm not even saying I could. Just that I wouldn't. Ever. I love you. You're my sister. My family. That means everything to me."

Darcy went from feeling like a worm to feeling like slime. Slime was definitely worse. "I know. I'm sorry. I'm not worried about you trying anything, Lauren. You'd never do that." Had never done that. "It's not you. It's . . . them. Him. Everyone likes you better. Most of the time I don't care, but this time it would really hurt."

"But I never did anything wrong," Lauren whispered.

Darcy rolled onto her side and pulled her knees to her chest. "I'm sorry. This is all about me. I'm the one who's insecure and stupid and acting like a child. I'm sorry."

"I'd never try to take Joe away from you.

Or anybody. I don't want to love that much again. Ever."

"You're going to have to let him go eventually," Darcy said.

Lauren's breath caught. "I can't. I loved him so much. I could never love anyone else like that. I don't think my heart's big enough."

"You could date. That would be fun."

"I'm okay by myself. I have my memories, and that's enough."

Darcy thought about pointing out that Lauren was only twenty-seven. A little young to be settling for mere memories.

"Anyway, how did this get to be about me and my lack of love life?" Lauren asked. "We were talking about you."

"Right. How stupid and jealous I am. Not my favorite topic."

"You're not the only one," Lauren said. "You think I don't get jealous of your life and your freedom?"

Darcy rolled onto her back and opened her eyes. "What? You're jealous of me?"

"Sure. You have a lot more privacy than me. No one expects you to be a saint, so you're not always getting judged. I love how you can tell the world to piss off if you're not in the mood."

Darcy couldn't believe it. Lauren wanted

to tell the world to piss off? "A lot of that's just a facade," she said cautiously.

"Who cares. You can do it. All I can do is cut ribbons at opening ceremonies and raise money. The moneyraising part is good, but the rest of it? Sometimes I just want to curl up with a good book or watch *Oprah.*"

Darcy realized she was free to do that and a lot more. Funny how she'd never seen herself as the lucky one before.

"I can TiVo *Oprah* for you if you'd like," she offered.

Lauren started to laugh. "That would be great. Although I'm catching up on reruns while I'm here. It's really fun."

"I miss you," Darcy said.

"I miss you, too."

She cleared her throat. "I think you should come visit me here. When it's safe for us to travel."

Lauren sighed. "No, it's okay."

The slime feeling returned. "I mean it, Lauren. Please. Come visit. It will be great."

"I'll think about it."

They talked a few more minutes, then hung up. Darcy sat up and thought about what her sister had said. That she thought Darcy had the better life. Impossible. But it was good to know she wasn't the only one who got jealous and crazy about her world.

As for Lauren coming here, maybe it was a good idea. It would force Darcy to face her demons. If the Marcellis liked Lauren better, well, Darcy would just get over it. And if Joe wanted her . . . Darcy grinned. Then she would just have to beat the crap out of him.

Joe left the guesthouse after the daily security briefing. Progress had been made — kidnappers caught. Not all of them, but a couple. And if they talked, he would soon be out of here and back where he belonged. Assuming the admiral had cooled down.

"Joseph. Joe."

He looked up and saw Lorenzo limping toward him. The old man leaned heavily on his cane.

"Come," he said. "Walk with me."

"No, thanks," Joe told him. "I'm not interested in more conversations about changing my name, learning about the wine, or accepting this as my destiny."

Lorenzo nodded. "All right. Walk with me anyway."

"Why?"

"Can't a grandfather want to spend time with his grandson?"

Joe swore under his breath, then fell into step with the old man as they headed toward the vineyards.

"We have good weather," Lorenzo said. "It makes for good grapes. Brenna wants to be a part of all of it this year, but I think her baby has other plans."

"I hope so," Joe said, remembering how huge she'd been the last time he'd seen her. "It looks painful."

Lorenzo grinned. "Women are strong. Never tell them, but I would not want to give birth. With Tessa, it was only twice. First Marco, then a little girl. She died."

Joe glanced at him. "I didn't know. I'm sorry."

He shrugged. "God gives and then he takes. It is always that way." He raised his cane and pointed toward the horizon. "I can remember when there were no vines up there. When we needed only one crew to pick the grapes. Now I can't even walk the land, there is so much." He winked. "But not too much, eh? There can never be too much."

"Land is wealth," Joe agreed.

"But it is more than money. It's about who we are. When I was a boy, I dreamed of when I would run Marcelli. My father was a stern man. Difficult to please. But I knew I would and one day this would all be mine. I have lived a long time, long enough to see my great-grandchildren born. Tessa speaks of blessings, and she is right."

Joe didn't know what to say so he nodded. "You have a good family."

"More to come. Brenna and Nic's baby will have wine in his veins. He'll be strong."

"He might be a she."

Lorenzo shrugged. "If God wishes. But there will be sons, too. And more children. The families will join. We will grow. I wanted that for you."

Joe didn't know if he meant children, family, or what. He'd meant what he said about not wanting to argue anymore so he kept quiet.

"I wanted so many things," Lorenzo said as they stopped by a row of grapes. The old man bent down and fingered a leaf. "All those years ago, when Marco told me he'd gotten a girl pregnant, I was angry. I thought he'd thrown his future away. She's Irish, you know."

"I'd heard," Joe said dryly.

"I wanted Marco to marry a nice Italian girl. But he loved Colleen, and I couldn't make him stop. But I could force them to send the baby away." Lorenzo looked at him. "I was stubborn and a fool and I've paid every day since. You've paid. So much lost. I'm sorry."

Joe had expected a lot of screaming but not an apology. He started to speak and found his throat had gotten tight and the words wouldn't come. Before he could make them, Lorenzo spoke again.

"Now I give you advice. I know you think I'm an old man who doesn't know much, but I've lived a long time. Get married. Not because of the family or because I've told you to but because it will make you happy. It's not good for a man to be alone so much."

"I already tried that and it didn't work," Joe told him. He wouldn't go through it again. Not the caring, the wanting more, the hope that maybe it could work only to come home and find a letter and an empty house.

"You didn't love her," Grandpa Lorenzo said flatly. "When a Marcelli man loves, it's forever."

"I don't think —"

"I know!" Lorenzo yelled as he thumped his cane. "Love like that never dies. It is who we are — like the land."

"All the more reason to avoid it," Joe told him. "I'm fine. I have what I need."

"Ah, yes. Your navy. There are things a woman can do to a man your navy will never do to you."

"Agreed, but I don't have to be married to get laid."

Lorenzo's expression hardened. "You think I'm talking about sex? Marriage is about the soul and the heart. It's about one person who knows everything and still reaches for you in the night. Love like that is a gift." He paused and the anger faded. "Joseph, don't have regrets. I've lived with them for thirty-three years and they're a heavy burden. I want so much for you. I want you to be happy. I want —"

"There you are!"

They both turned and saw Katie hurrying toward them, a red-haired toddler in her arms.

Katie Marcelli Stryker was the oldest of the Marcelli daughters. She and her husband, Zach, lived in Los Angeles, where he was a big-time lawyer and she ran a party-planning business.

"Look," Lorenzo said pointing. "Two beautiful women want to talk to us. We are lucky men."

Joe smiled. "I agree."

Katie stopped in front of them and laughed. "Look what she can do," she said proudly, then turned to her daughter. "Come on, honey. What did you want to say?"

The green-eyed beauty held out her arms to Lorenzo and said, "Gram."

The old man pulled her close and hugged her. "How are you? Such a little princess. Have you been practicing my name?"

Valerie nodded shyly and wrapped her arms around his neck. Katie turned to Joe.

"Where's my hug, big guy?"

He gathered her close. "Good to see you."

Katie squeezed him hard. "I heard we've got famous company."

"That's right."

She straightened and smiled. "Gee, Joe, did you have to have sex with the president's daughter on her very first visit?"

Darcy had been through enough Marcelli meals to expect insanity, but this beat all records. Leaves had been added to the already massive table in the dining room so that the whole family could sit together.

She'd been introduced to Katie and her family. Francesca, Sam, and the twins had arrived, along with Brenna and Nic. Only Mia was missing, and as Colleen had whispered in the kitchen, the blessing behind that was no Ian.

"Katie, you take that end," Colleen said. "We'll put Valerie in her high chair next to you. Francesca, I'll take one of the twins by me."

"I'll take the other," Brenna said. "I might as well practice. Unless you think *being* a twin and sitting next to another twin might make me have twins."

Nic leaned over and kissed her cheek. "It doesn't work that way. Whatever you've got, you've got."

Brenna patted her huge stomach. "I'm thinking a really big baby and a beach ball."

Everyone took their seats. Darcy found herself in the middle of the table, next to Grammy M and across from Joe. High chairs were slid into place and toddlers settled. Most of the food was already on the table, although Tessa carried in the last few dishes.

Lorenzo passed open bottles of cabernet down both sides of the table.

"It's good to have family here," he said. "We eat, we drink."

"We talk," Tessa said. "What did I forget?"

"The bread," Grammy M told her.

The two old women scowled at each other before Tessa returned to the kitchen.

Darcy took the wine Marco passed to her. She poured a glass, then filled Grammy M's. Gabriel took the bottle from her and winked.

Lorenzo pushed to his feet. "To my family," he said, raising his glass.

Darcy instantly looked at Joe, who hesitated before picking up his glass. Darcy picked up hers as well, knowing that while she wasn't part of the Marcellis, she was happy to wish them the best. They had been more than kind to her.

As soon as the toast was over, Tessa ordered everyone to "Eat. Eat before it gets cold."

Serving dishes circled the table. Darcy took small portions of everything. Despite her working out, she'd managed to put on enough weight to make half her wardrobe too tight to wear. But it was hard to care about that when she was having such a good time. Funny how just a few short weeks ago she'd arrived feeling scared and angry. It was as if she'd been nothing but sharp edges, and now she was all rounded corners and curves.

"What do you think of life on a winery, Darcy?" Katie asked. "It must be different for you."

"It is. I really like it."

"Did you see her designs?" Tessa asked. "So beautiful."

"I'm thrilled to finally have new wine labels," Brenna said. "So please accept my heartfelt thanks."

"I enjoyed working on the labels. And it was my first paying job in the graphic design business."

"Good for you," Katie said. "Is that what you studied at college?"

"Actually I was an art major. Painting — oils mostly. Then I discovered I wasn't very good and switched to graphic design and marketing."

Grammy M patted her hand. "I'm sure your pictures were delightful."

"Thank you. I tried, but I didn't have the talent."

"You have plenty of talent," Lorenzo intoned. "You should have seen the labels Brenna has brought me over the years. Goats. Who puts goats on wine bottles?"

Brenna shook her head. "They weren't goats."

"Animals then."

"Stop it, you two," Katie said mildly. "They're always like that, but I'm sure you're used to it by now."

"Pretty much," Darcy said with a laugh.

"It was worse before," Francesca said. "When Brenna moved back here, before she and Nic got together, wow, did she and Grandpa Lorenzo go at it."

"I had to be sure," the old man said. "Sure

that she wanted to devote herself to the winery. Now she has, and all will be well."

"We're a living, breathing soap opera," Colleen said. "We should be on daytime television."

"But you hate daytime TV," Marco said.

"Oh, I wouldn't watch," Colleen told him. "I'd like the money though."

She laughed and everyone joined in. Darcy glanced around the table, then spotted Katie watching her.

"Sorry," Katie said. "I know everyone else is used to you being here, but I'm still getting over the strangeness of the president's daughter sitting in the dining room of the house where I grew up. Until now the closest I've ever come to seeing you is in magazines."

"Occupational hazard," Darcy said.

"I guess. It would be so strange. People thinking they know you when they don't. Of course I think I know you because of what everyone has told me."

Darcy instantly glanced at Joe, then away. Katie grinned. "Oh, yeah, I know about that, too."

"Katie!" Colleen said, scolding her daughter. "Leave Darcy alone."

"It's okay," Darcy said, fighting a blush and having a bad feeling she was losing.

"It's not her fault," Francesca said. "Please don't take this the wrong way, Darcy, but we're all much more interested in Joe's part in this than yours. We assume you're normal, but to the best of our knowledge, our big brother has never dated. No one knew about his ex-wife until recently. Intellectually we know there must be dozens of women, but we've never *seen* him with one before. So we're all curious about how this is working."

"I'm not a freak of nature," Joe growled. "I've had girlfriends before."

Conversation ceased. Darcy didn't mind, because she didn't have anything to say either. Girlfriends? As in women in relationships? As in, she was one of them? She was his *girlfriend?*

Her insides got all warm and squishy. Was it true? And if it was, did it matter? Joe wasn't exactly a commitment-type guy. He handed out crumbs when she wanted a banquet. Had she somehow gotten past his emotional wall, or was she just fooling herself?

Joe shifted uncomfortably in the silence. Brenna opened her mouth, no doubt to say something funny but potentially embarrassing. Fortunately just then Valerie spilled her milk and Eric threw carrots at his sister.

Shrieks and tears erupted and Colleen, Francesca, and Katie all jumped to their feet and grabbed for extra napkins. The conversation was forgotten by everyone except Darcy, who found herself staring at Joe. And in a quirk of fate she couldn't explain, he was staring back. Just looking at her in a way that made her wonder about possibilities and romance and hope and if maybe, just this once, she was going to get it right.

After lunch there was discussion about going for a walk. In the end only Darcy, Grandpa Lorenzo, Brenna, and Nic started out into the vineyards.

"I'll accept the back pain, being unable to sleep, and the soccer games played in my belly, but why do I have to swell up like a toad?" Brenna asked as they strolled along a shady lane. "My shoes barely fit, I haven't been able to wear my wedding ring in three months, and we won't even discuss clothes."

"It will be worth it," Nic assured her as he helped her along.

"Ha. Want to trade?"

"Not really."

Brenna turned to Darcy. "A piece of advice — pass on the whole pregnancy thing. It's so much more disgusting than anyone tells you. There are things going on in my body that make it feel as if it's been taken over by aliens."

"So much talking," Lorenzo scolded mildly.

"You try carrying around a watermelon in your stomach for nine months." She came to a stop and rubbed her back. "Okay. This is as far as I go. You two have a nice walk."

Darcy glanced at Lorenzo. "Do you want to go back?"

He stared out at the horizon, then shook his head. "No. Let's see how far we can go."

"I hope you feel better," Darcy told Brenna.

"Not as much as I do." Brenna waved, then leaned heavily on Nic, who led the way back to the house.

Darcy moved next to Lorenzo. The old man surprised her by taking her hand and squeezing it.

"We'll be happy to have you in the family," he said.

She winced. "I appreciate that, but Joe and I aren't . . . That is to say we haven't . . . I'm not sure what's going on with him."

"I think my grandson is thinking about giving his heart."

Darcy wasn't sure about that, although it sounded nice.

"Do you love him?" Lorenzo asked.

Darcy stepped back and smiled. "Okay, I can't answer that, and maybe we should change the subject."

"You think I'm an old man who asks too many questions."

"Pretty much."

Lorenzo chuckled. They started walking again. The afternoon was still and clear. There were only the calls of birds to break the silence. After another ten or fifteen minutes, Lorenzo stopped, then looked around.

"I must sit down," he said.

They were in the middle of a row of grapes.

"Right here?" Darcy asked, then gasped as Lorenzo sank to the ground. She rushed over to him and crouched beside him. "Lorenzo?"

He didn't say anything, but something was very wrong. She could tell by his rapid, shallow breathing and lack of color in his skin.

Oh God. What should she do? She stood and looked around. Where was her Secret Service agent?

But no matter how she scanned the horizon, no one appeared.

She bent down and touched Lorenzo's hand. "I'll go get help," she said. "I'll be back as soon as I can."

"No." He gripped her fingers. "Don't go. It's too late."

Panic became fear. She felt for his pulse but couldn't find it. Tears filled her eyes and made it impossible to see.

She knelt on the dirt and looked around. "Help!" she yelled. "Someone help us."

"Shh." Lorenzo gave her a slight smile. "Don't worry, Darcy. It's all right."

It wasn't all right, but she didn't know what to do. She sat on the ground and lifted his head onto her lap. She held his hand until she realized the only breathing she heard was her own.

"Help," she called again, knowing it was too late. Over and over she called, but no one answered. For the first time in as long as she could remember, she was well and truly alone.

# 15

Joe put down the phone and reviewed the list in front of him. Even though several things had been checked off, the pile of things to do was getting longer, not shorter. He knew part of the problem was that no one could concentrate. Even he was having trouble staying mentally on task.

It had been two days. Only forty-eight hours since the Marcelli world as he knew it had changed forever. He couldn't think of this place existing without Lorenzo running things. The old man's gruff pronouncements were as integral as the house or the vines. How could he be gone?

Everyone had the same question. Everyone wanted to know what to do next. While it made sense for Marco to be in charge, Lorenzo's only child had turned to Joe when he'd heard the news. The shock in Marco's eyes had told Joe he was in no shape to make any decisions.

There was a knock at the open library door. Darcy entered and handed him a list.

"The rest of the phone calls have been made," she told him. "Everyone has been notified. The funeral home will take the body as soon as it's released, and the church has been arranged for the services Friday morning."

Joe ignored the list and looked at her. The shadows that had finally started to fade had returned. She looked thin and pale and unbearably sad.

"You shouldn't be making calls," he said. "What if someone recognized your voice?"

"I had to help." She moved into the room and sat down across from his desk. "I didn't call any friends or family members. Then I would have had to explain who I was. But I took care of the church and the catering. Tessa is saying she wants to cook, but I spoke to Colleen and Marco and they agree it's just too much for her. They're expecting nearly five hundred people at the funeral and nearly that many back here. Katie told me who to call, and they're going to be ready on time. I'm working on getting tents set up in the backyard, along with tables. I should have confirmation before five."

"You're good at this," he said, appreciative of the help. What did he know about putting together a funeral for a man who had been a part of the community for nearly eighty years?

"I grew up in politics," she said with a shrug. "I know how to organize parties. I know Katie was the more logical choice, but she's pretty broken up. They all are. Oh, and Mia just got here."

The youngest Marcelli sister had been missing for the past two days. "Where was she?" he asked.

"She and Ian went down to Mexico and didn't tell anyone. She got to her hotel in San Diego this morning and got the message. They drove right back. I'm sure she'll be in to see you in a second."

He leaned back in his chair and rubbed his eyes. "There's too much to do."

There wasn't. He'd organized tactical assignments for entire SEAL teams. This was nothing, in the logistics department. But emotionally — it was hell.

"It'll get done," Darcy said. "There are plenty of hands to lighten the load."

"When did you get philosophical?"

"When Lorenzo Marcelli died in my arms."

"I want to talk to you about that."

She looked away. "I'm okay."

He doubted that, but before he could say

anything, Mia ran into the room. Tears poured down her cheeks as she headed directly for Joe. He pushed back from the desk in time for her to drop into his lap and rest her face against his shoulder.

"I can't believe he's gone," she cried. "I loved him so much and I never told him."

"He knew," Joe told her as he awkwardly put his arms around her.

She cried until he felt the moisture seep through his shirt. He patted her back and looked at Darcy, desperate to know what to do next.

"It was very quick," Darcy said. "He was at peace."

Mia straightened and looked at her. "You swear? He wasn't in pain."

"Not at all."

"I'm glad." The tears made her face all blotchy.

Ian walked into the room, and Mia left Joe to hurry into his arms. "I can't believe it," she said. "He was fine when we left. Just fine."

For once Ian didn't seem to have anything to say. He gave them a sympathetic smile and ushered a sobbing Mia out of the library.

"Too much emotion," Joe said when she'd left.

"Mia leads with her heart," Darcy told him. "I'm going to guess she'll keep doing that until someone breaks it."

He didn't want to think about that happening. Honestly, he didn't want to think about anything. Right now he would sell his left nut for a military crisis calling him back to duty. He didn't care where, just so long as it was away from here.

But the phone didn't ring and Tessa entered the room with a tray of sandwiches and a pot of coffee.

"You've been in here so long," she said quietly. "You missed lunch."

She seemed smaller and more frail. As if the essence of who she was had been lost. As she set the tray down, she began to tremble. Joe stood, then looked helplessly at Darcy.

"Hold her," she mouthed.

Joe stared at the tiny woman, then opened his arms to her. Tessa stepped into his embrace and began to cry. He pulled her close and stroked her back. She barely came to the center of his chest, and he was afraid if he held her too tightly, she would snap in two.

Darcy stood and moved to the bookcase, where she grabbed a box of tissues and passed them to him. He offered a couple to

Tessa, who took them and wiped her face.

"I'm a foolish old woman," she murmured.

Darcy hugged her. "You're wonderful and you miss your husband. Of course there are tears. We're all sad. Lorenzo would probably tell us we were being foolish, crying over what we can't change. Then he'd want to know if anyone is checking on the grapes."

Tessa looked at her. A slight smiled pulled at the corners of her mouth. "Yes, you are right. That is what he would have said. But he would have been happy, too, to know how much we miss him."

She touched the large, carved desk. "He would sit here sometimes in the evening. He would do the books and I would read to Marco, or knit. In the winter we'd have a fire." Tears filled her eyes again. She opened her mouth, closed it, then quickly left.

Joe sank back onto his chair. "I've reached my limit. When is this going to be over?"

"Not for a long time."

He didn't like the sound of that. "Marco should be running things. Everyone's looking to me."

"Because you're the strong one. Those with natural leadership ability always rise to a position of authority."

"It's *his* family."

She walked around the desk and crouched in front of him. After taking both his hands in hers, she looked at him. Just looked.

He knew what she wanted — for him to admit it was his family, too. But he couldn't. Accepting the Marcellis as his own changed too much.

"I'm not one of them," he said stubbornly. "I know that makes me a real bastard, but I'm okay with that."

"Denial doesn't change reality."

"This isn't my reality."

She rose and, still holding his hands, leaned forward and lightly kissed him.

"Don't keep pushing them away. Learn from your past."

He jerked free. "You don't know what the hell you're talking about."

He hadn't pushed Alicia away. She'd gone on her own.

Darcy shrugged. "Have it your way." She left.

Alone in the silence, he thought. It was all he wanted. All he'd ever wanted.


Thursday morning Darcy reported for kitchen duty. Grandma Tessa had found out about the caterers and had a fit. She'd called in all the Marcelli women and Darcy to prepare everything. A menu had been posted on the refrigerator, Mia, Colleen, and Ian had been sent out for supplies, and now Grandma Tessa assigned tasks.

"Brenna, you'll need to stay off your feet," she said. "You can sit at the table and chop. Nothing more."

Brenna nodded. "Anything you want. You know that."

Her grandmother glared at her. "Stop being so nice to me. It makes me want to cry. No tears today. Today we cook. Tomorrow all those people will come to pay their respects to Lorenzo. They'll drink Marcelli wine and they'll eat Marcelli food. Nothing else." Her gaze narrowed as she turned her attention to Katie.

"I was only trying to help," her granddaughter said. "I thought I was helping."

"No. Helping is washing all the chickens when Mia brings them back."

The back door opened and Grammy M walked into the kitchen. Tessa stared at her for a long moment, then held open her arms. The two old ladies rushed together and hugged tightly.

"I'm sorry," Grammy M murmured. "Oh, Tessa, your pain. I would have come sooner, but I was thinkin' . . ." She gave a little sob. "I don't know what I was thinkin'. I can't believe he's gone. I've barely seen him these past three years. I regret that. And not seein' you."

They rocked back and forth.

"No," Tessa said. "I'm sorry. My harsh words."

Grammy M straightened and looked at her friend. " 'Tis no matter. I'll be moving back in. Gabriel's packin' my things. It'll be like it was before."

Tessa stared at her. "What did you say?"

"I'm movin' back in. Oh, Tessa, you need me now. I feel so horrible about what I did. You made me mad with your talk of the good Lord punishin' me, so I vowed not to come back until you apologized. Now I see I was an old fool. We're not gettin' any younger. We need to take advantage of the time we have left."

"Do you love him?" Tessa asked fiercely.

"Gabriel? Of course I love him."

Tessa marched to the phone and picked it up. "Then you call him right now and tell him to stop packing. You're staying there. If you love him, Mary, then hold on to him for as long as you have together. I don't care if you're married or not. I was mad because you seemed to leave so easily. As if I didn't matter."

"You matter," Grammy M said, throwing

herself at her friend. "You matter more than anyone."

Brenna was already weeping. The Grands cried, Katie cried, Francesca had put aside the flour she was measuring and searched for tissues. Darcy felt her own emotions give way.

Brenna pushed herself to her feet and waddled over to the Grands. "Group girl hug," she said, motioning Darcy in. Katie and Francesca joined them.

For Darcy, the pain of loss combined with the sweetness of feeling as if she belonged. In this time of family tragedy, the Marcellis reached out to include her.

Later, when the groceries had arrived and the tasks were assigned, she went with Grandma Tessa to collect the family silver from a pantry under the main staircase.

"We'll need all the serving pieces," Grandma Tessa said. "Bowls, chafing dishes."

She stepped aside so Darcy could duck into the small room. Shelves filled the space, and each shelf was crowded with beautiful pieces in silver, silver and glass, and crystal.

"This is all so incredible," Darcy breathed. "I've been to the White House, and I have to tell you, this is just as lovely."

Tessa smiled. "You're kind to say so. Bring

everything to the dining room table. Don't worry, I won't put you to work washing it all. You're helpful in the kitchen. Francesca will be in charge of washing and polishing. She never was very handy with a knife."

Darcy nodded. She would have to put the leaves in the table first, or there wouldn't be room. But then five hundred was a lot of people to feed, especially on three days' notice.

Tessa turned to leave. Darcy hesitated, then stopped her. "I know I probably shouldn't say anything, but I. . . ." She cleared her throat. "I'm sorry I didn't come get you or anyone. I wanted to, but then he said he didn't want to be alone. I screamed for help, but no one heard me. I just . . ." She had to swallow against the tightness and the tears. "I'm sorry he wasn't with family. At the end, I mean."

Tessa looked at her for a long time, then patted her arm. "Lorenzo died with someone he cared about very much, Darcy. That makes you family. I'm glad you were with him. So very glad."

Darcy nodded, but she couldn't see or speak. There were too many tears and no way to stop them.

Paige was prepared to go to the mat on this

one. "Darcy's request isn't unreasonable," she said, striving for patience, when she really wanted to hit Alex over the head and tie him up in the closet for a couple of days.

"No one is supposed to know the president's daughter is here. You don't think one of the five hundred people at the funeral will notice?" Alex demanded in a tone that told her he thought she was an idiot.

"She's hardly going to be parading herself around. She'll be in a hat with a heavy veil. We'll walk her in at the end and she'll duck out a side door right before the services end. She's not asking to go to the graveside and she's going to stay in her room with the door locked until the wake is over. That's more than reasonable."

"What's reasonable is not going out at all. We're talking five hundred people, Paige. Do you know what kind of security nightmare this is? We should move her to a secure location until all this mess is over. Typical Darcy, she's refusing to leave."

Paige took a step toward him and raised her chin. "Typical Darcy? What does that mean? How has she even once been difficult? How has she made your job harder? The only goddamn time she was left on her own was because of a shift change and the fact that you forgot to schedule overlap.

Which happened to be the exact moment Lorenzo Marcelli died." She poked him in the chest with her index finger. "Darcy was on her own with a dying man and no one around her. Did she come to you and point out the screwup? Did she threaten you? Not even close. So don't you dare tell me that she's been difficult."

Temper flared in his dark blue eyes. He carefully pushed her finger away. "Why is this so important?"

"Because she cares about these people. Because they mean something to her. An emotion you've probably never experienced, but it's there for the rest of the world."

Alex glared at her. "We do things by the book on my watch."

"Right. And sometimes mistakes get made."

He didn't respond. Paige knew it had to be killing him that he'd messed up. Such a minor thing, not assigning any overlap. It could have happened to anyone. But it had happened to Alex, and she was more than willing to press that point home.

"She will be completely covered and unrecognizable," Paige said more calmly. "I will be with her every second. You can have agents in the church. But she's going to that funeral."

"Fine," he said curtly. "Straight to the church and straight back. Nothing graveside, and I'll post agents on the stairs so no one gets up to her floor during the wake."

The victory surprised Paige. What had caused Alex to give in? She'd thought they'd have to fight a lot longer and she would have to threaten him with Darcy calling her father.

As it was, she was all charged up for a fight that had ended too soon. Lucky for her — there was still one more thing.

She moved in close again and glared at him. "Just so we're all clear on this — don't start something with me unless you intend to finish it. I'm not a toy, and this is not a game."

Under other circumstances his bewilderment would have been amusing. Right now it just pissed her off.

"What on earth are you talking about?" he asked.

"Figure it out," she told him, then stalked away.

The Catholic church closest to the Marcelli vineyards usually held three hundred. On a foggy, cool, Friday morning, nearly twice that many squeezed inside. Colleen had given Joe an idea of whom to expect. Even so, he was surprised to see so many unfamiliar faces.

Some were old — contemporaries of Lorenzo's. Others were much younger. Distant relatives, employees, fellow vintners. A half a dozen politicians sat in the pews.

There had been over two hundred requests to speak at the funeral. Last night Colleen and her daughters had gone through them and picked thirty. Twenty would speak in the church, the other ten by the graveside.

Joe listened to the religious service, then to the first few mourners. He heard stories about a Lorenzo he had never known. In some ways the tales made the old man seem alive again.

Tessa sat next to him, with Marco beside her. She cried through the service, seeming to shrink with every minute that passed. Unable to stand her quiet tears, he put an arm around her and pulled her close.

She looked up at him. "Your grandfather was so proud of you," she whispered from beneath her veil. "So proud."

His grandfather. He'd never claimed that relationship with Lorenzo. Joe had been careful to avoid calling him by name, much as he did with Marco and Colleen and Tessa. Grammy M had escaped the name stigma because her title didn't seem to be about any familial relationship.

There were too many people, Joe thought, wanting to bolt. He forced himself to stay in place, trying to think about other things. He felt Darcy's presence in the church. She sat in the back, on the side, where she would be whisked away before the service ended. She'd insisted on coming, saying she wanted to be there for the family and for herself.

He knew in his head funerals were supposed to help. That the ceremony clarified the moment of death and allowed those still living to move on. It had never worked that way for Joe. He'd been to funerals of guys he'd worked with, and the pomp and circumstance had only pissed him off, as it did now.

Nic stood and walked to the front of the church. He nodded at Tessa and Marco, then introduced himself.

"I first met Lorenzo when I was ten. I'd walked over from Wild Sea to taste some of his grapes. I was a kid — what did I know?" Nic smiled sadly. "Lorenzo found me snooping and took me back to the winery, where we did some barrel tasting. He listened to my opinion and told me his. I was terrified, of course. He was a Marcelli and we weren't supposed to get along, but he was kind that day and made me wish I could be a part of his family."

Nic paused and stared into the crowded church. "Years later, I met and fell in love with his granddaughter Brenna. After a little complaining because I was a Giovanni, Lorenzo welcomed me into the family. And there I've stayed, grateful to have known him. He was a man bound by tradition, yet farsighted enough to see what the future would require of those around him. He has given us all room to succeed, while offering us a haven of support and caring."

Joe let the words wash over him. Speaker after speaker spoke of a man Joe had barely allowed himself to know. He thought of all the times Lorenzo had pressed him to be part of the family, and of all the times Joe had refused. Lorenzo had wanted little more than a chance to get to know his grandson, but Joe had been determined to make sure that never happened.

Why? What was the point of disappointing an old man? What had he gained by resisting?

And now it was too late. He couldn't go to Lorenzo and say he understood why he, Joe, had been sent away all those years ago. He couldn't acknowledge that whatever his last name might be, Marcelli blood flowed in his veins. He couldn't stop rejecting what had been offered because the man who refused to give up was finally gone.

Several hours later Joe moved through the crowded kitchen. The guests were being kept outside by a combination of family and Secret Service agents gently ushering them in that direction. Tessa held court over the stove, accepting the condolences of those who stopped by to see her and share stories. Colleen and Grammy M stayed close, while Marco, Francesca, Katie, and Mia circulated with the guests. Nic had taken Brenna home. She'd been inconsolable after the funeral, and with her due date so close, everyone had agreed she needed to rest.

For the first time, Joe felt out of place. He didn't know where to go or what to do. Several family friends had spoken with him about his grandfather, but he hadn't known what he should say in return. He had no stories to share, no fond memories. He'd spent the last three years resisting.

Finally he made his way to the back of the house and went upstairs. The agent on the landing nodded, then stepped aside to let Joe pass. He walked to Darcy's room, knocked once, and entered when she called for him to come in.

She sat on her bed. The plain black dress was still in place, but she'd kicked off her shoes and removed the veil. Her skin was pale, her eyes large and filled with pain.

"How are you holding up?" he asked.

"That's my question for you," she told him as she stood and stepped toward him. "Are you okay?"

She wasn't mad. Typical Darcy. She liked to act tough, but she was all heart.

"I'm getting through it."

She studied his face, then touched her fingers to his cheeks. "I don't think so."

He swallowed. "I never told him it was okay. A couple of days before he died, he apologized to me for forcing Colleen and Marco to give me up for adoption. I never said I forgave him. He thinks I'm still mad at him for that."

She pressed herself against him. "No, he doesn't. He knows what's in your heart, Joe."

If only that were true. But in his book, it was a bunch of crap. "I never said I cared. I never admitted that I was one of them. A Marcelli. I wouldn't say it. I wouldn't even call him my grandfather."

Tears filled her eyes and spilled down her cheeks. He touched the moisture. "Hey, I'm

the one who screwed up. Why are you crying?"

"Because you can't."

# 16

Joe couldn't remember anyone ever crying *for* him. He didn't know what to say, so instead of trying to speak, he bent down and kissed her.

The gesture was supposed to offer comfort and thanks, but the second his mouth brushed hers, heat exploded inside of him. The wanting was as instant as it was powerful. Need took over, making him grab her and pull her close.

Darcy responded by clinging to him, urging him on. She parted her lips, and when he slipped his tongue inside, she welcomed him.

Blood raced south, making him hard in a heartbeat. He reached for the zipper at the back of her dress. One long pull had it free. A quick tug at her shoulders and it fell down her arms, exposing her black lacy bra.

He pulled back enough to get a good look. Soft, pale skin, black lace, tight nipples. If he'd had thoughts about turning back, one eyeful took care of that. Still, there was enough sanity left for him to remember where he was and what was happening.

"What the hell am I thinking?" he asked, more of himself than of her.

"Don't think," she said. She lowered her arms and stepped out of the dress. Underneath she wore a pair of tiny, black panties, her bra, and nothing else. How was he supposed to resist that?

As he watched, she crossed to the door and turned the old-fashioned lock. Then she drew the curtains so the room was in semidarkness. She moved back in front of him and gently pushed his suit jacket off his shoulders.

"Allow me," she whispered.

"Darcy," he began, but she shook her head.

"No talking," she told him. "No thinking. No analyzing. Just feel my touch. What I'm doing to you. Nothing else. Clear your mind."

She loosened his tie and pulled it off, then went to work on his shirt buttons. He stood there, feeling strange and awkward, not sure what was going on. Oh, he understood they were both about to be naked, but this was different from his usual lovemaking, although he couldn't say why.

There was something in her eyes, something in the way she seemed so solemn, yet determined. Something in her touch that kept him quiet and immobile.

When she'd tossed his shirt on the chair, she walked behind him and pressed her mouth to his back. He felt her tongue slip across an old scar.

"What happened?" she asked.

"Knife fight. I rolled when I should have ducked."

She nipped the area, sending a jolt of fire right down to his crotch. She moved her hands to his waist, then to his chest, where she stroked him from shoulder to belly, getting close to his erection, but never touching him.

"And this one?" she asked before tonguing another spot on his back.

"Not a clue." He picked up one of her hands and brought it to his mouth, where he bit down on the swell of flesh below her thumb and licked her palm.

"You can't remember?" she asked, her voice breathless.

"I have a lot of scars."

"So I see. Sit down and take off your shoes and socks."

He stepped away and did as she requested.

Then he stood again and removed his slacks and briefs. When he was naked, he turned toward her, waiting for more instructions.

Her gaze swept his body, pausing on his erection.

"Nice," she said with a smile. "Lie down on your stomach."

He did and watched as she slipped off her bra and panties. He had about two seconds to enjoy the view before she moved onto the bed, then straddled him just below his butt.

She leaned forward so the very tips of her breasts brushed across his back. The light touch drove him crazy, especially as she rocked her hips slightly, grinding his dick into the bed. It was just enough friction to be dangerous.

But he didn't tell her to stop. Not when she kissed and nibbled her way across his shoulders.

"You're so strong," she whispered. "You carry so much weight and worry. You can let it go, just for a few minutes. Just for now."

Under any other circumstances, he probably would have told her to keep her emotional mumbo jumbo to herself, but right then, the words made sense. He did want to give up the burden for a little while. To not think about anything except how she made him feel. But kisses on his shoulders and back weren't going to get it done, despite how nice they were.

In one quick move, he flipped over. He grabbed her around the waist, keeping her in place. Only now her hot, wet center was directly on his.

She sighed. "That's what I get for playing with an expert, huh?"

"Exactly."

He could have pushed inside of her. A large part of his body wanted just that. To bury himself inside and let the feelings take him away. But not just yet, he thought, thinking about things he could do to her and how good they would feel.

So he stayed in place, and when she moved up his body so she could kiss him, he didn't stop her.

Instead he claimed her with a deep kiss. He traced her tongue with his, to explore the soft sweetness of her mouth. He slid his hands to her breasts and cupped them. When he teased her tight nipples, she groaned.

That throaty, hungry sound was his undoing. Suddenly he had to have all of her. He had to touch her and taste her everywhere, except he didn't want to stop kissing her. Not yet.

He ignored the throbbing between his legs and concentrated on her pleasure. When she raised her head to catch her breath, he drew her up so that he could suck on her breasts.

First one and then the other. Her breathing increased and he felt her body tremble. He urged her up onto her knees as he slid down a little. For the first time, she hesitated.

"No, that's okay."

Joe looked at the beautiful naked woman straddling his chest and knew he needed her more than he'd ever needed anyone before.

"I want to," he told her.

She made a vague motion with her hands. "It's um . . . just . . . I don't know. I'm fine."

He didn't want her fine. He wanted her writhing and panting and completely out of control. Had some guy refused, saying it wasn't his thing? Had some bastard hurt her by going down on her? Or was this her first time?

He had a fantasy of her straddling his face, hanging on to the headboard and riding him to heaven. But that would have to wait for another time. In one quick series of grabs, shifts, and drops, he had her on her back with him between her legs.

"Jeez, how do you do that?" she asked. "I need more self-defense lessons if I'm going to keep up with you."

He thought about telling her she couldn't possibly keep up, but that it was okay because he had no intention of leaving her behind. He opened his mouth to say just that, but instead he realized he was inches above her belly and that any conversation could be had another time. Right now he had important erotic work to do.

He kissed her stomach, then along the top of her thighs. She squirmed, but it wasn't in a good way. Her hands pushed at him.

"Please," she said.

He braced himself on one elbow and looked at her. "What's wrong?" he asked.

Color stained her cheeks. "Nothing. It's not important."

"It is to me."

She closed her eyes. "I've only slept with a couple of guys. I was always afraid of who would talk and what they'd say. Maybe to the press or something."

"Makes sense."

"Well, the first one was someone from college. I thought he was really special. I thought I was in love with him." She opened her eyes and looked at him. "I wasn't. But before I found that out, I suggested we try, you know, oral sex. He got all disgusted and said it was gross and he couldn't believe I'd asked."

"Which made you embarrassed."

"Among other things. It was a couple of days before Christmas and I was taking him home to meet my family. On Christmas afternoon I overheard him coming on to my sister. He said that he and I were only friends, that he had a real thing for her, and that he wanted to make love with her. Then he detailed exactly what he wanted to do with her, including that."

Joe wanted to go find the bastard and pound him into a bloodstain on the sand. Instead he kissed her thigh and asked, "What did Lauren do?"

"Slapped him as hard as she could, called him a sex-crazed asshole, and told him to get out of the house."

He thought about saying he liked Lauren, but he figured Darcy would misunderstand his words.

"I've been a little sensitive about the whole thing ever since," she said.

"Makes sense. Give me five minutes."

"Joe, don't."

He moved between her thighs. "Five minutes and if you hate it, I'll stop."

She twisted away. "But you don't have to —"

"I got that. I want to, and I took this correspondence class on some real interesting techniques. You might like them."

Her eyes widened, then she started to laugh. "You did not," she said.

"I can show you my certificate. I graduated at the top of my class."

Then while she was still laughing, he used his fingers to part her and lightly stroke his tongue against her swollen center.

Darcy had big plans to endure the five minutes, then push him away. Sure she'd heard that some men liked that sort of thing and she was curious, but Greg's reaction had scarred her in a way she'd never forgotten. The look of absolute disgust and horror on his face had pretty much shattered her tiny burst of confidence.

With her second lover, she'd been passive, not daring to ask for anything in case he reacted the same way. Joe had been her third foray into sexuality, and their passionate encounter hadn't left any time for doubts.

But now she could think, and once she started, it was impossible to stop her brain.

The first brush of his tongue felt good. Really good. The second set nerve endings to humming in a way she'd never felt before.

Her legs fell open, her hips tilted toward him, and suddenly breathing didn't seem all that important.

He licked her over and over. It was different from being touched by his fingers. More intimate. Softer, but more direct. She could feel his breath. His shoulders pushed against her thighs. She was torn, wanting him inside of her and never, ever wanting this to stop.

Which, of course, it did.

She opened her eyes and stared at him. Fear swept through her. He hadn't liked it. He hadn't liked doing it to her. He hadn't —

"Relax," he said. "Give me your hands. Hold yourself open."

He positioned her fingers so she parted herself for him. She felt exposed and stupid, but before she could ask what he was doing, he returned his mouth to her body and rational thought fled.

The licking, gentle sucking, circling, breathing all continued. Tension moved through her body, starting at her toes and working its way up. At one point she thought she might have felt his teeth lightly graze that one most sensitive spot, but then there was his tongue again and a slight pressure at the opening.

Then she was caught up in a whirlwind of

sensation. Even as he continued to use his mouth on her, he slipped in first one finger, then another. He filled her in a slow, steady rhythm designed to make her scream and beg.

She drew her legs back and dug her heels into the mattress. She rocked her hips and tried to catch her breath. Need swept through her. It was hot and thick and too powerful to ignore. Closer, she thought as pleasure tightened and grew. She was so close.

His fingers moved faster, sliding in and out of her. His tongue kept pace. Suddenly her body was out of her control. She shuddered into her release as incredible sensations washed through her. She bucked against him, desperate to keep him there, touching her everywhere.

He read her mind, slowing but not stopping. Again and again she came until the climaxes slowed and her body relaxed.

She opened her eyes and saw him smiling at her.

"Not bad for a rookie," he told her, then he pushed into a kneeling position and shifted closer. He thrust into her, filling her completely.

Understanding dawned.

"You're still hard," she whispered.

"Very hard. I liked doing that. A lot."

Difficult not to believe him when the proof pushed in deep enough to make her clench around him.

Gratitude made her ache. Not only because he'd pleasured her, but also because he'd replaced a horrible memory with one that bordered on spectacular.

In a matter of seconds, the steady rhythm had her on the edge again. She wrapped her legs around him, drawing him closer, then quickly lost herself in more waves of release. Two thrusts later, he followed, groaning her name and hanging on as if he would never let go.

When they'd recovered enough to speak, Joe rolled off her and pulled her against him. He settled her head on his shoulder and wrapped his arm around her.

"Thank you," he said.

Darcy snuggled close. "I believe that's my line," she whispered. "You were great." With more than just sex, she thought. In all of it.

"I needed to be with you."

His words did a funny thing to her heart. It sort of stuttered a beat, before returning to the regular pace.

Danger, she told herself. This was the wrong man. She needed someone to love her back, not run for the emotional hills.

Oh but she wanted him to be different. She wanted him to care. But Joe had pushed away one wife and the entire Marcelli family. Why would she be any different?

"You need to get back," she said, giving him a little shove, knowing that if he stayed with her much longer, she was at risk of saying something that could embarrass them both.

"I don't want to."

"Perfectly understandable, but I'm not excited at the thought of someone in your family coming looking for you and finding you here. They already know about the last time."

"Good point." He kissed her, then sat up and reached for his clothes. "I wish you could come."

"Me, too. But Paige and Alex are right. Better for me to stay securely hidden away."

He dressed quickly and left. When she was alone again, Darcy dressed in shorts and a T-shirt, then stretched out on the bed. Now what? Everything had changed, and she didn't know how to make it go back. Falling in love with Joe was a huge mistake. Was it too late to protect herself? And even if she could stop herself from caring about him, however was she going to get over falling for his whole family?

Three days after the funeral Darcy walked into the kitchen and found Grandma Tessa sitting alone at the kitchen table. It was so strange to see the tiny woman simply sitting. Grandma Tessa was always on the move — carrying, chopping, stirring, serving.

When she saw Darcy, she stood up. "It's nearly lunchtime," she said briskly. "I'll fix you something."

Darcy knew the whole "food is love" talk. She'd given it to Joe more than once. But just this once she couldn't listen to her own advice.

"No," she said gently, pushing Tessa back in her chair. "Let me bring *you* something."

Tears filled Tessa's eyes, although she did her best to blink them away. "You're a good girl, Darcy. It's been a blessing to have you here." She fingered the rosary beads on the table in front of her. "Honestly, I'm not hungry. I know I have to eat, but not yet. I miss him too much."

Darcy sank down next to her and took her free hand. "I know. You've loved him a whole lifetime. It's only been a few days. You're allowed to grieve."

Tessa nodded and squeezed her fingers. "I

keep expecting to see him walk into the room. I can't sleep. The bed, it's so big. When did it get so big?"

Not knowing what else to do, Darcy hugged her. Tessa held on tight.

"I'm glad you're here," she said. "With the girls all gone, the house is so quiet. You bring us life again."

Darcy thought that might be an exaggeration, but she knew having people around gave Tessa something to think about other than her sadness. She wished she had something to say, something that would help ease the other woman's pain. But there weren't any words.

So they sat together, hugging and rocking, not speaking. Darcy breathed in the scent of spices and rose soap and did her best to be strong.

The back door opened. She glanced up, hoping to see Joe. He'd been busy with family stuff for the past couple of days, and they hadn't had any time alone. But instead of him, Paige walked into the kitchen.

"I have news," she said.

Tessa straightened and turned. "Paige. Are you hungry?"

Paige walked to the older woman and crouched in front of her. "You've got to stop feeding me," she teased. "I've gained twenty pounds."

Tessa cupped her face. "Maybe, but on you they're beautiful pounds."

"That's not what my supervisor's going to say after my next physical." She straightened and glanced at Darcy. "They've caught the last of the kidnappers. Your father will be calling in the next minute or so. The call will be put through here."

Darcy wondered if she looked as surprised as she felt. Caught? "Already?"

Paige smiled. "It's been nearly four weeks. But the ringleaders had gone pretty far underground."

Tessa stood and patted her hair. "The president?" she asked, sounding stunned. "Phoning here?"

"You look fine," Paige said with a grin.

Darcy tried to enjoy the humor of Tessa worried about her appearance for a phone call that wasn't for her, but she could only deal with her rising panic.

No! It couldn't be true. If the men were caught then she was free to leave. Actually, she *had* to leave. The Marcellis would want their house back.

But she wasn't ready. She and Brenna hadn't finalized the label designs, and the family was still in mourning, and what about Joe? They had to talk and she had to tell him that she. . . .

The phone rang. Paige reached for it.

"Agent Newberry," she said crisply, then nodded at Darcy. "Yes. She's right here." She held out the phone.

Darcy took it. "Hello?"

"Please hold for the president," a female voice said as Paige left the kitchen.

Darcy waited a second, then heard, "Darcy?"

"Hi, Dad."

"You've been told?"

"Uh-huh."

"Good news all-around. The last of them was rounded up this morning." He laughed gruffly. "I'll sleep better at night knowing my girls are safe now."

Two months ago Darcy would have dismissed the statement or at least reinterpreted it to mean he was glad Lauren was safe. Now she wasn't so sure. Maybe he meant it. Maybe she did matter to him.

"I've been talking to your sister," he continued. "She mentioned you'd like to get more involved with things here at the White House."

Darcy winced. That wasn't *exactly* what she'd said. "I thought it would be nice to do more."

"I'm glad," he said, sounding as if he meant it. "I always knew your space was important to you." He hesitated. "Do you young people still talk about having your own space?"

She smiled. "Not really. But I know what you mean."

"Good. When you come home, we can talk. I'd like to have you around more, Darcy. You're very important to me."

"Thanks." She shifted awkwardly. "Um, you, too," she mumbled.

"All right. I have to run. Let me know your travel plans. I can have a plane pick you up whenever you'd like. Maybe in the morning?"

So soon? She wasn't ready to go. "I'll let you know, Dad. Thanks."

"All right. Talk to you soon."

The line went dead. Darcy handed the phone back to Paige. "He's ready to have me home."

Grandma Tessa stared at her. "Of course you want to go be with your family," she said. "If you're safe now."

Darcy nodded. Tears burned, but she refused to give in to them. It wasn't right. "You've all been very kind."

"Kind." Tessa dismissed the word. "We like having you here."

"I've liked being here."

"You have things to do, yes? A life?" Tessa asked.

Darcy shrugged. "I guess."

The old woman took her hand. "If you don't have anything special waiting, you could stay a few days. Maybe a couple of weeks."

Darcy wanted to so much it hurt. "But I'm an intrusion. I have a Secret Service team. Less now, but at least two agents."

"Two. It's nothing." Tessa squeezed her fingers. "Say you'll stay. We want you here."

"But Marco and Colleen may not be happy about —"

"Of course they'll be happy," Tessa said. "I know my own children."

Just then Joe walked into the kitchen. Tessa turned to him. "Tell her to stay."

He frowned. "You're leaving?"

"They've found the rest of the kidnappers," Darcy told him. "Your assignment is over."

The second she said the words, horror washed over her. Of course. Joe was only here because of her. Now he was free to return to the naval base and continue his regular life. The one that didn't include her.

"But she should stay," Tessa said. "Tell her. A few weeks. For the harvest and the first pressing. To bring life to this house. For you, Joe. She can stay for you."

Darcy braced herself to hear that he was leaving as well. Emotions crossed his face, but they went so quickly, she couldn't read them.

Tessa's eyes widened. "You're not going, are you?" she asked, sounding frightened. "Joseph, your family needs you."

Time stood still until Joe nodded. "I know. I'll ask for compassionate leave and I'll stay a few more weeks." He looked at Darcy. "You should stay, too. Unless you have something else you should be doing."

That would mean having an actual life, which she didn't.

"Not really."

"Then we'll both stay."

Four simple words. They shouldn't have given her heart wings, and yet they had.

# 17

"You'll be leaving soon," Paige said. "That must make you happy."

Alex shrugged. "I didn't mind the assignment."

"But it's not very high profile. When you get back to D.C. maybe you can get assigned to the president."

He had the feeling she was talking about something other than the topic at hand, but then conversations with Paige were always filled with undercurrents.

"I enjoyed the opportunity to protect Darcy," he said carefully, wondering why he cared about Paige's opinion on anything. She was the one who'd pointed out the unfairness of his attitude — that if they got married, she would be the one to give up her job, not him. While he understood her intellectual argument, he resented the implication that he was the jerk in all this. Even if maybe he was.

Not that he gave a damn. Whatever they'd had was long over. They'd each gone their separate ways, and they would again.

"Hey, guys."

Alex turned and saw Darcy standing at the entrance to the guesthouse. "You heard the good news?" he asked.

"About the kidnappers? Yes, Paige told me." Darcy smiled at her. "I wanted to let you know, I'm not leaving here. Not just yet. There's so much going on, and well, Tessa asked me to stay and I said yes. I'm thinking for maybe two weeks. I don't know who my regular detail will be, so that's why I'm telling you."

"Not a problem," Paige told her. "I'll make the arrangements."

"Thanks."

Darcy waved and left.

Paige watched her go. "She's changed," she said, more to herself than him. "She used to be distant and sarcastic. Now she is warmer. Happier. I'm not sure how much of it is Joe and how much of it is the family, but I'm thrilled for her." She turned to Alex. "I'd like to stay."

"Here?"

"Yes, here. With Darcy. I'd like to be assigned to her. With the threat gone, she'll go back to a normal-size team. I want to be a part of that."

He'd thought they would both return to Washington. He'd thought they would have a long plane ride to discuss what she'd said to him about this not being a game.

"So that's it?" he asked, angry but not sure why.

"What else is there?" she asked. "You want your high-powered career. You want to be the best agent ever, to be alone. I don't want that anymore. Oh, I want to do a good job, but I want a life, too. I want people around me I love."

Not him. She didn't want him. Which was fine. The hell with her.

Joe had claimed the library as his office. He didn't want to work in the winery, and there weren't any other rooms that had desks and file cabinets.

Over the past couple of weeks, he'd settled into a rhythm of dealing with winery business in the morning and Lorenzo's personal papers in the afternoon. The will reading was at the end of the week. That was his cutoff date, he told himself. The Monday after the will was read, he was out of here.

He hadn't told anyone yet, although he didn't know why he was putting it off. No one would be surprised. The family understood his stay was only temporary.

Only they weren't acting like it. Assumptions had been made, and he needed to make sure they got unmade.

Darcy walked into the office, took one look at him, and collapsed into a chair. "Okay, you're looking fierce about something. Are you planning a revolt?"

As always, the sight of her eased the band of tension around his chest. Her easy smile welcomed him, and the sway of her body made him think of hot nights — an excellent distraction. She was the one person here who didn't want something from him.

"Not a revolt, an escape."

"Going anywhere interesting?"

"I haven't decided. You want to pick?"

She wore a short black and white skirt and a black sleeveless top. Her time here had added color to her skin and while she was still too skinny by far, there was a bit more meat on her bones.

He liked the changes. He liked her — which confused him, but in a good way.

"I've never been to Hawaii," she said. "Living on the East Coast, our escape for sun and sand is usually Florida or the Caribbean. But Hawaii sounds really nice."

"I know a couple of places. Quiet. Secluded. You could go naked."

"Joe!" She glanced over her shoulder toward the closed library door. "You have a family of lurkers. I love them to pieces, but they don't grasp the concept of privacy."

She was cute when she blushed, cuter still in his bed. They hadn't had much opportunity to make love. Not with so many people in and out of the house. But soon, he promised himself. Soon.

"How's it going?" she asked in an obvious attempt to change the subject.

He decided to go along with it. "Not bad. Running a winery is a lot of work. Sometimes I can feel the walls closing in."

Her concern turned sympathetic. "Your family is dependent on you in a way they've never been before."

He nodded.

"That makes you feel funny," she said. "You thought it would be different. That they were strong on their own. But things aren't always as they seem."

He looked at her. There was something in his voice. "We're not talking about the Marcellis, are we?"

She shook her head. "I was thinking about my situation."

"Lauren?"

"No. My father. He's . . ." She looked out the window. "I haven't felt a part of his life for a long time. I thought he didn't care about me, but now I wonder if that was just an excuse for me to stay mad and not try."

He didn't know what they were talking about but knew Darcy would explain further if she wanted him to know.

She returned her attention to him. "As a naval officer, are you legally and morally obligated to keep the president's secrets?"

He hadn't seen that coming. "Yes. I have top secret clearance. I'm a good security risk."

"You have to be better than good," she said. "You have to be. . . ." She swallowed. "You can't tell anyone."

She was serious. Joe leaned forward. "I give you my word, Darcy. But if you're not sure, don't tell me."

She smiled. "I appreciate that. But I want to talk about it. I never have. Not even with Lauren. Oh, I know she knows, but we never discuss it. It's our elephant on the table. The one we all carefully ignore."

"All right."

He stood and crossed the library, where he carefully locked the door. Then he returned to the desk, but this time he sat on her side of it, in the chair closest to hers. He took her hand and laced their fingers together.

She glanced from the door to him. "Gee, no pressure."

"I told you — don't tell me if you don't want to."

"I do. It's just, I don't even know where to begin."

"How about with 'It was a dark and stormy night.' "

She burst out laughing, then leaned toward him and kissed him.

"Thank you. I feel better now." She laughed again. "Okay, it was a dark and stormy night. My mom was dying. She'd come home from the hospital because she wanted to die at home. I was sixteen, Lauren was seventeen. We were scared and waiting to hear she was gone. Lauren fell asleep, but I couldn't. I went downstairs — a hospital room had been set up in the study of our house — and I sat in the hallway. I don't know how long. It felt like hours. I remember it was so cold, but I didn't want to leave to go get a blanket or a sweater."

Joe had known that Darcy had lost her mother at an early age, but he hadn't known the details.

"Didn't you have anyone to sit with you?" he asked. "Other family members?"

"I don't remember. That night it was just me. Finally my dad came out. I could tell

325

from the look on his face she was gone. I started to cry and go to him. He . . ." She paused, then continued. "He pushed me away. I tried to cling to him, and he told me not to touch him. That I wasn't his daughter. He never wanted to see me again."

Joe hadn't had any idea what she'd been going to tell him, but he hadn't expected this. Horror filled him, but nothing he felt could match the pain in her eyes.

"I didn't know what to do," she said in a whisper. "What to think. I ran to my room. I was crying too hard to speak. Lauren woke up and she got that Mom was gone. We cried together." Darcy tightened her grip on his hand. "Later my dad came to me. He said he was sorry about what he'd done, what he'd said. He told me it wasn't about me."

Joe moved his chair closer and wrapped his arm around her. "You don't have to talk about this."

She blinked away tears. "I'm kind of into it now, so you're going to have to hear the rest."

He kissed her forehead and rubbed her back. "Sure thing."

She drew in a deep breath. "He told me that my mom had had an affair. She'd met this bright young lawyer at some campaign event, and they'd had a torrid affair. She'd gotten pregnant and had been prepared to leave her husband and baby daughter, only the guy died. So she stayed and they patched up the marriage."

Darcy looked at him. "I'm the baby. The child of her lover. No one ever told me until that night. I never guessed. My dad — the man who raised me, not my biological father — never let on. Until the night she died, he loved Lauren and me exactly the same. Or at least he acted that way. But when my mom was dying, she called out for her lover. She died speaking his name. So that's what upset my dad — so much. When I went to him, he was thinking of her and what she'd done. That's why he was angry."

She brushed away tears. "He told me he was sorry and that I was still his daughter. He did everything he could to make it up to me. But I didn't believe him. I wasn't angry, exactly, but I was scared and hurt. I shut down. For weeks I wouldn't talk to him. At some point he told Lauren, but we never discussed it either. He kept reaching out to me, and I kept turning away. One day he stopped trying and when I was ready, I didn't know how to reach out to him. We sort of reached an impasse, which is where we've stayed. And in the middle of that is Lauren."

"All this family crap. Now you know why I want out of here."

She clutched his hand tighter. "No, I don't. You have wonderful people here who love you. There is nothing more important than that in the world."

He didn't want to have this conversation with her, but he knew she was vulnerable, and he didn't want to lash out at her.

"You don't understand," he said, determined not to get angry. "It's not forever. It's never forever. Why should I walk away from the work I do, the career I love, for this?"

She stared at him. "What are you saying? The Marcellis will change their mind? They'll wake up one morning and decide they don't want you in the family?"

He pulled free of her and stared out the window. "They already did that once."

Her breath caught. "The circumstances were completely different. You were a baby."

"Yeah, and now I can fight back."

He felt her gaze on him. When he finally looked at her, pain darkened her eyes.

"This isn't about them, as much as it is about her," Darcy murmured. "Your ex-wife. The one who left."

"That was years ago."

"What happened?"

He shrugged. There was no point in rehashing that old news, yet he found himself starting to speak. "I'd been gone nearly five months. I'd shipped out without warning. I couldn't get in touch with her while I was away. I got back after midnight. When I walked in the house, it was dark. It took me a minute to figure out it was mostly empty. She'd gone a few weeks before. Moved out, took the kids. She left a note and the divorce papers on the kitchen counter."

Darcy made a noise low in her throat. He saw tears fill her eyes.

"Don't sweat it," he told her. "I'd told her the life was rough. She didn't believe me until she lived it herself."

"Did you talk to her?" Darcy asked, her voice thick.

"I called to let her know I'd signed the papers and sent them back to the lawyer." He'd wanted to ask about seeing the kids but had figured it would only make things harder for them. Still, he wished he could have let them know he missed them.

"You didn't ask her to come back?"

"No. If she'd wanted to be with me, she would have stayed."

Darcy wiped her cheeks. "Maybe she wanted to know she mattered. Maybe she was trying to get your attention."

He looked at her. "I'd married her with the idea I'd spend the rest of my life with her. How much more attention did she need?"

His heart, Darcy thought, trying not to give in to the sobs rising inside of her. Joe told the story so casually, as if it had all happened to someone else. But she didn't believe that. She believed he'd been blind-sided. Oh, sure, he had a part in the divorce. It took two to screw up a marriage, but for him, this blow would wound deeper than most. Yet one more person had shown him that love wasn't something to be counted on.

He was trapped — unable to give emotionally because he believed there was no point, and unable to learn otherwise because he wouldn't give.

She wanted to hold him and somehow convince him everything could be different. All he needed was a step of faith. But he was a powerful, capable man. What did he need with faith?

Which left her where? Falling in love with a man who could never love her back?

■ ■ ■ ■

"Are you sure you're okay with this?" Lauren asked. "I don't have to come visit."

Darcy rolled onto her back and stared at the ceiling. "It will be great to have you here," she said and nearly meant it.

"It's just you've made everyone sound so wonderful, and I'm dying to meet Joe." She lowered her voice. "You know I'm not going to do anything to get in the way of your relationship, right?"

"Of course. So not your style."

Besides, Joe was avoiding everyone and since their conversation the previous day, they didn't seem to have much of a relationship.

"I'll let Grandma Tessa know that it's for sure. She'll be beside herself. The president's daughters. She'll be cooking up a storm."

"Okay. See you Friday afternoon."

"I'll be here."

She hung up, walked out of her room, and headed for the kitchen. Although she'd already asked the Marcellis about Lauren coming for a couple of days, she wanted to let them know that it was for sure. And someone was always in the kitchen.

Grandma Tessa stood by the stove. She smiled when she saw Darcy. "There you are. Are you hungry?"

Darcy laughed. "I can't wear most of my pants and shorts. I'm barely squeezing into skirts I brought."

"You're too skinny."

Darcy patted her stomach. "Not for long." She cheered at the thought of Lauren packing on a few pounds. That was the one place where her sister had more of a problem. Then she scolded herself for being so shallow.

"I talked to my sister. She'll be here Friday afternoon, after the reading of the will."

Tessa clapped her hands. "Good. Good. We'll plan a special dinner, eh? I'll call Mary and have her come help. You can help with the menu. We'll have wine. Such fun. We can . . ." She frowned. "You're not happy, Darcy. Why?"

"It's nothing. Really. This is great."

The tiny woman walked over and put her hands on her hips. "I've had children in this house nearly all my life and I know when something's wrong."

Darcy figured she might be too old to be considered a child, but she was certainly acting like one. She sighed. "It's just . . ."

She shifted her feet. "This is really stupid." Even more stupid when the first tear slipped down her cheek.

Tessa led her to the table and motioned to a chair. "Tell me."

Darcy sank into the seat, then covered her face with her hands. "I love it here," she said as the tears really let loose. "You've all been so good to me, and I really love this family so much. But Lauren is really a much better person. She's nicer and prettier and more fun to be with. You're all going to like her better and Joe isn't talking to me and I'm not going to have anyone and I found you guys first. Which makes me sound like a three-year-old. Plus, you're still mourning Lorenzo and me talking about something so selfish and stupid is really bad."

She braced herself for the scolding or at least a disapproving silence. Instead she heard a soft laugh. She looked at Tessa, who grinned at her.

"Is that all?" the elderly woman asked.

"All? It's a ton."

"I know. Poor Darcy." Tessa wiped her tears. "You're a good girl. You try hard and you give with your whole heart. Of course we'll like you best. You're one of us now. Who is this Lauren anyway?"

Darcy sniffed. "She's really great. Trust

me. Everyone adores her."

"Maybe, but she's not you, eh?"

Because her life was one entertainment after the other, Joe chose that moment to walk into the kitchen. He took one look at her tear-stained face and started to back out. Tessa stopped him with a glance.

"Joseph. Come here. Darcy is worried about her sister visiting. Tell her that she'll always be first in our hearts. And you should make up with her. She's a good girl. You're lucky to have her. But do you tell her? No."

Darcy winced. This was so not the way to win Joe's affections.

"I'm okay," she said quickly.

Not surprisingly, Joe ducked out without speaking.

"He's been doing a lot of that lately," she murmured.

"He'll come around," Tessa assured her.

Darcy wanted to believe it was true, but she had her doubts. So far he'd been doing a fabulous imitation of a man doing his best to bolt for freedom.

Paige considered the contents of the refrigerator, but it was really tough to get worked up about cooking when all she had to do was walk up to the main house and collect some of the best leftovers on the planet.

She didn't know the secret ingredient Grandma Tessa and Grammy M put into their meals, but it was worth millions. Paige was willing to give up a large percent of her pension to get daily access to Grammy M's scones alone. And Tessa's marinara sauce was worthy of stardom.

There was, however, the calorie issue. She was already five pounds over her normal weight. So a salad for dinner made sense. The fact that there was an entire platter of chicken marsala with a side of grilled potatoes less than a hundred yards away was meaningless. Salad was the far healthier choice.

She closed the refrigerator and looked longingly at the door. Okay, principle over self-indulgence. Which would win? Alex walked into the kitchen. "I'm not leaving," he announced.

The unexpected statement left her blinking. She banished thoughts of flavorful chicken and considered his words.

"Not leaving here?" she asked.

"Right. I'm on the team. With you."

"Okay. That begs the question of why. Isn't there something more important for you to be doing with your day?"

"I'm not always interested in the high-profile cases," he told her. "I'm not in this for the glory."

"Agreed, but nobody even knows Darcy's here. The odds of something happening to her are pretty close to zero. So you're setting yourself up for some long days when nothing is going to happen. That isn't exactly your style."

"Maybe my style is changing."

Funny how she wanted to believe that. Being around Alex had a way of making her remember the past — their past. But to what end?

"I'm thinking of leaving," she said.

"This job?"

"The agency. When Darcy returns to D.C. I'm going to resign."

Nothing about his expression changed. She'd thought he might be disappointed, but she was wrong. He wasn't anything.

"Why?" he asked, although she wasn't sure why he bothered.

"We've discussed this before. I want a life. I want to belong to something other than my job. I want a personal worldview that doesn't include daily concerns that someone I care about is going to be shot or kidnapped."

"So you're leaving me again?"

She stared at him. "This has nothing to do with you."

"It has everything to do with me," he said. "You told me not to play games, or start something I wasn't prepared to finish. I'm going to tell you the same thing."

He left. Paige gave in to the inevitable and headed for the main house, where she would drown her confusion in sweet sauce and perfectly cooked chicken.

She and Alex seemed to have mastered the art of the cryptic conversation, which made for an entertaining afternoon but didn't really get them anywhere.

Did she want to change that? Did she want to talk to him about what was in her heart? Did she know what was in her heart? All those years ago, life had been both harder and easier. With her late husband, she'd learned what loving someone really meant. She wanted that again. But did she want it with Alex, and if she did, was he willing to make the sacrifices love required?

The reading of the will took place in the living room. The family lawyer was a young woman of thirty or so, which surprised Joe. He'd expected some old and dusty family retainer. Good to know that Lorenzo still had the power to shock him, even after he was gone.

The entire family gathered on sofas and

chairs. As this was the Marcellis, there was plenty of food, although wine was noticeably absent.

Joe listened to the lawyer, who explained the nature of the will. There were several provisions for charities, a significant trust fund for Marco and Colleen and the great-grandchildren. But the biggie, the winery itself, was left for last.

The lawyer flipped the page and cleared her throat.

"Marcelli Wines," she read, "is my pride and joy. Four generations have worked the land. Soon that will be five. It is my dearest wish that the winery go on forever. To ensure that, I leave it in capable hands. Hands I trust. I leave each of my granddaughters fifteen percent of the winery and to my grandson, Joseph Larson, I leave forty percent. The majority share."

# 18

After the reading of the will, Joe sat in the library until the lawyer and most of the family had filed out. Marco and Brenna stayed behind.

Joe took one look at their calm faces and said, "You knew."

Marco sat on the sofa across from Joe's chair and nodded. "My father told me what he wanted to do about a year ago. We discussed it and agreed it was a good idea."

Joe didn't know who the "we" was in the conversation, nor did he care. "It's not a good idea for me."

"He wanted you to be a part of the family," Marco said. "He wanted you to belong."

"You can't force me to do this," Joe told him. "What was he thinking of, leaving me the majority share?"

"It's what he wanted. What we all want," Brenna said from her seat at the opposite end of the sofa. "Partners, Joe. Remember?"

"You run the winery," Joe told her. "You have for years. You should be in charge."

"I will be." Brenna rubbed her stomach. "But Four Sisters winery is growing. That's going to take more and more of my time. Plus, honest to God, some of the choices Nic wants to make at Wild Sea. He needs me. You don't have to panic, Joe. We're going to hire a manager to run Marcelli until you learn what you need to and get your feet under you."

"You're deciding for me? In case you've forgotten, I have a career. One I've worked for. One I want. Not here."

He stood and glared at them both. "You think you can finish what he started?" he asked, furious with the change of events. "It's not going to happen. I'm leaving on Monday, and right now I have no plans to come back."

Brenna paled. Marco looked as if he'd been shot. Before either could react, Darcy stepped into the library.

"Sorry to interrupt," she said.

"This is not the time," Joe told her, his voice cold.

She narrowed her gaze. "Amazingly enough, everything isn't about you, Joe. As requested, I'm letting Brenna and Marco know that my sister is due to arrive any second. And just in case it's of interest to you, your captain left a message to say he would be delighted to join us for dinner tonight and it's formal. So you'll need your dress whites."

He felt like a jerk. "Darcy," he said as he reached for her.

She sidestepped him. "I have to go see my sister."

Darcy headed for the kitchen. She appreciated that Joe was under a lot of strain, but she wanted to walk back to the library and smack him upside the head.

Katie had already told her what had happened when the will was read, so she knew he couldn't be happy about that. While she was willing to offer friendly support, she didn't appreciate him turning on her as though she was the enemy.

Mia and Ian were in the kitchen, while Grandma Tessa was nowhere to be seen. Had the ever chatty Ian driven away the matriarch of the family?

"I can't wait to meet your sister," Ian said. "I've seen lots of pictures of her. She's really pretty. Is she that pretty in person? I've heard she's really nice. Is she nice? I sent money to that children's charity she supports. Only a few dollars because I'm a student, right? It's not like I have a ton of cash. But still, it was something."

Darcy walked to the coffeepot and tried to block out Ian's incessant conversation. Mia joined her.

"I know he's a little hard to take," she whispered. "I'm going to dump him as soon as we get back to D.C. He's starting to get on my nerves, too. It's just been nice to have him around, especially after Grandpa Lorenzo died, you know?"

Darcy nodded. She heard a car pull up outside and hurried to the back door.

She walked out onto the back porch just as the rear door of the SUV opened. Lauren stepped out into the early afternoon light. Sunlight brightened her hair to the color of spun gold and made her features seem as if they'd been touched with starlight. Her tailored cotton blouse topped a trim khaki skirt that showed off her voluptuous curves to perfection. Darcy tugged at her black dress and suddenly felt like a grandmother in mourning.

Lauren spotted her and grinned. Darcy smiled in return. As she took a step forward, she had a moment of complete clarity. It was what Oprah always called a lightbulb moment.

She didn't want to *be* Lauren. She'd never actually envied her sister. She'd envied what her sister had — a life she adored, a great love, a close family. Darcy didn't want to be blond, she wanted connections. A sense of belonging.

The downside was falling for a man incapable of committing, but whose life was perfect?

Grandma Tessa hovered. There was no other word to describe the older woman's anxious, quivering movement as she motioned to the room in question.

"If we'd had more time," she murmured, gesturing to the floral wallpaper and fifteen-year-old rock star posters, "we could have decorated."

Lauren hugged the tiny woman. "It's lovely. Just like my room back in high school. You're so sweet to take me in on a moment's notice. I could have stayed at a hotel. This is such an inconvenience and I apologize. It's just I've missed Darcy so much, and she's made all of you sound so wonderful that I couldn't resist the opportunity to crash the party. Is that horribly rude?"

As Darcy watched, Tessa, Grammy M, and

Colleen were completely charmed by Lauren.

"We're delighted to have you here," Colleen said.

" 'Tis no trouble a'tall," Grammy M assured her.

"Stay as long as you like," Grandma Tessa requested.

Lauren laughed. "You might want to be careful with invitations like that. What if I never want to leave?"

Being who they were, and Lauren who she was, the Marcelli women only looked delighted at the prospect.

Her sister was gracious, Darcy thought. She wasn't sure if she'd been born that way or had developed the skill over time, but it was something she was going to have to cultivate. It seemed to smooth over rough patches. There were other changes she could make, she thought. She could get more involved in her father's life. Go to the White House more. Her stubbornness was costing her a once-in-a-lifetime opportunity.

That decided, she completed the tour of the amenities, showing Lauren the bathroom across the hall.

"At least we won't be sharing," Mia said as she raced up the stairs with one of Lauren's small suitcases. "Good thing. I'm not too bad, but Ian hogs the mirror for hours."

Lauren looked at her and smiled. "Mia, right? All these names. I'll never get them straight."

Mia set down the suitcase. "Oh, I'm easy to remember. I'm the fun sister. And the only one who isn't married." She frowned. "How on earth did that happen? Oh, yeah. Right. Didn't want to be tied down."

She grinned, and Lauren laughed. Colleen welcomed her again, then ushered the Grands away.

"We'll let you girls help Lauren unpack. Don't forget dinner tonight is formal. Mia, you know what that means."

Mia rolled her eyes. "Yes, Mom. I'll tone down the makeup and wear something nice. And I'll be polite to Joe's captain." She watched as her mother went down the stairs with the Grands, then leaned in close.

"She's afraid I'll ask about the sexy SEALs. I tease Joe about it all the time and it makes him crazy."

"How do you tease him?" Lauren asked.

"Pretending I want to sleep with them all."

Darcy eyed her. "I don't think it's much of a pretense."

Mia grinned. "Sometimes it's not."

They returned to Lauren's temporary quarters. Lauren closed the door, put her hands on her hips, and shook her head. "Do you have to always wear black?" she asked.

Darcy laughed, then hugged her. "I missed you, too."

Mia looked between them. "You're right. Darcy *is* always in black. I never noticed before. It's very city chic."

"You hear that?" Darcy asked. "I'm chic, and you're an Easter egg."

Mia flopped down on one of the beds. "Hey, don't pull me into a family argument. Lauren looks fabulous, too. But in a different way."

"I'm much more wholesome," Lauren said primly. She picked up one of her suitcases and put it on the other bed. "And I wear colors."

Mia looked at the pile of luggage. "Do you have a maid or something to take care of your clothes?"

"No. Just me. Well, back home there is a full laundry and dry cleaning service, so I don't have to worry about that."

Mia sat up. "You mean back home at the White House."

Darcy sat next to her. "I can't believe you're starstruck. I figured you were too cool for that."

Mia laughed. "I only pretend to be cool. I've never known anyone who's been related to a president before I met you two." She leaned toward Lauren. "So tell me everything."

"Hey." Darcy bumped her shoulder against Mia's. "You didn't ask me questions about the White House."

"I know." Mia looked at her. "I guess I just think of you as one of us."

Darcy felt her whole body relax as Mia's words sank in. It was about the nicest thing anyone had ever said to her.

Mia squinted at Lauren. "I see the resemblance a little, but you guys are pretty different."

"Lauren's the beauty," Darcy said easily.

Lauren threw a pair of socks at her. "You're very attractive."

Mia glanced between them. "Lauren's the classic beauty," she said thoughtfully, "but Darcy has the face you can't look away from. At least my brother can't."

Darcy rolled her eyes. "Don't you start with me."

"I can if I want to." She leaned toward Lauren. "They're having sex. We all know about it, but we're pretting we don't."

Darcy groaned. "You weren't supposed to say anything."

"Why not?" Lauren asked. "I already know you have sex with him. Although she won't give me details. I hate that. I want specifics."

Mia shook her head. "Normally I would, too, but he's my brother. He's going to look gorgeous tonight," she added. "You'll both have to control yourselves."

Lauren hung up yet another pastel-colored skirt. "Because of the formal dinner?"

"Dress whites," Darcy said. "He'll be impressive."

"Then we'll all have to look nice," Lauren said. "So he can be impressed, too."

# 19

Joe was downstairs fifteen minutes before his captain was due to arrive. As per his custom, Owen Phillips was ten minutes early. Joe stood at attention by the house and waited until Phillips stepped out of his fully restored '68 Mustang and closed the door.

"Sir," Joe said, saluting.

Phillips returned the salute, then said, "Good to see you, Joe. Sorry about your grandfather."

"Thank you, sir."

His captain smiled. "It's a family dinner. I think we should ease off on the formalities."

Joe nodded, thinking if they weren't standing on ceremony then why were they both wearing ice cream suits.

"Great place," Phillips said as he looked around at the vineyard. "I've always enjoyed this part of the state. Very pretty."

"Yes, ah, it is. The vineyards do well. We'll

be having Marcelli wine with dinner."

Phillips looked at him. "You told me you'll be back on base on Monday. It's only been a couple of weeks since your grandfather died. You're welcome to take more leave."

"I appreciate that, but I'm ready to get back to work. My team needs me."

"The admiral has cooled down enough that you should be safe to return to duty, but I have to tell you. If I had a home like this, I don't think I'd be so quick to leave it. A man could search all over the world and never find anything quite like this."

Before Joe could respond, the back door opened and the Grands hurried down the stairs. For two old ladies, they sure moved fast.

"We heard the car," Grammy M said, beaming at the captain. "We were thinkin' it was your friend."

Joe winced. "Captain Phillips, may I present the matriarchs of my family? This is Tessa Marcelli and Mary-Margaret O'Shea. Better known as Grandma Tessa and Grammy M."

Phillips nodded at them both, then took Tessa's small hand in his. "I'm so sorry about your loss," he said quietly. "I hope I'm not imposing too soon."

"Not at all," Tessa told him. "We invited

you so we could meet you. Besides, I like the company." Then, before Joe could warn the other man or stop her, Tessa reached up and pinched Phillips's cheek. "You're a handsome one. Married, I suppose?"

Phillips looked stunned. "Yes, ma'am. Nearly twenty years now."

"It's all right. You're too old for Mia."

Grammy M stepped forward and managed something that looked suspiciously like a curtsey. "We're all so happy to be havin' a friend of Joe's here. You work with him, do you?"

"Ah, yes." The captain still seemed shell-shocked.

Colleen and Marco came out next. "We heard you were here," Colleen said as she smoothed the front of her silk dress. "Welcome."

"So much for trying to get you in the door before you meet everyone," Joe told his commanding officer. "I did warn you."

"Yes, you did." Phillips grinned. "I'm liking them."

Joe looked at the couple and opened his mouth to introduce them. "Marco and Colleen Marcelli," he said. Then without planning the words in advance, he added, "My parents."

There was a moment of silence. The

Grands, Colleen, and Marco turned to stare at him. Colleen recovered first.

"It's a long drive, Captain. Thank you so much for making it."

"My pleasure, ma'am."

"Please, call me Colleen."

He shook her hand. "And you must call me Owen. All of you." He glanced at Joe. "Not you."

Joe grinned. "Yes, sir. Understood."

Joe finally got everyone in the house. Katie, Zach, and Valerie were in Los Angeles, but the rest of the family had come for dinner. He made introductions, then realized not everyone was there.

"Where's Darcy?" he asked.

"With her sister," Mia said smugly. "They were trying to figure out what to wear. It could be hours."

"Not likely," Colleen said, chiding her youngest. "Darcy is always on time." She smiled at Owen. "Very polite and simply charming. I'll admit we were a little nervous about hosting a daughter of the president."

"Too much like royalty," Mia joked.

"Actually, that's true," Colleen said. "But she's been a delight. We'll all be sorry to see her go."

Mia jabbed Joe in the ribs. "You could do something about that."

Before he could tell her to shut up, he heard something on the stairs and glanced up. Darcy and the sister he'd yet to meet started down the stairs. He had a vague impression of long blond hair and curves, but neither interested him. Instead he couldn't stop staring at Darcy.

She wore a long, silky-looking dress in a pale peach color. The cut or style or something emphasized her slender body in a way that got his blood boiling. Thin straps were all that held it up, he thought, knowing he could make quick work of them.

Her large eyes seemed to glow and her mouth was soft and pouty-looking. Pearl earrings hung nearly to her bare shoulders, while a twisted strand hugged her neck.

She was beautiful. More than beautiful — she was spectacular. Feminine, sexy as hell, and if he remembered correctly, he'd spent the last few days acting like a complete idiot around her.

Colleen moved toward the two women. "You're both so lovely," she said with a smile. "Allow me to present our dinner guest. Captain Owen Phillips. Captain, this is Darcy Jensen and Lauren Jensen-Smith."

"Nice to meet you," Darcy said as she shook his hand.

Lauren did the same and pleasantries were

exchanged. Colleen ushered everyone into the living room for a predinner drink, but Joe lingered in the hallway. He touched Darcy's arm before she could follow the family.

"You look great," he said, when they were alone.

She gave him a once-over, then shrugged. "Not bad, yourself. I always did like dress whites."

Emotions swelled up inside him. The sensations were unfamiliar and uncomfortable and all unnamed. But they made him want to say something, do something.

"Darcy, I —"

"Comin' through," Grammy M said as she walked toward them with a tray of appetizers. "Hot food here."

Joe moved to one side and let his grandmother pass. He tried to think of what to say when Marco came out of the living room.

"Your captain wants to start with our wines." He grinned. "It's going to be a long night. Good thing we booked him a room at the hotel down the road."

When Marco had passed, Darcy touched his hand. "It's okay," she told him. "I understand."

An interesting concept, when he didn't

understand himself.

"Now will you believe me?" Lauren asked sometime close to midnight as she sprawled across Darcy's bed. "I swear, Joe looked like something out of a cartoon the way his mouth dropped open when he saw you. I thought he was going to dislocate his jaw or something."

Darcy curled up in a chair in the corner of the room. She'd traded in the dress she'd borrowed from her sister for shorts and a T-shirt, but she could still remember the sensual feel of the silk on her body and the stunned appreciation in Joe's eyes.

"He was pretty surprised."

Lauren grinned. "Color is our friend. When we go home, I want to go shopping with you and you're not allowed to buy anything black."

"Except for lingerie."

"Okay. Yeah, that can be black, but nothing else." Lauren sat up and faced her. "He's really great. I can see the appeal. And when you look at him, there are stars in your eyes."

"Not stars."

"Something. You're in love with him."

Darcy nodded. "Which doesn't mean anything."

"Of course it does. You've never been in love before."

"My track record with men isn't the greatest, and I don't think this time is going to work out any better."

Lauren shook her head. "You're wrong. Joe couldn't stop looking at you all through dinner."

"I know, and it was really cool, but how much does that mean? He finds me attractive, and okay, the sex is hot, but that's not a real relationship."

"It's not a bad start."

Darcy wished that were true. "He's not like other guys. He holds back. No one touches his heart. He let his wife go without a word. It's been three years and he's still resisting the Marcellis. How long will he resist me?"

"Maybe he won't. Maybe he's starting to get it."

Darcy wished that were true, but she didn't have any evidence to back it up. "He's a good man. Strong and loyal. I'd trust him with my life and even my heart, but I don't think he's interested in either. I've learned so much being here. About myself and life and people. I'll be okay when it's time to leave. I'll . . ."

"Survive?" Lauren asked, her face serious,

but her eyes bright with humor.

"Don't you dare disco me. Yes. I'll survive. Better than that. I want to get closer to you and Dad. I want to come to the White House and find a charity I can support and get involved in."

"What about Joe?"

"What do you mean?"

"Are you going to tell him how you feel?" Lauren asked. "Before you leave."

"I can't decide. It's not that I want to keep the truth from him, it's that I'm not sure letting him know how I feel is very kind. I don't think he can take one more person wanting him to love her back."

"I don't agree. He seems like a pretty tough guy."

Someone knocked on the door.

"I'll get it," Lauren said as she stood and crossed the room.

She pulled open the door, and Darcy saw Joe standing there. He looked between the women.

Before he could speak, Lauren grinned and stepped into the hallway. "I was just leaving. You kids have a good time. Don't stay up too late."

With that, she was gone.

Joe hovered awkwardly in the hallway. "She didn't have to leave," he said.

Darcy laughed. "Okay. That could make things interesting."

He stepped into the room and closed the door behind him. "I meant I didn't want to run her off."

He stood in the center of the room and stared at her. There was a sadness in his eyes she hadn't seen before. She rose and faced him.

"What's wrong?" she asked.

"Hell if I know." He took a step toward her. "I'm sorry. I've been difficult and a jerk. Whatever I have going on isn't your fault. I've always been good at moving on. At taking the next assignment. I don't know what to do. But I do know that this is the only place where I can draw a breath."

"My room?" she asked, surprised it was anything close to a haven for him. "It's not as if your family won't think to look for you here."

He reached for her and pulled her close. "Not your room. Being with you. It doesn't matter where."

Alex paced outside the guesthouse. The night was clear and cool. There was a forecast of rain, but he didn't believe it. Not that it mattered one way or the other. Rain, snow, sleet, weather wasn't his problem. Paige was.

He didn't understand her. He'd stayed because . . . because. He swore. He didn't know why. Because leaving hadn't felt right. Because they'd had unfinished business. Or so he'd thought. But in the past couple of days, she'd acted as if he didn't exist. Or matter. If he lived to be a thousand he would never understand women. Why did they have to be so damn complicated?

He turned and stared at the front door. He could talk to her. That was something women really seemed to like. Talking. Endless talking.

But about what? She was going to want to ask a bunch of questions, and he didn't have the answers. She was like that. Tricky. Sly. Beautiful.

He stared up at the stars and thought about how she moved and the sound of her laughter. That in all the years they'd been apart, he'd never forgotten her or wanted anyone the way he'd wanted her.

Alex swore under his breath and walked into the guesthouse. He headed directly for Paige's bedroom and opened the door without knocking.

She lay on her bed, reading. Her hair was mussed, her face free of makeup. The tank top she wore over pj bottoms looked thin and worn. Not the least bit sexy — but that didn't stop him from wanting her.

They stared at each other. Neither spoke. Paige put down her book, then slid down on the bed and smiled.

That's all it took. One smile.

Even as he jerked off his T-shirt, he moved toward her. He reached for her as she reached for him, and then he was in her arms. She felt soft and feminine and so familiar that he ached inside. Their mouths locked in a deep, hungry kiss. It had been so long, he thought as need rocketed through him. Too long.

Even as their tongues tangled and brushed and circled, they tore at each other's clothes. He needed her naked — he had to touch her or die.

There were no gentle preliminaries, no murmured words, no light touches. Just reaching and getting naked and kissing. And then she was on her back and he was between her legs. She stared at him, her green eyes dark with passion.

"I want you," she breathed.

"I've missed you," he told her, right before he claimed her.

Tessa sat alone in the dark. Her room was

quiet, even with the window open. Moonlight allowed her to see the vineyard and nearly to the ocean. Hints of salt air mingled with the heavy fragrance of the ripening grapes.

The chardonnay harvest had begun. Soon the machinery in the pressing room would clank to life, and the cycle would begin again.

Across from her chair stood the big, empty bed where she and Lorenzo had slept for so many years. She'd avoided it, spending her nights dozing in her chair. But tonight she felt differently. More at peace.

"Are you here?" she asked the quiet darkness. "Lorenzo?"

As she asked the question, she smiled. Even if her husband could reach her from the great beyond, he was just stubborn enough to refuse to speak to her.

"I miss you, Lorenzo," she whispered. "So much."

There was no response.

Tessa stood and made her way to the bed. As she lay down on the cool sheets, she waited for the knot of fear and panic that had driven her from this bed the first night after he died. It didn't come. Instead she felt somehow safe and comforted. And a slight dipping of the mattress, as if someone had joined her.

No one had, of course. When she turned to look, she was still alone. But not so lonely anymore.

Four hours later, Darcy was asleep, but Joe couldn't relax enough to stay in bed. He dressed and quietly left her room. Instead of returning to his own, he walked out of the house and into the night.

The sky was clear, the moon nearly full. He walked into the vineyards, brushing against the heavy grapes.

The leaves were dry from lack of rain, but dry, warm conditions were supposed to be good for harvesting. Or was it less sun and no —

He shook his head. None of it mattered, he told himself. He was leaving on Monday and he wasn't coming back for a long time. He had SEAL teams to get ready. Plans had to be made, training implemented. There was a whole world outside of the vineyard, and he intended to be a part of it.

"Anywhere but here," he murmured into the night.

But even as he spoke the words, he felt a heavy weight on his shoulders. Brenna's baby was due anytime now. How would she hire a manager before she gave birth? What about Marco and Colleen? They were sticking around to help when they really wanted to be on the road, selling the wines. There was the harvest, the pressing, the bottling. So many responsibilities and he —

"No!" he roared, glaring up at the heavens. "I don't know where you are, Lorenzo, but you couldn't make me care before and you can't make me care now. I'm not staying. This isn't where I belong. I've never belonged here. I don't blame you for this — it's simply the truth. Not here."

His words drifted into the night. There was no response, and he felt a little foolish after his outburst. Yelling at ghosts wasn't going to accomplish anything.

He turned to walk back to the house, only to pause. There was something . . .

He inhaled deeply and realized what it was.

Smoke.

# 20

Darcy woke to a loud shrieking sound she couldn't place. Joe wasn't in her bed and there was no way the alarm signaled good news.

She'd barely thrown back the covers when Mia burst into her room.

"It's a fire," Mia yelled. "There's a fire in the vineyards."

Fire? How could that happen? Sure it had been dry, but what on earth could start a fire in the middle of grapevines?

Rather than consider an answer, she grabbed clothes and pulled them on. Lauren ran into her room.

"What's going on?" her sister asked.

"A fire in the vineyard. Get dressed. We'll go downstairs and see if we can help."

In a matter of a couple of minutes, everyone had assembled in the kitchen. The emergency siren had been turned off, but there was still a sense of urgency.

Grandma Tessa was already making coffee. Joe paced back and forth, talking to Marco in a low voice and making notes on a pad of paper. Marco left the kitchen and Joe glanced at everyone else.

"There's a fire in the east field. I can't tell how big it is, but it's spreading fast. Everything is just dry enough to burn. The fire department is on its way. They're sending three companies, and at dawn we'll get air support."

"What about Brenna?" Darcy asked. "She'll want to know."

Joe nodded. "I've already spoken with Nic, and they're on their way."

"A fire," Ian said. "Wow. Do you know how it started? There hasn't been any lightning, has there? I didn't think you got a lot of lightning in this part of the country. Maybe some homeless guy smoking or something. Could a match have started the fire? Or a downed electrical wire. Only why would it be down. There are —"

Joe, Colleen, Marco, and Mia all turned to Ian.

"Shut up," they said together.

Ian took a step back. "Sorry. I was just trying to help."

"Help silently," Joe said.

The back door opened and Alex and Paige

raced inside. "You know about the fire, right?" Alex asked.

Joe nodded. Marco returned. He had several rolled sheets of paper in his hands.

"Maps," Joe said. "We need to help the fire department find the best places to fight the fire."

Marco spread out the large maps on the kitchen table, anchoring the edges with salt and pepper shakers and a bowl of sugar.

"Here's the house," the elder Marcelli said. "Here's the east field."

Everyone gathered around the table.

"There's a service road," Joe said, tracing a dark line on the map. "Where are the water connections?"

Marco pointed to several triangular icons. "These show them. The trucks can hook up directly to our main water supply."

Joe straightened and counted heads. "We'll split up into teams and take maps with us. Tessa, I'll tell you where to send Nic when he arrives. You'll stay here with Brenna, Lauren, and Darcy."

"I'm not staying," Darcy told him. "And before you start arguing, I've spent the last five weeks walking all over this vineyard. I know it better than you do. I know what the water stations look like. I'm going to help."

His dark gaze locked with hers, then he

nodded once. "Alex, you're with Darcy. Mia and Ian, as well. I want this fire stopped, but even more than that, I want Darcy kept safe."

"That goes for everyone," he added, before she could wonder if his concern was about her, Darcy, the woman he shared a bed with, or her, Darcy, the president's daughter.

"I know the vineyard is important, but it's just grapes. They can be replanted, but none of you can be. Stay safe and think before you do anything rash. Agreed?"

Everyone nodded.

Sirens could be heard in the distance. A car pulled up and squealed to a stop.

"Let's get ready," Joe said.

The next fifteen minutes passed in a blur. Brenna was helped inside where Grandma Tessa did her best to keep her calm. The various teams went out to join the firefighters, which was how Darcy found herself seated in a large truck, staring at a map by flashlight and calling out when she thought they were close to a water connection.

"It's here," she said, looking up and pointing.

The truck stopped on the service road. She waited for the firefighters to scramble out, then she eased to the ground and got her first good look at the fire.

It stretched across what looked like miles. Bright, hot flames consumed the vines much more quickly than she could have imagined. Every now and then a column rose to salute the sky, as if in victory.

"No, you don't," Darcy murmured, even as she inhaled the sharp scent of scorched grapes and burned leaves.

The firefighters went to work with their hoses. Darcy circled around the back of the truck and found Mia.

"We have to go locate the next water station," Darcy said. "For the next truck. It shouldn't be that far."

"Lead on," Mia told her. "Alex, we're going up to find the next water connection."

He nodded and joined them. In the distance Darcy saw another truck pull up. Several people climbed out. She thought she saw Joe, but in the swirling smoke, it was hard to be sure. Still, her heart jumped a little, as if it recognized its one true love.

And then she knew she had to tell him the truth. She couldn't leave without admitting she loved him. To do so would be to dishonor the connection she felt with him.

But first, there was a fire to fight and a

vineyard to save.

For a Navy SEAL, water was a safe haven. Joe didn't like this new enemy that consumed without conscience. The flames grew and stretched and took. It didn't seem to matter how much water they sprayed, the fire lived on.

He stayed close to the fire chief, giving information when he could and helping with hoses. As he worked, he eyed the sky. How long until dawn? How long until the air support could join them?

Time seemed to stand still until the world was simply heat and flames and water. He sweated and coughed from the smoke and hoped everyone was staying safe.

Too many civilians, he thought. Too many people who didn't have the training. It wasn't supposed to be like this. The winery was supposed to be easy. *Not on my watch,* he thought. *Not on my watch.*

Frustration became anger. Lorenzo had left him the winery so he would stay. The old man had wanted him to care. Now, with the fire destroying all that four generations of Marcellis had built, Joe found himself cursing his own worry and concern.

"Good news," the fire chief said as he handed Joe a bottle of water. "The fog's coming in."

Joe unscrewed the top of the bottle and swallowed half the contents in one long drink. Then he turned to the west and saw the stars had disappeared behind a bank of heavy fog. The air was less dry, the flying ash and cinders less hot.

"Will this make a difference?" he asked.

"It'll help," the chief told him. "A heavy fog bank will combine with the smoke and make it a bitch to see, but there isn't any wind. If we can get the humidity high enough, we'll get a handle on this son of a bitch."

Joe finished the water. "I want to know how it started."

"You and me, both," the chief told him. "I have a feeling you're not going to like what we find."

"Arson?"

"Could be. You have cultivated vineyards up here. No power lines, no lightning strikes. The ground is dry, but not parched, and the heavy fruit doesn't burn easily."

Joe couldn't think of anyone who would want to burn down Marcelli Wines. They were successful, but not a major holding. Not like Wild Sea.

He reminded himself this wasn't the time or the way to find answers. Instead he went back to work on the fire. When the firefighters came and asked him to help pull up several rows of grapes to widen a fire break, he reached for a shovel and dug in.

Time passed. The moments were measured in sweat and sparks and smoke. The fog continued to roll in until some of it reached behind the fire, creating an eerie backdrop for the dancing flames.

He heard a horn honk and turned to look. Paige and Lauren drove up on a golf cart.

"We have food and water," Lauren yelled. "Take a break."

He joined the other men as the women handed out thick sandwiches and chilly bottles of water.

"How's it going?" he asked.

"Good." Paige tucked a bottle of water into his jeans pocket. "The other teams are making progress, too. The fog's helping. We're hoping for rain."

"I'm going to go check on them," he told the chief.

"You know where to find us."

Joe hopped on the back of the cart and directed Paige toward the other teams.

"Thanks for helping," he said. "You didn't have to."

She glanced at him over her shoulder. "I've put in my time here, too," she said. "I

care about the Marcellis as much as you."
She faced front and shrugged. "They're
good people."

They *were* good people, he thought as he
jumped out of the cart and walked over to
another group of firefighters. Marco and
Colleen were studying maps spread on the
ground.

"Here," Marco said, pointing. "Above it is
the steepest terrain we have. I wouldn't risk
going any higher. If we make our stand
there, we should be fine." He glanced up
and saw Joe. "We're winning."

"You think?"

Marco motioned to the thickening fog.
"Pop wouldn't have it any other way."

Joe wanted to point out that the fog was a
weather phenomenon common to the area,
not proof of ghostly interference, but he
couldn't seem to say the words. Maybe
because he'd felt Lorenzo's presence as
well. Four generations of Marcellis had
worked the line. There was no way the old
man would let that be lost.

The smoke was less thick here. He could
see the acres of grapes yet to be touched by
the flames.

"If we can get a protective break around
them," he said, thinking out loud.

"Exactly," Marco said. "We can save most

of them. Still have a decent year."

There was, Joe realized, a point when a soldier knew to give up the battle. When the victory or the loss became inevitable. Casualties could still occur on both sides, but the outcome had been determined.

When had that happened to him? He'd been fighting long enough, but against what? His destiny? What was so bad about claiming this as his heritage? What did he resent about it?

He liked it here, he admitted to himself. He liked the family and the location. Darcy loved it and them. She was . . .

Colleen touched his arm. "What are you thinking about? You're smiling."

"Darcy," he admitted, wondering when exactly he'd let Darcy in.

"Really? I knew you two were getting along, but I didn't think things were that serious. She's the president's daughter."

"Yeah. I figured that out already."

"I only meant that there will be complications." She smiled. "We're here for you, Joe. You know that, right?"

He nodded. "Okay, back to the fire. I'm going to check on the other teams."

His mother hugged him. "On Darcy, you mean."

"That, too."

Suddenly he was eager to see her. This wasn't the time or place to discuss anything, but he needed to hear her voice and know she was all right.

Darcy had never fought a fire before, and she made a mental note to keep it off her to-do list. So far the firefighters had kept them back, relegating them to behind the truck activities. Even so, carting water and supplies, showing the way to the next hose hookup was hard, hot work. The smoke made it tough to breathe easily, and even with the fog rolling in there were still sparks flying everywhere.

But she wasn't going to give up, especially when it seemed as if they were making progress. The flames didn't seem to reach as high, and every now and then she thought she could see a little farther into the vineyard.

She walked back to the trucks and reached for one of the sandwiches Paige and Lauren had brought. She'd just taken her first bite when Ian came running up.

"Joe's looking for you," he said.

"Really? Is he all right?"

Ian grinned. "I think he wants to make sure that you are. Come on. This way."

He led her around the trucks and into the

vineyard. They were heading away from the fire.

"Joe's out here?" she asked.

Just then someone called her name. She turned back and saw someone running after them, but she couldn't see who it was. A man, but who?

"Wait," Darcy told Ian. "Is that Joe?"

Ian moved beside her and took her arm in his left hand. Then, before she realized what was happening, he pulled a gun out of his jacket, took aim on the approaching man, and pulled the trigger.

The world slowed. Later, Darcy would swear that she could actually see the bullet burst out of the barrel. She saw the man stop in midstride. He twisted and then he was falling to the ground.

"Joe!" she screamed in horror. Not him. It couldn't be him.

She started to run but found she couldn't move. She turned to see what was holding her in place. Ian had a grip on her arm. Other men appeared out of the darkness. There were four of them. Just like before.

"No!" she screamed into the night.

The men didn't stop. One of them tackled her, and she found herself flat on her back. She couldn't breathe, and no matter how she squirmed and clawed and kicked, they didn't let go. Her arms were yanked behind her back, and ropes were fastened around her hands. More ties bound her ankles. She screamed again and one of them stuffed a handkerchief into her mouth. The dry, dirty cotton made her gag.

Joe! Joe! Was he shot? Bleeding? Dead?

Two of them half dragged, half carried her to a van. Past and present blended until she wasn't sure what was real and what was from before.

She bucked and twisted and lashed out as best she could. One of the men released her. She hit the ground on her side. Pain shot through her shoulder, but she didn't give in to it. Instead she rolled toward the vines, intent on hiding, on getting away.

Then the men were around her. They picked her up. One of them used bolt cutters to remove her security bracelet. Ian held a gun to her cheek.

"Try escaping again and I'll splatter your brains all over the place. Got me?"

Ian, she thought. How could it be him? He was harmless. He was Mia's annoying boyfriend. It couldn't be Ian.

But it was, and the gun in his hand told her he was deadly serious.

"They're right over here," Paige said as she

stopped the cart. "We should be able to find them by following Ian's chatter."

Joe nodded as he got out of the cart. He looked around. The firefighters were clearly visible, but not anyone else.

Without warning, his gut clenched. There was no reason, but he'd learned to trust the sensation.

"Something's wrong," he told Paige. "Get backup."

"What?"

"Now," he ordered, even as he headed out into the vineyards. "Darcy," he yelled. "Darcy?"

It was hard to hear anything with the roar of the fire in the background, but he listened intently. A groan caught his attention.

He raced toward the sound only to find Mia on all fours. She'd just finished vomiting.

"My head," she said weakly. "That bastard hit me on the head."

"Who?" Joe asked, although he already knew.

"Ian. What the hell is wrong with him?" she demanded.

Joe felt her pulse, then touched the bump on her head. He stood and called for Lauren. "Mia's been hurt," he told her. "Get her to the cart."

"Where's Darcy?" Lauren asked frantically. "Where's my sister?"

Joe didn't know and thinking about the possibilities made his blood run cold. Who else had been part of the team? "Alex," he yelled. "Alex!"

Paige joined him. "Where are they? Where are Alex and Darcy?"

Rather than answer, Joe hurried to the edge of the vineyard. There he saw the broken vines, ripped leaves. A struggle. He reached down and picked up Darcy's security bracelet. Paige was behind him and to his left. She screamed.

"Alex's been shot. He's been shot."

# 21

Once again Darcy found herself tied up in the back of a van. There was just enough predawn light coming through the back window for her to see the filthy floor, complete with a hole about eight inches across.

What was it with kidnappers that they couldn't afford decent vehicles? she wondered, trying to be disgusted and angry instead of terrified. And if they had to buy some beat-up piece of crap, couldn't they at least keep it clean?

The van took a corner at high speed. Darcy went sliding, along with candy wrappers, sheets of paper, and who knows what else. She didn't want to think about things like rats and bugs, nor did she want to remember the easy way Ian had shot someone.

Not Joe, she prayed. Not anyone, but especially not Joe.

Ian! A kidnapper! It wasn't possible. How had he ever shut up enough to plan anything? Oh God. Joe. Be alive.

She didn't want to consider any other possibility, so she forced herself to think about something else. Like how she was gagging on the handkerchief. She pushed her tongue against the cloth and worked her mouth until she was able to spit it out. The cloth hit the floor, rolled, and fell out the hole in the bottom of the van.

As she watched it go, she wished she were small enough to simply fall out the bottom of the van. Any bumps and bruises from hitting the road would be better than what Ian had in mind for her.

Oh God. Fear exploded inside of her. She turned and twisted on the dirty floor as she tried to free herself. She screamed and screamed but knew no one could hear her. It was five or six in the morning on a narrow road in the middle of nowhere. Who was going to be around to listen?

Worse, did anyone even know she was gone? With the fire and everyone busy with that, it could be hours before they noticed she was missing.

Tears burned her eyes but she refused to give in to them. Be strong, she told herself. Tough. She'd already survived one kidnapping. Of course those kidnappers hadn't wanted her, they'd wanted Lauren and —

Darcy sat up. Lauren had been right there at the winery. Ian could have taken her just as easily, but he hadn't.

"This is not how I wanted to be the special daughter," she screamed, kicking at the side of the van. "I was thinking more of an award or something."

A few candy wrappers fluttered out the hole. Great. Now she was littering.

"Wait a minute."

She stared at the hole, then at all the garbage in the back of the van. Could she use it to signal where they were going, or at least where they'd been?

She scooted so her back was against one of the walls of the van, and kicked a candy wrapper toward the hole. After counting to sixty, she pushed it out. Another minute later, she pushed out a rag.

Would anyone realize it wasn't just trash? she wondered. Would the trash get blown away? She needed something bigger. Something more significant.

She looked around at the back of the van. Nothing came to mind until she looked at her feet. Her shoes.

While she didn't like the thought of being barefoot, she liked the thought of being dead even less. She toed off one of her shoes and nudged it toward the opening. It slipped through and fell to the road. She would continue with the trash, then put out the other shoe in another ten minutes or so.

If only she knew how long they would be driving, she thought. Should she wait longer than ten minutes? What would happen when they got wherever they were going?

"Don't think about it," she told herself. "Don't think about it."

But there was little else to occupy her mind. Fearing and wondering if Joe were alive. After dumping out more trash, she debated removing her other shoe. Before she could decide, the van came to a stop. The fear returned and with it a certain sense of dread.

"Towels," Joe yelled. "Thick towels."

"They're not sterile," Tessa told him as she and Grammy M hurried around the kitchen.

"It's fine. We need pressure." He took the towel Tessa handed him and held it over the wound in Alex's side.

The Secret Service agent looked up at him. "I didn't see it coming. Should have."

His color was nonexistent, his breathing labored. From what Joe could tell, the bullet had gone in and out cleanly. But what it had done while passing through remained to be seen.

He looked around at the frantic faces in the kitchen. Paige was on the phone, detailing what had happened. He felt a burning need to hunt down Ian and kill him. But until Paige was done, he was the only one in the house with the training to keep Alex alive.

"What should we do?" Colleen asked, her expression both worried and grim. "I can't believe Ian took Darcy. Should we start searching the buildings?"

"No point. They're gone. I saw tracks heading west."

"Toward the interstate," Marco said. "They could be anywhere."

Goddamn son of a bitch, when he got his hands on Ian, he was going to rip him apart and watch him bleed to death.

Mia crouched in a chair. She was still woozy from being hit on the head and needed to be checked out. There was too much to do, he thought grimly.

Paige hung up the phone. "Okay, the team's coming. Local, state, and federal law enforcement have been notified. Road blocks will be up within the half hour. We'll have full tactical support in less time. The president has been notified."

Joe didn't want to think about that phone call or what the other man must be feeling. Joe had enough trouble battling his own worry, and he was a trained professional.

"I should have known," he muttered.

Paige hurried to the kitchen table where she stared down at Alex. "We all should have known."

"He checked out clean," Alex said, his voice heavy with pain.

"Too clean," Joe said. "I never liked him."

Someone began to cry. He turned and saw Lauren. Grammy M and Colleen hurried to her. Lauren looked at him.

"She'll be all right, won't she? You'll get Darcy back."

He didn't have an answer to that, but he nodded. "Of course we will." He turned to Paige. "Get her team back here."

The extra Secret Service agents had been at the hotel in town, the same one Captain Phillips had retired to the previous evening.

"I've already called them. The rest of Darcy's team will be assigned to Lauren until we can get her out of here."

"No," Lauren said. "I'm not leaving. I want to know what's going on."

Paige shook her head. "You'll be safer somewhere else."

"No. You can protect me here. I want to know what's happening."

"We'll all be here to protect her," Marco said. "Anyone trying to kidnap Lauren will have to come through us."

Joe appreciated the sentiment, but it wasn't going to be much help against trained experts.

He replaced the blood-soaked towel with a fresh one. "We don't have time to argue," he told Paige. "She's staying until the team arrives. Then let them deal with her."

"I'm not leaving," Lauren said stubbornly.

Joe glanced at her. It was the first time she'd reminded him of Darcy.

Darcy. Fear crashed in on him. He'd never felt anything like it before. Sure, he'd worried about his team, but he'd never felt this icy, crushing sensation in his chest. If something happened to her . . .

Brenna limped into the kitchen. She cradled her belly with one hand and leaned against Nic. "So, ah, how is Alex getting to the hospital?"

"Helicopter," Paige said, pressing on the bleeding wound from the underside.

"Is it big enough for two?"

Joe turned to look at her. Really looked. It was only then he noticed the dark stain down the front of her maternity dress.

"My water broke," she said. "I guess I'm in labor."

In the second between when the van stopped and Ian opened one of the doors, Darcy heard an odd sound. It was familiar, but she couldn't place it. Something rhythmic and swooshy. Then the door swung open and she saw they were parked on the beach. The thick fog added a sense of the macabre to the otherwise perfect view.

Why here? Why not some airport or a freeway?

"Come on, Darcy," Ian said. "Let's get going."

Her instinct was to fight them. There were only two of them. Then Ian pulled out his gun and smiled.

"I'd prefer you didn't make trouble, but if you do, I'll shoot you. Not to kill, you understand. Just enough to slow you down. I've never been shot, but I'd think it really hurts. Especially if I mess up and it goes through bone. So you don't want to be a problem, right?"

She looked at him and nodded slowly.

"Then get out of the van."

She did as he said, sliding forward on her butt until she reached the open door. The other man, tall, with dark hair and cold eyes, grabbed her arm and pulled her to her feet.

Darcy looked between them as a horrifying thought occurred to her. She could see their faces. Which meant she could easily identify them. Which led to the logical conclusion that they didn't plan for that ever to happen. They weren't going to let her go.

She wasn't ready to die, she thought frantically. Not now. Not like this. Joe was . . .

Joe might be dead. No, she couldn't think like that. He was strong; she would be strong, too.

Instinctively, she twisted away from the man. She managed to get free, but with her feet tied, she couldn't run. She teetered, then fell to the sand. Seconds later, something hard slammed into her ribs as Ian kicked her. She screamed.

"That was a warning," Ian said coldly. "Next time I *will* shoot you."

She couldn't catch her breath. The pain was incredible. It was like fire along her rib cage. Had he broken something?

Ian stood over her. "Here's the thing, Darcy. You're our prisoner, and there's nothing you can do about it. If you cooperate, I promise to make your time with us as pleasant as possible. If you don't, I'll hurt you. Those are simple rules, right? You can understand them."

She nodded slowly. "What do you want?"

"To use you as a bargaining chip."

Not good, she thought as she sucked in air. Not good at all. "The president doesn't negotiate with terrorists."

"Yeah, I've heard that. I'm guessing I can change his mind. See, it's a great policy right up until someone you love is kidnapped. We'll start with polite requests, and if that doesn't work, we'll send you back to him in pieces. I know that sounds scary and I'm sorry about that. We'll give you something for the pain, but it's probably still going to hurt. We can't help that. The point is when we send your finger or your ear or your hand to the press, your dad is going to be a whole lot more willing to give us what we want."

She was going to pass out. The good news was, she wouldn't have to listen to Ian anymore. He was speaking so calmly, she thought, unable to believe any of this was really happening. How could Ian be doing this? Ian, who had stayed at the Marcelli house. Ian, who had dated Mia and driven them all crazy with his talking.

"They'll find you," she said.

"I don't think so. They won't know where we are, and I've found a spot they'll never even look."

He nodded at the other man, who then pulled her to her feet, bent down, and shoved his shoulder into her midsection. When he stood, the pain of her bruised side nearly made her pass out. She thought she was going to throw up.

They started walking toward a small boat pulled up on the sand. She didn't like boats, especially small ones. She didn't like being kidnapped, either, she thought grimly.

"We're going to a cave," Ian said. "I found it years ago, when I went fishing around here with my grandfather. I used to think it was a really cool hideout, but I never thought I'd use it for a headquarters."

She slipped free of the man's shoulder and felt herself falling and falling. When she hit the boat, the impact was hard. Her head cracked against a wooden seat.

"Watch it, Jesse. We don't want to kill her."

Not yet, she thought as the world started to fold in at the corners and then fade to black. Not yet.

Joe stared at the maps spread out on the counter of the kitchen. Where would they take Darcy? They had an hour's head start, which gave them a lot of leeway. Still roadblocks were already up, and the heavy fog meant all regional airports were closed.

Would they try to get distance between themselves and the winery or were they holing up close by? What would he do?

Joe touched the largest map, but he couldn't think, couldn't figure out the plan. Ian had done this. He'd been the enemy all along, and no one had noticed.

Had he planned this from the beginning? Joe didn't think that was possible. No one had known Darcy was coming here more than forty-eight hours before it had happened. Which meant Ian had taken advantage of a lucky break.

Who was he? The name had to be false, along with the identity. He'd been completely clean. No one that clean pulled off something like this.

"The bleeding's slowed," Paige said, sounding relieved. "Hold on, Alex. The helicopter will be here soon. You, too, Brenna."

Brenna waved from her sprawled position on a kitchen chair. "Don't worry about me. I'm sure I'll be in labor for hours. I appreciate the ride, though. Right now the thought of a thirty-minute car trip is very disheartening."

Nic crouched next to her and held her hand. "Just breathe, okay."

She smiled at him. "I can breathe and scream. I'm good at both of those. It's the whole birthing process I'm worried about. And the fact that I swear I can feel more than two feet pressing against me."

Joe blocked out the conversation and concentrated on the maps. But before he could figure anything out, Mia walked over and touched his arm.

"I'm sorry," she whispered.

He took a second to give her a hug. "It's not your fault."

"Yes, it is. I'm the one who brought him here. I can't believe I didn't know who he really was. I traveled with him, I slept with him. I should have guessed."

"You can only see what you see. You can't read minds."

She shook her head. "I should have known. Somehow."

Joe led her into the dining room. "Did he ever say anything about his family? About friends? Do you have any names?"

Mia stared at him. "No. He talked about his grandfather all the time. The one who took him fishing. But not his parents. He was more interested in mine. I just . . ." She stifled a sob. "He was so excited about meeting Darcy. I thought he was starstruck. Then, later, he asked me all kinds of questions. I figured he had a crush on her or something. But it wasn't that. Now Alex is shot, and they have Darcy, and it's all my fault."

She began to cry. Joe pulled her close and kept his mouth shut. A part of him did want to blame Mia, but he was as guilty as she.

Darcy regained consciousness when she was carried from the small boat and put onto a canvas chair in the middle of a cave. Her hands and feet were still tied and her ribs ached, along with her head. If this kept up much longer, she was going to be one big bruise.

She waited until Ian and someone she hadn't seen before walked away, then she raised her head and looked around. The cave was larger than it looked from the outside, for which she was grateful. She'd grown to dislike small, dark spaces.

The boat had been tied up next to one just like it on the side of the cave, not that far from where she sat. On the other side were a couple of tables covered with electronic equipment. Bottled water and canned foods filled a pallet by the rock wall.

She could hear men talking, which made

her nervous. She didn't want to know who they were. She wanted to be set free and not be able to identify them later so they wouldn't have to kill her.

The cave itself seemed to bend around, perhaps creating a second room. She wasn't sure, as she couldn't see it, but that's where the voices came from. Maybe the rest of them would stay there, she thought.

Ian reappeared. He walked toward her and held out a length of chain with bands at each end. "For your ankles," he said cheerfully. "So you can't get away. Oh, in case you're wondering, these are heavy. If you head for the water, you'll sink right to the bottom. No swimming for freedom, Darcy."

He was so calm, she thought. Calm to the point of pleasant, which just wasn't right.

When he bent at her feet, she thought about kicking him but decided it wasn't the time for an escape. Not when she was tied up and didn't know how many other men were around. He secured the chains around her ankles, then unfastened the ropes. Finally he used a smaller chain to attach her left arm to the chair itself, leaving her right arm and hand free.

"Thirsty?" he asked, motioning to the bottles.

She nodded.

He brought her water and opened it, then crossed to the table of communication equipment. "I'm going to call your dad," he said as he put on a headset. "I don't mind you screaming, but you can't tell them where we are. And as I don't trust you . . ."

He motioned with his hands. Jesse appeared with a gag. Darcy tried pulling away, but she was weighed down by the chains and the chair. Jesse quickly secured the gag, effectively silencing her.

Ian hit a button on a console. Instantly the sound of a dial tone filled the cave. He punched in a phone number, then waited until a woman said, "This is the White House operator. How may I direct your call?"

"I need to speak to the man in charge," Ian told her. "President Jensen. I'm the guy who has his daughter. She's right here. I'd let you talk to her, but she's all tied up."

He laughed at his own joke.

"One minute, sir."

There was a moment of silence, then a man picked up. "This is Special Agent in Charge Allister. Who is this?"

"I'm Ian Welton, Allister, but you already knew that. I'm sure the folks back at the ranch, or winery in this case, have already told you all about me. And you're not who

I want to speak with. I called for the president."

"He's not here right now."

Ian glanced at Darcy and raised his eyebrows. "Daddy's not home. Where do you think he is?"

Darcy didn't have a clue.

"I'm sure you can patch me through to him," Ian said, returning his attention to the call. "Which I want you to do. I have a list of demands. And before you tell me you don't negotiate with terrorists, I'll remind you I have his daughter here. He only has the two, so I think he'd miss this one if we had to return her in pieces."

Stay calm, Darcy told herself. Stay calm. People were looking for her and they would find her. She would be okay. She had to be. For Joe. Because if he'd been shot, he would need her. And if he hadn't, then he would come find her.

"Threats don't help your cause," Allister said. "What do you want?"

"Right now I'd like a really good burger, but instead I'll take the release of Jonathan Misner from prison. He is to be picked up by helicopter and taken to the county airport. There you will have a plane waiting, along with two million dollars in cash."

Misner, Misner. The name was familiar,

but she couldn't place it at first.

"The domestic terrorist?" Allister asked.

Then she remembered. Jonathan Misner was responsible for the bombing of a large suburban Chicago mall nearly three years ago. Dozens of people had been killed and hundreds injured. He and his men had been opposed to money being sent abroad for foreign aid. They'd wanted the funds to stay home, along with jobs and technology. Their demands had been for the United States to isolate itself from the rest of the world.

Misner had been captured nearly a year after the bombing. It had been one of those quirks of fate — a routine traffic stop had brought him to the attention of a small-town deputy. Later, the deputy had followed him to a local motel and called in federal authorities. Several of Misner's men had gotten away, but the leader had been captured. He had been arrested and convicted, and was on death row in federal prison.

"We see him as a revolutionary," Ian said calmly. "Imagine what the king of England thought of the signers of the Declaration of Independence. Not an original argument, I'll grant you, but accurate. You have twelve hours. If I don't see Misner starring on CNN as he's led out of prison, I'll have to hurt Darcy."

Ian glanced at her and gave her an apologetic smile. "Funny thing is, I really don't want to do it. I like her a lot. But the cause is bigger, and I want Misner out of prison. If he's not released by" — Ian glanced at his watch — "seven-forty-three P.M. Pacific Time, I'll have to make my point. We'll start small. Her little finger from her left hand. She'll be gagged, so you won't hear her screaming, but trust me, she will be."

# 22

The task force arrived by air. Shortly after eight in the morning, three Sikorsky Super-hawk helicopters descended from the sky and landed on the open grassy area by the long driveway leading up to the house.

Most of the personnel were navy, with a few Secret Service agents thrown in the mix. Joe knew that other members of the team would arrive as soon as they could be flown in from other parts of the country. Captain Phillips had driven from his hotel to act as a liaison.

Joe stood by the front of the house as the helicopters shut down. When the team was assembled, he stepped forward to lead them toward the winery. He'd already com-mandeered the conference room and had Marco call the office staff to tell them not to come in to work. The team could spread out into the various offices and have access to the phone lines if necessary, although it wouldn't take long for them to establish their own communications system.

"Through here," Joe said as they walked into the main building of the winery.

One of the team members, Admiral Grant, moved next to Joe. "The fire was started as a diversion?" he asked.

Joe nodded. "We have preliminary confirmation of arson. A final report will take some time, but there's enough evidence for our purposes."

"There were two Secret Service agents with Darcy?"

"No. Just Alex. Alex Vanmeter. The agent who was shot."

The admiral raised his eyebrows. Yes, Darcy should have been protected by two agents. She also shouldn't have been sent off with the very man trying to kidnap her. Joe had already beaten himself up about it a dozen times.

"Lauren was with Paige," Joe continued.

"No doubt the reason only Darcy was taken," the admiral said.

Joe wasn't so sure. Ian and his group had planned their kidnapping very well. If they'd wanted Lauren, he didn't doubt they could have taken her. The fire had put everyone in a panic.

"You've given your report to Captain Phillips?" the admiral asked.

Joe nodded. They'd reached the conference room. He pointed out the maps of the area and the contact list, which included local law enforcement officials, the fire chief, and the main number of the house.

Joe started to step into the room, but the admiral blocked his way.

"That will be all," the man told him.

Joe glared at him. "Sir, I know I screwed up. I know the kidnapping is my fault. But I'm still the best tactical officer you have."

The admiral shook his head. "A good tactical officer doesn't let his subject get kidnapped. You're relieved of duty, sailor."

The door closed in his face.

There was no lock. Joe could have stepped inside and forced them to listen, but to what end? He didn't have anything to say. Nothing useful, anyway. Telling them that he wanted to trade himself for Darcy was meaningless. Letting them know that he would give his life for hers a hundred times over would only get in the way.

He turned from the conference room and headed for Lorenzo's office. There he could stare at the maps on the wall and will them to reveal their secrets to him. Where had Ian taken her? What would the little shithead do with her?

An hour later, he was no closer to a solution. He slumped in Lorenzo's chair and endured the frustration of having no way to act. Nearly as bad as imagining what Darcy must be going through was the reality of knowing that he had had Ian within his grasp and had never considered him a danger. If he had, he would have cheerfully ripped him into a dozen pieces.

But he hadn't. Instead he'd listened to Ian talk on and on about everything from his opinion of the growing world economy to his seemingly endless anecdotal stories about his studies, his various roommates, and the time he spent locally with his —

Joe stared at the map. Ian had talked about his grandfather taking him fishing around here. He'd talked about caves.

He reached for the phone and called the main house. "Marco," he barked, when Tessa answered.

Marco came on the line.

"Meet me in the conference room right now," he ordered. "Hurry."

Joe slammed down the phone and raced to the conference room. He burst in without knocking. The fourteen people sitting around the table all looked at him.

Captain Phillips stood. "Joe, you're screwing up here," he began, his voice cold.

"I don't give a good goddamn about that," Joe told him. "I know where Ian's taken her."

Phillips stared at him. "What are you talking about?"

"You haven't caught him, have you? Not with any of the roadblocks. You're not going to. He's already off the road. He's taken her to a boat somewhere close. There are caves on the coast, some of them big enough to hide in. He'll wait until dark, then use a boat to get her away."

Phillips and the admiral exchanged a glance. The Secret Service agent in charge nodded.

"We've found the van," Phillips told him. "It was abandoned on the beach. Apparently there was a hole in the rear floor because we also found a trail of trash, rags, and one of Darcy's shoes."

Joe felt a flash of pride. As scared as she must have been, she hadn't lost her head. Good for her.

The conference room door opened and Marco stepped in. "My father," Joe said. "Marco Marcelli." He crossed to the maps pinned to the walls. "We think Ian took her by boat to a cave. Which ones are big enough to hold a dozen or so people and equipment?"

402

Marco joined him at the map. He studied it for a second, then pointed. "Here. There are three caves big enough. I used to play in them when I was a kid. A couple of these have several rooms."

Three was manageable, Joe thought. Three caves, three teams. "What's the deadline?" he asked.

Phillips shook his head. "Joe, this isn't your fight."

"Yes, it is. This happened on my watch. What are his demands and how long do we have?"

Phillips considered the question, then explained Ian's demands for Misner's release. "The first deadline is seven-forty-three tonight."

Not much time, Joe thought, calculating the travel time from San Diego to here. But enough. "We'll have three SEAL teams, one on each cave. They can be here by one, and we'll put together our plan."

Phillips looked at the admiral. "It's what he's best at."

Admiral Grant nodded. "All right, Joe. You take charge of your SEALs. Everything comes through me." He glanced at his watch. "The president will be landing in a couple of hours, and he'll want a full briefing."

"Can we make Ian think we're giving in to his demands?" Joe asked. "Having him monitor that will provide a distraction and keep Darcy safe."

The admiral picked up a phone. "Let me see what I can do."

Despite Ian removing the gag and offering Darcy more water, she still felt nauseated and faint. She wanted to cradle her left hand against her stomach and protect her suddenly vulnerable fingers. She wanted to run screaming out of the dark cave, into safety. She wanted to be back at the Marcelli house, with Grandma Tessa offering her food and Joe tempting her into his bed. She wanted to live, fingers and all.

Fear grabbed at her and refused to let go. The need to scream built until she had to press her hand to her mouth to hold it inside. Focus, she told herself. She had to focus. Be calm. Relax.

Tears burned, but she held them in. Eventually the need to scream faded to a whimper. She thought about Joe and how tough he was, how he would want her to be tough, too. She thought about Lauren and knew however much she loved her sister, Lauren couldn't possibly handle being kidnapped. She would be too scared.

Darcy nearly laughed. After all these years had she just realized she was the strong one, emotionally? What a time to have a self-actualization-type breakthrough.

Sometime around noon, Ian offered her a sandwich. She didn't want to eat, but she knew she needed to keep up her strength. Later, she was allowed to use the Porta Potti in the back of the cave. There was no escaping from that route, she thought as she glanced around at rock walls.

She returned to her chair, was chained in place, and waited to see what would happen. Ian kept the television turned to CNN, but there was no mention of her kidnapping at all. The first hint of news came a little before three when the phone rang.

Ian picked it up and flipped on the speaker. "Welton here," he said.

"Ian, how are you?"

Darcy watched as Ian grinned and waved toward the back of the cave. "Jonathan?"

"Yeah." The other man chuckled. "I don't know how you did it, but they're letting me out. Hell of a job, kid. Hell of a job."

Ian squared his shoulders. "I told you I wouldn't let you rot in jail. I'd planned on kidnapping the British prime minister when he came to San Francisco in three months, but then someone dumped a better idea in my lap."

"They won't tell me anything. What have you done?"

Ian glanced at Darcy and winked. "Kidnapped the president's daughter."

"Lauren?"

"No. Darcy. She's right here. Couldn't have been easier." He explained how he'd been dating Mia and had gone to meet her family, only to discover Darcy in residence.

"Luck like that doesn't happen every day," Ian said. "What could I do?"

Jonathan laughed. "Good for you, Ian. Now you know this could be a trick."

"Already got that covered."

Darcy didn't know what to think. There was no way she believed her father would agree to release a prisoner on death row. He couldn't. Which meant it *was* a trick, or someone was lying. She shivered from fear and cold, even though it was warm in the cave.

She stared at the lapping water only a few feet away. If not for the heavy chains, she would take her chances in the ocean. Maybe she could swim to shore.

Ian ended his call and disappeared into the other room of the cave. She heard the men cheering as they discussed the good news. A few minutes later he came back with something in his hands. Something that looked like a vest.

"You're going to have to wear this," he said, holding it out to her. "I know it looks scary, but it's perfectly safe. There isn't even a manual detonation. It has to be done by remote control, so you can't trigger it yourself by sneezing or something. See?"

The fear became tangible. She felt it deaden her arms and legs. She could barely breathe as she stared at the vest.

Strips of gray material had been sewn into rows of pockets on the outside of the vest. She'd seen enough action movies to know the claylike substance was some kind of explosive.

Everything had been wired, with the colorful wires all meeting back at a common point that would be right above her left breast.

"Look. No boom." He smiled and shook it, then dropped it on the floor. As if that proved anything.

Hysterical laughter threatened. Right. Safe, right up until the minute someone pushed the little red button on the detonator and she exploded into a million pieces.

"I can't," she whispered.

"I know you don't want to, Darcy, but I'm

not giving you a choice. I'd like to. You're really nice. Lauren's okay, but you're prettier, and I like you better, which is why I wanted to kidnap you. Although I'll be real sad if I have to kill you."

She wanted to point out he was probably going to anyway, but what was the point?

"The thing is, we have a greater good to think about," he continued. "That's why I'm doing this. The government has to understand we're not responsible for the world. We have our own problems to deal with. Charity begins at home, right? We're not being especially charitable right now. Do you know how many children go to bed hungry every night right here in this country? Shouldn't we be taking care of them? So you see why I have to do this, don't you?"

He held out the vest. She leaned back and shook her head.

Ian sighed. "Jesse," he yelled. "We've got to get the vest on her."

Jesse appeared from the rear of the cave and roughly pulled her out of the chair. She twisted and turned and wished her feet weren't manacled together so she could kick the crap out of him. But they were, and the heavy chains didn't allow for much mobility.

"No!" she cried as he put one of her arms

through the vest.

Jesse raised his hand and slapped her hard across the face. The pain and shock immobilized her enough for them to unlock her hand and finish putting on the vest. Then they pushed her back into her seat and resecured her wrist to the chair.

The vest was thick and lighter than it looked. There was an odd smell that terrified her. Her heart beat so quickly she thought it might fly right out of her chest. This couldn't be happening to her. It couldn't. Her face throbbed from the slap, and she knew deep down in her heart she wasn't getting out of this alive. Not now. They were going to kill her, and there was no way anyone would ever find her in time.

Joe finished briefing the team, then picked up his diving gear and weapons. Everything felt good in his hands. Right.

He suited up, then climbed in the back of the truck for the short trip to the boats that would take them close to the caves. From there they would approach underwater.

At nearly five in the afternoon, he and his men waded out into the ocean and slipped onto the boats. Joe's headset crackled.

"Larson?"

"Yes, Captain."

"We just got word. They warned us not to try anything. They've wired her with an explosive. If anything happens they don't like, she's gone."

Joe heard the information but he refused to react to it. Now he was on a mission and it was all about doing the job. He wouldn't allow himself to think emotionally or feel. Darcy's life depended on his ability to disconnect from her.

"This changes everything," Phillips said. "You have to come back."

"No, sir," Joe told him. "We're still going forward. If they've got her wired, they're prepared to kill her. They'll probably do it anyway. We have to get her out."

"Larson?" Another man came on the line. "This is President Jensen."

Joe stiffened. "Yes, sir."

"That's my daughter we're talking about."

It was also the woman Joe loved. "I understand what she means to you, sir. I'll bring her back alive."

"You'd better."

"Sir, I will bring her back or die trying."

Jensen didn't respond. Phillips came on and gave a few last-minute instructions, then Joe motioned for the team to head out. As they moved north across the ocean, Joe breathed in the scent of salt air. The water had always been a haven, he thought. It was the one place a SEAL could feel safe, and where he performed best.

Three caves. He'd taken the team going into the largest one. His gut told him she was there. They had a plan and a willingness to do whatever it took to save her life. He loved her too much to let her die.

Darcy sat in her chair, shaking. She would have thought that over time the fear would lessen, but it hadn't. She held on by a thread.

Ian and Jesse stood in the rear of the cave, speaking in low voices. The acoustics were such that Darcy could hear them, and their words didn't make her feel any more comfortable.

"You think they're really going to release Jonathan?" Jesse asked.

"Sure. They don't want anything to happen to Darcy. We've got them. Once we get word he's released, we'll call the boat and get out of here."

Boat? They already had two. Darcy glanced at the small vessels in question and realized Ian was talking about something bigger. Of course. They were flying Jonathan to a rendezvous point and they would meet him there with a boat.

"Good," Jesse said. "When we've put this place behind us, we'll dump her overboard. No one will ever find her."

Darcy froze and waited for Ian to deny the statement. When he didn't, she knew she wasn't going to be able to hold it together much longer. A scream built up inside her.

Suddenly the television picture disappeared into snowy static. Ian ripped off his headset and yelled, "What the hell?" Cries of pain came from the back of the cave. Without warning, the water seemed to rise up and a shock wave blasted across the open space.

Darcy felt herself tossed around like a toy. She and the chair slammed into the wall and everything went black.

Joe and his men rushed out of the water. The jamming signal had rendered everything electronic inoperative, including the remote detonation for the bomb. He'd sent in the stun grenades such that Darcy received the least of the impact, but she'd still been blown back into the wall.

"No one gets out of the cave," Joe said into his headset.

The instruction was unnecessary — his team knew what to do, but he couldn't help it. There was too much at stake.

He ran to Darcy's side and checked her for injuries. No blood, although her head might have hit the wall. He saw the chains and cursed, then reached for the vest.

"Joe?"

"Hey, Darcy." She was awake. Thank God. He fingered the various wires, then reached for his small tool kit.

"You're not dead. I thought he shot you." Tears trickled from the corners of her eyes.

"That was Alex," he told her. "I'm okay and so are you."

"Alex?"

"He's in surgery."

"It was horrible. I was so scared." She touched the vest. "It's a bomb."

"I know. Trust me. I know what I'm doing." He managed a smile. "I've taught the class."

"I always knew you were a great guy to have around in a crisis."

He sorted through the wires, then cut three. "How do you feel?" he asked as he pulled off the vest and tossed it away.

"Like I was hit on the head with a hammer. You know, he could have detonated that remotely."

Joe wrapped his arms around her and pulled her close. She was still attached to the chair, but he didn't care.

"We jammed the signal."

"So that's why the TV went out."

"Yeah. Signals from the cavalry. You okay?"

She clung to him. As soon as he felt her hands on his back, he allowed himself to relax a little.

"Never better."

"You must have been scared."

She pulled back enough to look at him. "You can't imagine. Remember how last time you said I had to talk to someone?"

He nodded and touched the bruise on her cheek. "I have some names."

"I think I'm going to need them." Tears filled her eyes. "Oh, Joe. You're here."

"Yes, Darcy. I'm here."

"Don't let go."

"I won't. Not ever."

"You can't take me," Ian screamed as he ran out from the back of the cave and drew a gun.

Joe pushed Darcy behind him and, in one quick move, pulled out his gun. One of the guys on his team got there first. After a terse order to "freeze," three shots rang out in the cave. Ian stumbled then collapsed.

Joe ignored the bleeding body. "The rest?"

"All captured, sir."

"Call it in. Tell them to send the boat in for Darcy."

He turned back to her. She had her eyes closed. "I don't want to look," she whispered.

"You don't have to."

One of his men brought over a key for the chains. Joe released her and pulled her onto his lap. She huddled against him and started to cry.

"Hey," he said gently, smoothing her hair and kissing her face. "Don't do that. You'll want to look good for your dad."

She sniffed. "He's here?"

"Of course. The entire military is here. Lauren, too. The Marcellis are really worried about you. Oh, Brenna's in labor."

"You're kidding. Now?"

"Yeah. She's at the hospital. Last I heard, there's no baby, but plenty of screaming."

She chuckled. "I don't blame her. Nothing about the actual process of giving birth seems pleasant."

He cupped her face. "There's one more thing."

"What's that?"

He stared into her brown eyes and knew he'd finally found the one thing that had been missing his whole life.

"I love you."

She stared at him. "Excuse me?"

"I love you, Darcy."

She opened her mouth, but before she could say anything, Joe felt a tap on his shoulder.

"The boat is here, sir."

Joe shifted Darcy onto the ground, then stood and swept her into his arms. She grabbed him around his neck.

"What are you doing?" she asked.

"Saving you."

"You've already done that once today."

"I plan on doing it for a long time to come."

# 23

They were escorted out of the cave and back to shore by the Coast Guard. Darcy had expected a Secret Service agent or two to be waiting, but what she saw instead was something closer to the staging area for a space shuttle launch. There were five or six ships cruising the immediate area. At least two dozen cars were parked along the sand. Three helicopters sat on the road, and two trucks filled with military personnel stood watch a hundred or so feet away.

Joe took her arm and helped her step onto the sand. She looked from the staring crowd back to him. "All this for me?" she asked, not able to believe it.

"Of course."

"Wow."

The fear had faded, but in its place was a shaky feeling. Too much emotion in too short a time, she told herself. She clung to Joe, her only stable point in a spinning world, and promised herself that as soon as she caught her breath she would deal with his amazing and unexpected declaration of love. She would have guessed he cared, but not that he could admit he actually loved her.

The crowd parted and her father hurried toward her. "Darcy!"

He held out his arms.

The unexpected gesture made her hesitate at first, then she rushed forward to hug him. He pulled her close and squeezed so hard, she could barely breathe.

"I was scared to death," he murmured in her ear. "When I heard what had happened, I couldn't believe it."

"Me, either," she said.

He cupped her face in his hands. "I don't want anything to happen to you. I'd be lost without you."

She read the truth in his eyes and felt sadness for all the time they'd wasted.

"I love you, Daddy," she whispered.

He kissed her forehead. "I love you, too, Darcy. You're my daughter. You know that, right?"

She nodded, too close to crying to speak. Her father put his arm around her and led her to the waiting SUV. Before she climbed in, she looked back for Joe, but he was gone.

"Where is he?" she asked. "Joe Larson."

"Debriefing," her father told her. "Don't worry. You'll see him later, and you can thank him for rescuing you."

She planned to do a whole lot more than that but doubted her father wanted to hear about the details.

"Is Alex all right?" she asked as she slid onto the leather seat.

"Yes. He's already out of surgery."

"I'd like to go see him."

"Of course. We'll stop by the hospital on our way back to the Marcelli house."

The Marcellis. She'd nearly forgotten. "The fire. Is everyone all right? Did they get it out?"

"Yes. Just as you were kidnapped, it started to rain. That put out the rest of it. A few acres were burned, but I was told they can be replanted."

"Ian did that," she said. "He started the fire as a diversion."

"The authorities know."

"You're not letting that Jonathan person out of prison, are you?"

Her father pulled her close and put his arm around her. "Stop worrying, Darcy. I'm doing a good job of running the country. Just think about yourself and the fact that you're safe now."

She hadn't been held by her father in more years than she could count, but the sensation was still familiar and comforting. Funny how she'd spent so much time looking for a place to belong and it had been waiting for her all along.

Mia sat alone in the house. She couldn't remember the last occasion when she'd been the only person there. Usually Grandma Tessa or Grammy M were puttering around, but not this evening. Everyone had gone to the hospital to check on either Alex or Brenna. Mia had promised to come as soon as she could. But she'd needed to be alone. To think. To recover from the horror of what had happened.

Ian had betrayed her. He'd used her to do something horrific, and she'd never had a clue.

She'd trusted him, both in and out of her bed. She'd thought he was funny and smart, if a little too talkative. She'd been friends with him for nearly two years, lovers for three months, and she'd never guessed.

Paige had pointed out that she, Mia, was a civilian. She couldn't be expected to know. But Mia was used to being smarter than that. No one had ever fooled her so completely.

She reached for her backpack and pulled out her wallet. Tucked inside was a plain white business card. There was no name on it — just a phone number. She'd been given the card one of the many times someone had approached her about becoming a clandestine operative for the government.

She stared at the number for a long time before dialing it.

It rang twice.

"Yes?"

"Hi. I'm, ah, Mia Marcelli. I was given this card a few months ago."

"One moment, please."

Mia heard the man typing on a keyboard. "Yes, Mia. I have your file. How can I help you?"

File? She had a file? "I'm interested in what you do. In being, you know, a spy."

Paige sat by Alex and held his hand. He was still pretty out of it, but she wasn't going to let go. Not until he told her to go away, which, based on how out of it he was, wouldn't be happening anytime soon.

He stirred slightly. She rose and leaned over him.

"Hey, big guy. How are you feeling?"

His eyelids fluttered. "Paige?"

"I'm right here. You had surgery. They

poked around and made sure you're going to be okay. Apparently you got lucky. The bullet didn't damage anything you couldn't live without."

"Good to know." He stared into her eyes. "Where will you go?"

"After I leave the service?"

"Yeah."

"Texas. There's a little house I've been looking at outside of Austin. I'm thinking of getting my credentials and teaching."

"You'd be good at that." He opened his eyes and drew in a breath. "How small is the house?"

"About twelve hundred square feet."

"Not much room for anyone else."

Her heart stopped. She felt it stutter, then still completely. "I didn't think there would be anyone interested. I haven't bought the house yet. I could get something bigger, if you wanted."

He squeezed her hand. "I remember when you told me you didn't regret losing me. I want to be someone you'd regret losing."

She bent down and kissed him. "I was mad," she whispered. "I did regret losing you."

One corner of his mouth turned up. "I doubt that, but it's nice of you to say it. I want to change, Paige. I want to matter to you."

Emotions flooded her. They came on so quickly, she didn't know which one to experience first.

"You do matter. I love you, Alex."

The curve turned into a smile. "I love you more. Because you're a pain in the ass."

"You act like you've got a stick up yours."

"You're too emotional."

"You're too by the book."

He gazed at her. "Don't ever change," he said. "Promise."

"I won't, except I think I want to love you a little more each day. Are you all right with that?"

"Never better."

Joe wasn't sure what the other patients in the small hospital thought about the invasion. There were Marcellis everywhere, Secret Service agents, military personnel, the president, and his two daughters.

He'd been excused from his debriefing to visit Brenna, who'd just given birth. As he left her room, a marine stopped him and said the president would like to see him. Joe followed the man to a busy office on the ground floor of the building. But instead of hospital staff manning the phones, there were agents and military officers.

Joe walked up to the president and saluted.

Ryan Jensen looked him over. "You're the man who rescued my daughter."

"Yes, sir."

"Well done. Now, what exactly are your intentions toward her?"

The room went silent. For a split second, no one spoke, no one pretended not to be listening. Then a phone rang and the various staff members returned to their work, although Joe had a good idea they were all still waiting to hear his answer.

Joe squared his shoulders, looked his commander in chief in the eye, and said, "I love her and I intend to ask her to marry me, sir. I don't know if she'll have me."

Jensen didn't blink. "I see. And if she were to agree, where would you live? On base?"

"No, sir. I'll be leaving the navy to help run the Marcelli winery. I thought we could build a house near the hacienda. Darcy likes it there, sir. She likes my family. It's a good place to raise children."

Jensen's gaze narrowed. "My daughter is an extremely special young woman. You'd better take damn good care of her."

"Yes, sir. I will."

"Oh, Daddy."

Joe turned and saw Darcy standing in the doorway. She looked from him to her father and sighed.

"Stop interrogating Joe. What if he doesn't want to marry me? You can't make him."

"Want to bet?" the president asked.

"I doubt it's an executive order any of us would be proud of," she told him, then turned to Joe. "Don't worry. I'll get my father off your back."

He crossed to her and took her hands in his. "I don't want him off my back," he said, staring into her eyes and knowing he would never get tired of looking at her. "I want him monitoring everything I do because then he can see how happy I'm going to make you. And because you deserve that. I love you, Darcy. I want to marry you. I want you to have the wedding of your dreams and a life so filled with happiness, you can't stop telling people how lucky you are."

A single tear trickled down her cheek. He brushed it away with his thumb. "Why are you crying?"

"Because I'm already so happy." She threw herself at him. "I love you, Joe. I want to marry you. I want to get married in the gazebo on the winery grounds and have a dress made by the Marcelli women. I want to be a part of your family, and I want you to be a part of mine. I want to have kids and dogs and learn about wine and live with you until we're older than Grammy M and Gabriel."

He kissed her. "That's a pretty big list."

"You up to the task?"

"Absolutely. I can't wait to get started."

They kissed again and went on kissing until the sound of someone clearing his throat interrupted. Joe pulled back. "Think I should ask your dad's blessing?" he asked with a grin.

Darcy nodded. "He'll say yes, but it would be a nice gesture."

He turned to the president, who eyed him with two parts suspicion and one part acceptance.

"Oh, did you hear about Brenna?" Darcy asked.

Joe chuckled. "Oh, yeah. Twins. Brace yourself. They run in the family."

"We can handle it. We can handle anything."

# ABOUT THE AUTHOR

**Susan Mallery** is the *USA Today* bestselling author of more than eighty romance novels, including *Married for a Month*, *Sweet Success*, and her acclaimed trilogy featuring the Marcelli sisters: *The Sparkling One*, *The Sassy One*, and *The Seductive One*. The winner of the National Readers Choice Award, she has a Masters degree in Writing Popular Fiction. Susan makes her home in Los Angeles with her husband and two very charming cats. Visit her website at www.su sanmallery.com.